THE SPACES THAT HOLD YOU

The Spaces That Hold You

KARLA SELF

ARTEM & BELLUS BOOKS, LLC

First published in the United States by Artem & Bellus Books, LLC

Editing by Thornton Sully
Original front cover art and book design by Karla Self
Photography by Randy Self

Library of Congress Control Number: 2023939145

ISBN 979-8-9882206-0-2 (Paperback Edition)
ISBN 979-8-9882206-1-9 (ebook)

Printed in the United States of America
First printing 2023

Books are available for special quantity discounts. Please contact:

Artem & Bellus Books, LLC
PO Box 251
Jacksonville, OR 97530
info@artemandbellus.com
www.artemandbellus.com

This book is dedicated to all the children, and to those who reach out a loving hand to make their world a better place.

And it is for my family, my connections, who are all held eternally in the love of my grandmother, Alta Mae. For her, for holding me up like a newborn star, even when I was grown. For Mom and Dad, for taking that leap when you were so young, and for loving us through every storm. For Randy, for patiently listening to all of my wandering ideas, even when I'm wrong, for all these many years. For Josh, Colby and Tiffiny, I still marvel that I get the great privilege of being your mother. For Deanna, Russ and Uncle Ronnie, my first and forever friends. For Pat, Brycelaine, Lauren and Jimmy, my dear ones, I am so grateful that you said yes, which brought you to me. For Terri, my special gift from saying yes to your brother. And for my beautiful grandchildren, my newborn stars, who shine their light on me; Brier, Ellis, Riley, Hunter, Waylan, Calian, Holden and Hadley. May you always know that you are held eternally in my love for you.

Hope whispers in the darkness
And dances in the sun
It rides through every bitter storm
And lights your path, steer on

— Karla Self

Prologue

The life of a child is not truly his own. He merely exists, for a time, in the world that is created by those around him. Molded, mostly, by the unskilled hands of those whose own lives started in the same unknowing way.

My reality as a child was pretty much fabricated, and the hardest thing about it is remembering who that boy was amid the pool of memories that collide, still, with the truth.

Growing up, I worried mostly about my mother, who I loved, but she was a heavy load to carry. There was a weight to her that I didn't understand at the time. She tried with all she had, but everything was skewed for her, as if she were seeing the world through a different lens. We were both just hanging on for dear life, living on that lower rung of existence where mere survival was at the forefront of each day. Everything else was simply happenstance, with a little mix of wide-eyed wonder when I could peek at a different world between the covers of a book or imagine a perfect one in the melody of a song.

My mother needed help, but her secrets kept her trapped inside her suffering, holding that door closed with all her might. Her life was like a prison, and I know now, that she could see no way out. She spent most of her life in hiding, trying to avoid the pain of her *knowing*. Her efforts to soothe her torment became her only motive for existence, which took on a life of its own that bound her up in its fury. It became her state, her place in life, and that is the place where my mother lived, with me.

I am Levi and this is my story. I have placed the memories of my mother in a comfortable space within my heart where I can live with the enormity of the secrets she kept. The many secrets that finally found their way to me. It is not an enormous space that *holds me* any longer, but one that I choose to hold tenderly for her.

My boyhood self is like an old childhood friend who I hold dear. He is a valiant reminder that all things are possible, no matter the circumstances. He is the lionheart within me. I cherish him and cry, still, for his suffering.

Chapter 1

om and I sat near the front of the bus as it rolled down the dusty California highway, the landscape floating past like a scene in a movie. Each image blew by with the stifling heat as it swept across my sweaty face from the half-open window, providing a sense of cool. We drifted down the road, the tranquility only broken by a swift lane change as everyone's head leaned to the right with the acceleration to passing speed, then back to the left as we settled back into the slow lane. I couldn't help but overhear the two men in the seat behind us who were discussing President Kennedy thinking that he could put a man way up there on the moon. They both thought it was a hairbrained idea and that he needed to pull his head out of the clouds and tend to more important matters right here on planet earth.

"Momma? Can a man really fly to the moon?"

"If the president says so, I guess. Sounds like crazy talk to me though."

Wouldn't that be something? A man on the moon. That thought carried me around for many miles and I never looked at the moon the same way ever again. It wasn't just a light up there in the night sky, it was a place that a man might be able to go if he needed a better place to be.

I was suddenly intrigued by the idea of a real bathroom riding down the road with us when Mom headed back to use it. I followed, and waited for her on the empty back seat, leaning over it to peer out the rear window. The traffic trailed behind us like the tail of a kite. As I imagined us taking flight, I heard the door click and could have waited, but as Mom stepped out, I stepped in. She warned me not to touch the seat, which was a regular mantra. The marvel of the traveling restroom that lured me in was a trap. My curiosity quickly waned as I stepped inside and was nearly knocked back by the overwhelming vapors, my tear ducts trying to protect my eyes with a deluge. I moved quickly, holding my breath against the burning torrent of the stagnated air. I had lousy aim, on unsteady feet, as I peppered most of the surfaces on and around the streaky metal bowl. Each gentle sway of the bus became a heavy surf threatening to knock me off my feet. My shoes felt the stickiness of the floor, which I knew were the remnants of the countless others who had baptized the place before me. I contributed well to the stick, and finally made my escape, seriously disheartened by the dreadful thing. The germ count was the only true marvel.

Other details of the trip remain spotty, as I was young, not having started school yet. Our destination was unknown to me until Mom stood up and made her way to the bus driver to have a word. At her prompting, he stopped to let us off right there at a crossroad along the busy highway. We quickly grabbed our things and stepped out and into our new life. I don't remember much about the old one, but as our feet hit the pavement, my senses were piqued by the sweet smell of molasses that filled the air.

As the bus pulled out, a cloud of dust swelled up around us. We turned away from its threat to face the enormous feed mill that was billowing the sugary steam of molasses being cooked into the grain. We maneuvered across four lanes of traffic to reach the other side of the highway, with the heat sweltering up around our ankles from the scorching pavement. We walked along a frontage road that hugged a long bank of pink flowering oleanders that separated the two thoroughfares. Less than a mile down that road was Kelsey, well hidden from the world by the bank of heavy oleanders. No one would ever notice it unless they had been fairly warned.

I was raised on the streets of that little nothing of a town. It was one of those places that most would try to avoid for fear of the sorts who dwelled there. It was a rough spot in the road, a perfect place to hole up for those who were running away, hiding out, or simply never saw a greater design for their lives. It was the perfect place for my mother, a little net in which she fell that tangled around her like a cocoon, protecting her, and me, from the greater world outside.

Hardly anyone ever happened upon Kelsey by accident, and if they did, they would spin their car around, having quickly noticed that they were heading down the wrong road. Old shanties lined the dirt roads and alleyways of town, remnants of the dust bowl migrants who built this once-bustling township, as a fruitful stop on their long journey up and down the California corridor chasing the maturing crops.

Bill's Corner Store, aptly named, sat on the corner of Main Street and the frontage road, the only paved roads in Kelsey. Mr. Bill was famous in town for his fancy barbecue loaf, a sweet flavored bologna with cracked pepper lined along one edge like a zipper. There wasn't anything better than a thick slice of that fancy loaf, layered with barbecued potato chips in between two slices of soft white glue-bread. Glue-bread is that pasty white flour bread that you can mash together with a bit of water to form a paste for holding practically anything together.

The back door of Sydney's Beauty Parlor sat right on the alley in front of our ramshackle house. She had a sign to advertise her three-dollar shampoo/set special on the roof. It could be seen from the highway and did well to entice the ladies who lived in the bigger towns up and down the valley to travel the distance to become regulars. A shampoo/set included a shampooing, set in rollers, drying under the fancy hairdryers, back combing with a fine rat tail comb, a comb out and enough hairspray to last the week. She also did modern cuts, permanent waves, pin curls and fancy updos.

She had a steady stream of patrons who came like clockwork every single week and again for special occasions. Sydney worked real hard for her dollars, standing steady on her feet with a great ear for listening.

Next to Sydney's was the Black Hole Bar, another highly patronized establishment. Kelsey was literally crawling with entrepreneurial enterprises. We also had a small post office, a free library and an old schoolhouse that sat on 3rd Street, off Main. It seemed that almost everybody was poor in Kelsey. Most had a roof over their head, even if the rain did come pouring through in buckets. The warm scent of cookies baking in the oven all day, every day, from the feed mill gave our town a sweet sense of home. It gave the impression that mothers greeted their children after school, wearing their aprons, having just pulled the cookies from the oven.

When we walked into Kelsey that first day, we hid our things in some bushes out back of the corner store to have a look around. We roamed through the alleys, skirting the edges of town, wading through a thicket of tall weeds and overgrown shrubs, looking for a good spot to lay our pallets for the night. To our great surprise, we found an old abandoned shack tucked inside a stockade of suckers that had grown in a scatter from the giant trees that towered overhead. After we circled the old shanty, we made our way inside through the unlatched front door. It appeared to have been empty for a long while as dust, garbage and mouse droppings covered the floor. It was completely furnished, though the musky odor of its pesky squatters stole from its charm. We ducked through the cobwebs to find two small bedrooms, each with an old mattress on the floor. The smallest room was papered in cowboys riding through a desert filled with cactus. The light from the tiny window made it feel warmer than the rest of the house, as the hot afternoon sun burned right through it, making the desert feel bona fide. The kitchen was graced with a small refrigerator standing open. The handle was broken off with a screw driver stuck into the opening, which could be jockeyed around to maneuver the latch. A small silver and red dinette set sat against a wall of faded teapot motif wallpaper. There was a window over the sink with a yellowed lace curtain that threatened to tatter to shreds with the slightest breeze. A worn-out crushed velvet sofa sat sullen in the living room. It was red, with a brownish tenge from a lifetime of spills. There was a bathroom with a gritty tub and toilet that needed a good dousing with heavy bleach.

"We'll stay here tonight," Mom announced. "We'll see if we can find the owner tomorrow."

We ran and got our things and pulled up the mattress in the larger bedroom to kick off the mouse droppings and slept there uninvited and unnoticed, except by the mice who scampered and squeaked with their disapproval. I was awakened by a shriek when one of them hopped right onto Mom's leg as we slept. I tucked myself in under her arm and laid there in the darkness with the sounds of the tiny rodents moving about, just waiting for one of them to light up on me.

The following day we stashed our things in the bushes again and went into the corner store to find out who owned the abandoned shack. The clerk directed us to Mr. Cooper, who lived in a bright pink house on Main Street.

Mom stood back after knocking on the door. No one answered, so she knocked again. This time a thin elderly man eased the door open.

Mom spoke in a flowery tone. "Hi, my name's Katharine Strong. My friends call me Kat. And this here is my boy, Levi. We've just moved to town and would like to see about renting your house on the alley behind the beauty parlor."

"It ain't for rent." Mr. Cooper's voice was mighty disagreeable.

"What if I clean it up for you?"

"I ain't interested."

"Sir, me and my boy need a place to stay and can't afford much. It's just what I'm looking for."

He looked long at her. Then at me. His gaze was stern, like a gate keeper not wanting to let anybody in.

"I'm good at cleaning houses. I can make it look real nice."

He lifted his eyes up staring at someplace far away. There was a long silence. He looked forlorn. We were desperate.

"Please sir, we won't be any trouble," Mom pleaded.

"If the county comes around, it'll be condemned."

"Not when I'm through with it."

I looked up at my mother's pretty face, her short dishwater blonde hair tucked back behind her ears. She was wearing her sunny yellow dress, her blue eyes shimmering as she breathed in a long hopeful breath. As the seconds passed, I began to worry that she might fall apart. Sometimes, it didn't take much. She was unskilled in the art of coping. My hackles were beginning to lift with dread when Mr. Cooper finally melted under the pressure of our homelessness. To my relief, he and Mom worked out a deal and that little shanty became our humble home. Mr. Cooper turned on the electricity and we cleaned it up real nice just as Mom promised. It felt dreamy, like everything might just fall into place, for a time anyway.

Chapter 2

S oon after we settled into our house, Mom found some odd jobs and it wasn't long before she figured a way to deal with the difficulties of our life, which produced a problem with her drinking, which cultivated into a problem with the *gloss*, her secret spy word for her drugs. She wasn't particular about her gloss, as most anything would do: pills, powdery stuff, and then the wretched homemade methamphetamine. She didn't make the stuff herself, she simply befriended a cooker, Charlie Pratt, a member of a local motorcycle gang, who found Kelsey to be the perfect distribution center for his Kelsey Kocaine. He was an early adopter of the cheap, injectable form, having learned from a man who fought for Hitler in World War II. Charlie started out by peddling diet pills that he could easily buy from expired pharmaceutical sales samples that he bought in bulk from a sordid supplier. Charlie and his gang then created their own concoction from the German recipe. Ol' Charlie and his brew drew my mother in like a starving pup to a rotten egg, as it commenced the annihilation of her. She became Charlie Pratt's willing guinea pig and stayed awake for days on end, spinning like a top and working on how and when she was going to get her next granules of discontentment.

On those days when she ran the length of her gloss, she would crawl out of bed in search of something to drink. She would drink anything with alcohol in it, putting cough syrup in danger of being jerked. Those were desperate times. As I started school and learned a little bit about how *normal* people lived, I began to wonder how anyone could live like my mother did. Just sitting around letting the worst of life drag you right down into nothing. There was no way I was gonna let that kind of life catch hold of me. I would have left early on if I hadn't been afraid that my mother would just lay there and drink or gloss herself to death, alone. Sometimes I wondered what difference it would make if she did. It pained me to think like that. But sometimes the old devil would grab a hold of me, and I'd have to fight my way free. It's hard to remember Mom before the gloss. She was overtaken so long ago. It pillaged and reworked her brain until she believed it was omnipotent. It was her only hope for a moment's peace, which came at a heavy price. She lay deep in the shadows of my memory where I only glimpse who she might have been, only if. Deep down, I knew it wasn't her fault that she slowly disappeared. It was her effort to find some escape, within the gloss, from her insurmountable fear, loneliness, and the echoing voices in her own head that drove her further and further away. She believed all of their lies, as each raised up against her. She was no longer in charge of her own self. They made her do awful things. Secret things. I respected them, all of them, always on the lookout for what they might prod her to do. They became her truth bearers, and the architects of our lives.

I try to think back to a time when my mother could sit still in the shade on a warm summer day, quietly resting her mind, singing with the breeze. I always knew she was different from most people, but she once had an easy smile and a warmth that floated free on some days, kind of like it was being released from a faint memory of a better time.

I didn't have a dad and my mother proclaimed that she didn't even know who he was. She wouldn't even offer up a name. How could she not even know? I had learned enough about those birds and bees to know that this was nearly impossible. I used to dream of all the men who could have been my dad. Maybe that was why we moved to Kelsey, to be close to him. It could have been Jay Don, the owner of Cramer's Thrift Shop or Sheriff Bender, who had the same dirty brown hair as me, with a hint of copper when the light was just right. Joe Riley Lawson was another possible culprit. He was my best buddy Chance's dad. Wouldn't it be something if he and I were brothers? I fought myself not to confide my suspicions. It made sense, though. It could have been the reason that we got along so well. It didn't matter that we looked nothing alike, me and Joe Riley shared ways — ways of walking and moving our hands to tell a better story, and the way we could raise one eyebrow higher than the other when perplexed. I practiced my eyebrow lift in the mirror many times, solidifying the evidence. Then the thought occurred to me that my dad could just be old Eugene, one of the local town drunks. That thought always snapped me right out of that dreaming business. It didn't matter anyway. I didn't need no cranky old man telling me what to do. I was my own man and could take plenty good care of myself. But sometimes, I found myself longing for my dad, someone who was likely just a figment of my imagination and the fascination I had with the whole idea of such a man.

Chapter 3

I was playing in the dirt outside my house when I heard a cry. It sounded like a baby. I followed the whimpering to the alley. It was coming from behind a trash can, lying in wait for the garbage truck. My hands were shaking as I walked over to find a little yellow pup. It was cowered down inside the cup of a large red bra. It let out a howl when it saw me.

"Don't cry now. It's gonna be alright." I walked toward her and called out with a short kissy noise. The pup came to full attention and perked her ears, one held at half-mast. She ran straight to me, jumping into my arms like I was her long-lost brother. She tongue-kissed my whole face, enjoying the salt build up that had crusted over it. I must have smelled like something dead because she nearly rolled all over me.

"Well, hello little lady. I wish you could be *my* little lady." I ran to the house with her, "Look, Mom. Look what I found. Can I keep her?" I smiled my biggest smile, shining all my little teeth with my eyebrows lifted up to my hairline.

"You know we can't afford a dog."

I knew that was a fact. "Please, Mom. Please let me keep her. I'll take good care of her. You won't have to do nothing. Look, she likes you." I handed her to Mom, praying that my little lady would win her over. I closed my eyes and furrowed my brow real dramatic-like, lifting my shoulders up to my ears, smiling like the Cheshire Cat.

Mom held her close like a baby, rubbing her soft belly. The pup smiled her widest grin up at Mom, her dark eyes sparkling. Mom smiled back, "She *is* cute, isn't she?"

"She sure is." I shook my head. "She's really something."

Incredibly, I got to keep her, my very first and faithful friend, M'Lady. It wasn't really a decision, she just never left. She laid claim on me, keeping my feet warm at night, my belly laughing during the day, and did a fine job as a notifier of noises in the dark. She was my constant companion and taking care of her gave my life a new meaning. Mom and I both shared our food with her. I scrounged around the alley collecting scraps for my girl. I would have done anything for her. I loved that dog. I think Mr. Bill did too, because one day when I was looking through his trash, he came out and handed me a brown paper sack filled with dry dog food that had spilled from torn bags in his inventory. I think he liked us too, because sometimes he would ask if we would like to take some of the outdated canned goods or wilting fruits and vegetables off his hands. He had a way of making you feel like you were doing him a favor, not the other way around.

Chapter 4

Me and Chance started a little business venture when we were just finishing up the fourth grade. We would collect pop bottles from the side of the highway and redeem them at Mr. Bill's. We would split the profits . . . partners and blood-brothers for life. We also worked the cockfights at Red Harrington's barn some Saturday nights. It was a very popular venue. Red's clientele was rich with culture. There were shirtless field workers standing next to men in white business shirts, all hollering and wagering on the flopping fowl. Chance and me almost always bet on Waylon Mitchell's cocks. He had been breeding them for years; went clear down to Mexico to find the top breeding stock.

After the fights, we would climb up on Red's barn to watch whatever was playing at the Moonlight Drive In, which we could see in the distance. We spent many a night up on that barn watching the silence of Hollywood movies, some a little racy if we were lucky. And when its face was full,

I would stare up in amazement at the man in the moon, imagining myself riding one of President Kennedy's rockets clear on up there. I remember the day he was killed. I was watching TV when the news man announced that he had been shot. I yelled for my mother. She came running in and cried as we watched the scenes play out again and again on the screen. I understood the magnitude of what happened, and cried for the loss of my president, who dreamed so big, that he would someday put me up there on that moon.

Many nights me and Chance and our buddies would sit on the rail fence in my front yard on the alley, watching for action at the Black Hole. It was always a promising possibility that we could catch a good street brawl. On a slow night we would fan out and gather up all the half-smoked cigarettes out back of the Hole. We only gleaned the filtered butts so we could cut away the nasty slobbered ends, leaving clean low filtered smokes. We were incredibly cool as we held our fags between our thumb and forefinger, squinting our eyes through the thin white line of smoke, as we swapped stories from our colorful imaginations. After scavenging our smokes, we would sometimes clear a place for a game of marbles or take off running across the highway over to the feed mill. The grain tower stood high in the air like a gray metal fortress, with the moonlight glancing off it like giant searchlights. If the timing was in our favor, there would be train cars lined up for miles, just sitting there, inviting us in to see what fascinating items were being transported through town. We would go at night so as not to be seen by anyone, but the hobos and lost souls holed up in the dark corners of the multi-colored steel railroad cars. Our most lucrative summer at the mill was when we worked a barrel full of dill pickles from a train car, spilling hundreds of pickles on the ground. We pulled off our shirts, creating filthy cloth satchels to haul the pickles home in. It took us several trips back and forth across the highway, but we managed to tote home dozens of pickles from that barrel. We ate real good in that summer-of-the-pickles. That very same week, in one of the rail cars, we found dozens of crates of Army helmets. We broke one open and hauled two of the helmets home to our fabricated fort. Putting together a fitting army and battling for the fertile soil of Kelsey was our calling during that long hot summer. Who knows what would have happened to her if we hadn't been there to fight for her? The blistering heat tested our resilience and courage, but with our bellies full of pickles we soldiered on, protecting our land, and fighting for the only thing we had to believe in.

Chapter 5

You have to be careful when you live in a town like Kelsey, sorting out who you can trust. There are golden souls like Mr. Bill and Sydney Mello, at the beauty parlor, working right next door to sorts like Jess Davies, a glue-sniffer and petty thief. Everyone had to watch their backs on account of him and others like him who scuttled around like mice in the dark, on the prowl for an easy lift.

We never had much money, but for what Mom made selling gloss through the underworld, and what I could rustle up. It went mostly to pay the rent, always late, and for enough food to keep us breathing. Mom would skim the gloss, many times leaving her in debt from her scooping, until she started *stepping on them*, aiming to cut them into enough to make a living and enough to self-medicate from the reality of her fears, both a life-and-death endeavor. She kept us alive and in the leanest of times, we could always fall back on bologna sandwiches, gleaning harvested fields, and the charity of Mr.

Bill's unsellable goods. Every once in a while, we would get some spread to smear on the bread of our sandwiches. That salty bologna always tasted good though, especially if we could swing a bag of chips to go along with it. The county provided cheese and powdered milk, so we would never go hungry. We would just stand in line with the rest of the poor folks to get our staples. No strings attached, which was just to my mother's liking. Luckily, I had several places I could go for a bite if I got too hungry from the lack. Checking with Sydney and following my Buddy Chance home was always good for a meal.

Our old shack was rough and had never been painted as far as I could tell. It sat right down on the ground. No blocks to hold up the sagging floor. It was freezing in the winter and burning hot in the summer. Coats were always worn indoors in the winter. It was much like many of the other old worn-down shanties off the alleyways of our little town. Mr. Cooper always came knocking for the rent money. Mom would curse and swear about how the damn place wasn't worth a dime. Mr. Cooper would just say "yeah, yeah, just get me the money, Kat." She would finally hand it over and Mr. Cooper would just shake his head. He always wore a scowl on his face. Never smiled. I guessed it was because he lost his boy, Clinton, in a car wreck. He was on his way to the *Jumpin' Frog Jubilee* in Calaveras County when he took a turn too wide and rolled his old truck right over. Two boys died that day. They say there were kids sprawled all over the hill side. It scarred him. Losing his child seemed to take a part of him. There was a hole left there where the wind and chill was free to blow right through him. You could almost see it blowing. It was a quiet breeze though, cold and damp. Kind of like the air in an old musty cave. Keeping you cold and shivering all the time. Eventually, the hole would fill up, you'd think. But it may only fill up with pain and heartache, as seemed true for Mr. Cooper. I later observed the same, when such a gale blew right in on my mother. A blow of which I was forbidden to speak.

Pain and suffering are just cobbles in the road. You get enough of them, and they give you a solid place to rest your feet. If you didn't have those hard places, you'd just sink right down into the ground. I had cobbles enough to build a wall clear around myself. It protected me from all the days that blurred into the darkness of night. It took a while for me to see a greater design that might offer a glimmer of hope. Such are the consequences of the war that plays out in the turmoil of some lives. Makes it difficult to see the wonder in the very air we breathe. Life was just way too crazy to see the little things. What is hope anyway? Does it just happen on you? Can you really feel it, or see it? Why is it that some folks get upbringing, and some folks don't? The luck of the draw, I would guess, and some kids just get dealt a low-ball hand in a game of Texas Hold 'em. It is sad and difficult and just the way it is for some unlucky souls. But there is still magic out there. The magic of people and faces, who can make a difference in the lives of those around them. They are the ones who show up and have hope in us, no matter who we are.

Chapter 6

The good people of Kelsey became my family. Sydney, at the beauty parlor, was always there for me. She was nice to all us kids when we popped in just to say hello. Sometimes she would let me take in her pop bottles, letting me keep some of the money for my trouble. The first time I stepped into the shop to check it out, she walked toward me with a big smile and sparkles that spurt clean out of her eyes. She was short, not even five feet tall, wearing a bright pink smock. Her hair was done up in a perfect beehive, making her appear much taller. Her hair, black as night. I'm not sure if she had made it such, or if it was natural. Her lips were always painted to match her lively smocks, with teeth as white as snow. She was proudly Portuguese, her family coming to America from the Azores. She did free haircut clinics with the ladies from the Beauty Institute who were working toward their cosmetology licenses every fall, as us kids were preparing to start school. Those of us who couldn't afford a proper haircut could stand in line to get a decent trimming. The ladies would get good practice and we a new lease on life, well-coiffed. Sydney was a godsend to the whole town.

One day I concocted a plan to save my mother from the misery of her days. I needed a job to make some money so I could ease her away from the pushers. They had her in a Catch-22 where she needed their goods, which took most of the money that she made selling their goods. She had become a pusher herself as a means to make our ends meet. It had become a losing proposition as far as I could see. It was a vicious circle, like a merry-go-round spinning out of control, with my mother going through the motions of the ride as they tossed her up and down like a painted pony. Somehow, I had to get her off. If she could get off the gloss, maybe she could settle back to using only the drink to ward off the voices. She was losing all sense of herself. She had gotten so skinny. Her hair was growing thin and dull, and her face had little color left in it. Her days were spent doing all she had to do to ease the pain that lived inside her. She soared up and fell flat, all dependent on which type of gloss was on the market. If I could work hard enough, maybe I could get her free of it. I decided to go straight into the beauty parlor and ask Sydney for a job. I had put some thought into it, having showered and combed my hair over, trying to paste the curls down with water. I didn't know about the miracle of Dippity-Do, so water was my only choice at trying to control the girly curls. I put on my best pair of pants, a little bit high watery from my growing spirt, but I tucked them into a perfectly good pair of men's boots that I had found poking around at the dump. The toes were curled clean up so far that my feet stayed tucked down toward the heel. My favorite shirt was near the bottom of my clothes pile, but the orange color played off the color of my hair. I looked sharp.

I stood nervously at the front counter. Sydney was working on a lady's head as she looked over and gave me a nod. I nodded back and smiled real big, standing up as tall as I could. She excused herself and walked over noticing my boots right off. *Good choice.*

"What can I do for you today, Levi? Love your boots." She smiled as she looked down at the wonder of them. "Would you like a haircut?"

Darn, that would have been a good in, if I had had the money. "I can't today. I'm here on business. I'm looking for a job." I looked down at my boots, the points staring right back at me.

"What kind of work are you looking for?" she asked, interested.

"Whatever you need done, I can do it." I could tell she was impressed, as she nodded, smiling widely.

"Hmm . . . let me think." She looked around the shop, considering what I might be able to do for her as I started feeling hopeful. There were a couple of ladies sitting under hair dryers and another one reading a magazine, awaiting her turn. The front door opened and yet another patron walked through the front door.

"Hi Margaret. I'm a little behind today. Just have a seat. Would you like a cup of coffee?"

"No thank you. I'm fine." She picked up a hairstyling magazine. "I'll just sit here and see if there are any new styles I might want to try. I like this one here on the cover." She held it up. It was a picture of a smiling Debbie Reynolds. "But I guess that might be asking you to make a silk purse out of a sow's ear." All the ladies giggled at the notion.

"I'll do my best." Sydney was tickled, then looked back at me. "I've overbooked myself a bit today. Can you come back tomorrow afternoon? I'll slot you into my schedule so we can sit down and have a proper talk about your employment goals." She eyed me, grinning. The ladies in waiting chuckled again like what she said might be funny. I definitely had employment goals. There wasn't nothing funny about it.

"Okay," I said slowly, wearing my disappointment that my plan was more difficult than I thought.

"How about 4:00, after school tomorrow?"

"Okay." I tried to smile.

"Levi, thank you for coming in today. It's good to see you."

"You too. I'll see you tomorrow." I turned to walk out.

"Hey, you doing alright?" her voice lifted from behind me.

"Yeah, I'm good." *Just disappointed.* I walked out the door and headed on home.

I tossed and turned all night worrying about my employment goals. Maybe Sydney had lots of people stopping by to ask for work. There might be competition. My stomach rolled me over into despair. I was feeling desperate as it was the only way I could see to get my mother free of the gloss. This had to work, my working.

After a long day at school, I headed over to the shop wearing the same good clothes that I had worn the day before, including the boots, which caused quite a ruckus at school as everyone made fun of them. I didn't get it. I thought they might have been jealous that I had such a fine pair of grown men's boots to wear. A couple of the guys got in trouble for poking too much fun at me. I hated for anyone to lay their focus on me, good or bad. I preferred to keep a low profile. Staying out of trouble and not raising my hand, answering questions only if asked was my style. It was a long and exhausting day. I got to the shop at five minutes to four. Sydney was sitting at the front desk.

"Right on time," she grinned. "Thanks for coming back in. I'm sorry about yesterday. Some days are so busy that I can't see straight. Would you like a soda?"

I thought I should say no, but I really wanted one. "I would, thanks."

"Okay, go ahead and have a seat." She pointed to the reception chairs in the front of the shop and walked to the back room. I heard her pull off a bottle cap and she came out with a Coca Cola and a small bag of peanuts and sat down.

"So, you're wanting to make some extra money, huh?" She handed me the soda and nuts.

"Yeah." I took a swig and placed the nuts in the breast pocket of my shirt for later.

"Is your goal to buy something special?"

"No, not really. I just need a job."

"I see . . . you're looking for a steady job."

"Yeah, that's what I need."

"Okay." She looked me over real good. "How's your mom doing?"

"She's doing just fine." *The lie poured right on out.* I stirred in my seat.

"That's good to hear."

Sydney knew everybody in town. The beauty parlor was Gossip Central. Everyone's business ended up there. I wondered how much she knew about my mother's doings. Mom was slithery though and I hoped that she slid right down under the radar of the Kelsey tittle-tattle.

I wished that I could tell her that I needed some help with my mother, but I couldn't. I trusted Sydney, but Mom said it was important for us to keep our business to ourselves. She didn't take to any meddling of any kind. It was worrisome for her to let people in. That worry caused me to miss the whole first year that I should have been in school. The next year, she said *they* would come looking for me if I didn't get some schooling. There were a lot of *theys*. All the outsiders. She never had any friends come to our house and I was not allowed to bring anyone over, either. "Our home is our refuge," she would say. She felt safe, us being alone. But we still had to battle with the *outsiders* that showed up, unannounced, from inside her head.

"Is she having trouble making ends meet?"

"Sometimes it's hard." I said too much. "But we're doing good. I just have some free time and I'd like to help out a bit." This was getting dodgy.

"Your mom is a lucky lady to have a son like you."

I gave a sheepish grin as my face grew warm. I wasn't used to hearing compliments. "I guess."

"Well, I hadn't thought of having a good hand around here, but the more I think about it, it would be mighty nice to have some help."

I stared in near disbelief, half smiling. *Is she gonna hire me?* I sat up taller to catch her words more quickly.

She smiled and looked warmly into my eyes. "I would be so happy to have such a fine young man working here."

My eyes lit up and my mouth flew open. "Really?!"

"Yes. Really. I was thinking that with school and all, we could have a flexible schedule for you. Have your mom stop by so we can go over what she thinks is best, regarding school, your homework and how much time you may have to help me out around here."

Her words began to fade along with my hope as it spiraled down toward the floor. "I don't think she can . . . she's real busy."

Sydney held a pleasant expression, but stared deeply into my eyes, reading me. "Honey, I'll need your mom's permission for you to work for me. I'd be happy to walk over to talk to her."

My mind was racing for a way through this predicament. "She's so busy. Can I bring a note?" I thought fast.

"I'd feel better if she and I could talk."

I wouldn't. "Can I have her call you?" *Even though we have no phone and I have no idea how I'm gonna get my mother to call.*

"Of course. We just all need to be on board here." She shot me a warm smile through her eyes.

"Okay, I'll have her call you." My face grew warmer by the second as frustration was taking over. I stood up to go.

She got up and walked to her desk. "Here's my business card with the number on it."

I took the card. "Thanks. And thanks for the soda, and the nuts, and for the job." I gave her a crooked grin. It wasn't quite mine yet. It was wavering in front of me, with my mother holding a boulder high on the cliff, like Wile E. Coyote over the Road Runner. Threatening to squash my hopes. But maybe I could hop on the Road Runner's back, and we could outrun it.

"You're welcome. I'll look forward to hearing from your mom so we can get some work done around here," she said cheerily.

"Yeah, me too." I walked over to the door, opened it, and stepped out and into the worry of the dreaded phone call that was gonna be quite a feat to work out.

I spent the next few days trying to ponder up a scheme to get my mother to make that call. She could screw up the whole thing in a second if she was in the wrong mood. Finally, I just had to bring it up. She was sitting at the kitchen table smoking a cigarette, staring at the wallpaper.

"Mom?" I moved in slowly so I wouldn't startle her.

"Uh huh." She didn't look over at me. That was a sign that she was on the downside of a downer. Sometimes she would have to take a downer to downplay the upper. It was a complicated balance that she never got right. Up, down, up, down . . . sideways . . . on the floor. Repeat.

"I was over at Sydney's Beauty Parlor and asked her if I could do some work for her."

"Uh huh." She held her gaze on the teapots.

"She said I could, if you said it was alright."

"What?" She peered from the distance.

"I went and got myself a job . . . well, Sydney said I can work if it's okay with you."

"Hmm." She looked at the floor.

"Mom?" She looked up. "Can I do some work over at the beauty parlor?"

"I don't know why not?" Her voice was slow. She was in a double-down. Maybe it wasn't the best time. But it was better than the high extreme, which would make her talk and rock so fast that it was impossible to follow along.

"Oh good. Can you call Sydney at the shop to tell her it's alright with you if I work for her?"

She held her gaze, but chuckled. "We don't have a phone, silly."

"I know, but there's one out front of Mr. Bill's. We can use that one."

"Why don't we just talk in the alley?"

"Well, that would be good, I guess." I really didn't want a confrontation between the two of them face-to-face. It could go squirrely, but I was beginning to run out of time and options. I needed that job.

"You wanna go now, over to the shop?" I asked, half-way hoping she would say no.

She thought on it . . . s l o w l y. "Well, I guess I could." She was worn out by the gloss. That devilish stuff was beating the life right out of her. It made me feel more desperate.

My heart began to flutter in anticipation of everything going sideways, but the risk of losing her was much higher. "I'll run over first and make sure she's not too busy."

"Okay. I love you, Honey."

I yelled back as I ran out the front door, "I love you too, Mom."

I flew into the shop and Sydney was standing behind a blonde-haired lady, taking out curlers from her long hair. She shot me a smile as she turned to see that it was me.

"Hey Levi."

"Hi Sydney." I waved and motioned her over, kind of frantic-like.

"Is everything okay?" She looked at me puzzled.

"Yeah, sure. It's just that Mom would like to come over to talk to you about my job."

"Oh, that's great."

"Can she come now?" I asked, my face squinting.

Sydney looked at the blondie in the chair. "I'll be done in about twenty minutes. Tell her to come on over then."

"Okay. Great." I turned to run for the door and then spun around. "Sydney?"

"Yeah?"

"Mom hasn't been feeling well today and is on quite a bit of medicine so she might not be herself." *Yeah, that was good.* "She's a little groggy."

"Are you sure she feels like walking over? I can come that way if she'd like."

"No! I mean that's okay." *Dear God, no.* "She said she could come."

"Okay then. I'll see her in twenty."

I tore out toward home, my heart beating its way toward my new job. I had to work fast to outrun *Wile E.* The Road Runner stood at the ready, just in case. I gave him a salute as I ran by.

Mom was still sitting at the table. Her cigarette hanging in her mouth with a long bead of ash ready to fall into her lap. I looked at the clock on the wall. *4:24. Plus twenty. We should be there at 4:44.* "Mom, can we go in twenty minutes?" I concentrated to slow my words so they wouldn't try to keep up with my racing heartbeat.

"Sure Honey."

"Okay. You want a drink of water?"

"That'd be nice."

I ran her a full glass of cool water from the tap. She drank it in one long guzzling gulp. "Thanks. I needed that," she said weakly. I took the glass and hugged her. She leaned her head on me. I stayed there, missing her, even though she was sitting right there.

At 4:40, I grabbed my mother's hand. "Let's go on over."

"Where we goin?"

"To the beauty parlor Mom. About my job."

"Oh. Okay. The job."

I helped her to her feet as we shuffled out the door. I lead her to the front door of the shop. We were a few minutes late. Mom didn't move very fast in her current state. I opened the door to find Sydney at her desk and exposed my mother to her. It was a bold move, but I had no choice.

Sydney stood up half smiling. "Hi, Kat."

I didn't know when Mom and Sydney had last seen each other. Sydney worked the county food program sometimes, handing out cheese but I had been picking it up myself for a long while. I looked up at my mother's face and she looked about ready to fold over.

"Please. Have a seat." Sydney pointed to the reception chairs. I helped Mom to a chair and sat down next to her.

"Hi, Sydney," Mom slurred.

"It's been a long time, Kat. How're you doing?"

"I've seen better days." Mom chuckled and gave out a quick hack from the cigarette smoke that was fighting its way out.

Sydney forced a grin with a frown creasing along her forehead as my mother's condition was beginning to trouble her just as I had feared.

I spoke up loudly. "Mom said that I can work for you. Right, Mom?"

"Yeah. It's awful nice . . . you offering him a job." She spoke slowly and lifted her eyes up from the floor, looking at Sydney. She was sinking fast.

"Can he work after school sometimes or on the weekends?" Sydney got right to it, recognizing that the window of opportunity was short.

"That'd be fine by me . . . so long as he does good in school."

"I will Mom. Well, that's it! We gotta go." I stood up and grabbed my mother's arm, helping her to find her feet before she passed out right there.

"Okay, why don't you come in on Monday, after school?" Sydney spoke quickly.

I wanted to leap into the air and kick my heels together but didn't want to let go of my mother. "I'll be here."

"Thanks for giving my boy some work. He's my pride and joy. My everything. He'll make you proud, just like he does me." I watched the words fall slowly from her mouth as I smiled inside. I felt a pang of pride and deeply sorry for her.

"Bye, Sydney. See you Monday." I waved with my free hand.

"Bye." Sydney helped with the door as we headed on home. Me, already dreaming about earning enough money to save my mother.

I tucked Mom into bed and opened a can of chicken noodle soup for dinner. We had some saltines that I crushed into it. She was out cold so she couldn't join me. Then I watched an episode of Bonanza on TV. I was spent yet excited that my plan was finally coming together.

Though saving my mother was a pipe dream, that job, and Sydney, changed my life. When I came in to work, she always found something for me to do. I swept the floors, washed windows and learned to use the small washing machine that she used to wash the towels and capes and hang them on the line out back. She even let me throw some of our things in to give them a chance at clean. I helped to sanitize all the implements — combs, brushes, curlers, and yoyette clippies. Sydney kept a steady watch for lice. She had a few good scares, as she would always part her client's hair, gingerly behind the ears, before getting started, and without them knowing that she was on the hunt. If she found a single egg, she would have to send them on their way, until they were egg and lice free, while she sanitized the entire area to fend off an infestation. One day I dropped a whole gallon of cleaning solution on the floor of the shop, sending it flying off everywhere. I hit my knees and said out loud, "I'm so stupid!" Sydney ran over, pulling me up to my feet, staring straight into my eyes. She was mad as hell. Not about the spill, but about what I said. She told me that I was perfect, and that she didn't ever want to hear me talking about such a perfect boy like that ever again! That did something to me. I stood up a little taller and for the first time I felt like something.

My favorite job was helping Sydney with Penelope, the penguin lady. Penelope was a little person with no arms, just little stubs where they should have been. Her legs were really short with just a mangled-looking foot at each ankle. She waddled, just like a penguin, hence her alias. Sydney would clean Penelope's ears and fix her hair, while I would listen to her exciting stories of her circus adventures, and help out by scrubbing her bare feet, that she kept un-shoed so she could use her toes sort of like fingers to manipulate things. Sydney would clip her toenails to her liking, if they had grown too long, leaving a good amount so she could grab a better hold of smaller things. Penelope bragged about me being her personal assistant. I felt honored, as she was a celebrity, having a real live act with Barnum and Bailey during the circus season. One time she got tickets for me and Sydney when the circus travelled near. We got to go to her trailer and meet all the outrageous characters in the camp. There were clowns, a bearded lady, trapeze artists, a lion tamer, and even a giant! I could hardly control my excitement as we walked over to the animal cages. The lions paced back and forth as they growled, and the elephant was as big as a mountain up close. We had to stand back from the spitting camel, as he was a perfect shot, in his act of hitting the bullseye. I was so excited for the start of the show, as we got seated right there in the front row. It was magnificent! And finally, it was Penelope's turn to show her stuff. My stomach was flopping around like a caterpillar on a hot road as she came waddling in. Everyone began to roar with laughter. I was smiling and giggling right along with them. She waddled around the ring grinning from ear to ear. Sydney had done up her deep black hair into a mix of flowers, as they piled high upon her head.

She was so pretty wearing a cape of red velvet with puffs of white fur surrounding her neck and wrists, like a queen. She was leading a miniature pony behind her, who also wore a bouquet of flowers in its mane and tail. On the pony's back sat a Jack Russell Terrier, wearing a skirt and twirling like a dancer in perfect rhythm with each step. Someone behind me shouted, "FREAK! Look at the freaking midget!" As the roar of laughter accelerated, my elation began to falter. The caterpillar was dying a slow death. Anger swelled up, as my face grew hot. I always cried when I got mad. It was an affliction I had to battle throughout all my young life. I saw it as a weakness, but I realize now that it probably saved my life, as I had to deal with the fighting back of my tears always long enough for the anger itself to settle on down.

After the show, I told Sydney that I didn't like the way people made fun of Penelope. She tried to explain to me that the laughter was good for her job. Job security in effect. She had turned her misfortune into her key to success. As long as there was laughter, she would always have a job. I understood the whole money thing, but that still didn't make it right. Sometimes you've just got to draw the line on what's acceptable and making fun of somebody else's adversity was just plain wrong. It had to grieve her deep down. The thoughtless buffoons in the audience were paling the beauty of her with their belittlement, making her a target of their ignorance. This, I would never say to Penelope, but held in the quiver of my disgust.

Chapter 7

It felt like me and Chance had known each other forever. We were the same age and in the same grade, him doing a redo of first grade and me having started school a year late. We were almost always in the same class, except when he had to be pulled out for his reading. He just couldn't make words. He would stutter and spit, trying to make his mouth do justice to written terms. I didn't know why Chance had to have so much trouble picking up reading. I was lucky. It just made sense to me. I could just make the written words roll right over my tongue. It seemed like poor Chance was going to be destined to struggle through the ages, unable to read. Sometimes I would try to help him with his homework, but it made me so frustrated that my stomach would ache from the pain of it. And Chance would just sit back in despair with every attempt to read a sentence. "I'm just too stupid!"

"You are not!" I said, "You're just as smart as anybody else!" I learned, from Sydney, that hopeful words should always be applied. "Your brain just works different. That don't make you stupid." I did my best to help him form the words. "*Jane. See Jane run.* Come on, Chance. Say it, *Jane.*" It was nearly hopeless. I figured out what the patience of Job must have meant. And I believed that God may have left me a little shy of enough patience for Chance's difficulty with words. I still had hope, though. But that was all I had that was of any help.

We became best friends after Chance had the doorknob accident at Kelsey Elementary School. One day I was chasing him down the hallway when someone opened up one of the classroom doors just in time to smack poor Chance clean in the forehead with the doorknob. The knob was kind of hollowed out in the center so that the edges around the hollowed-out part formed a decent edge. I saw it coming and everything went into slow motion as I yelled, *Stop!* But it was too late. That decent edge of the doorknob cut its way clean into Chance's forehead, in a perfect circle. Blood was everywhere. I moaned, "Oh my God!" then quickly raised my hands to my mouth. Had I blasphemed? I had never used God's name quick out like that before. It scared me just about as much as the scene that lay before me. I was sure I was headed straight to hell, would probably make it there faster than Chance would make it to the hospital. Mr. Bridges was the culprit who had handled the door. He scooped Chance up in his arms and ran him to the office. After I prayed for my very soul, I prayed that Chance would be okay. Then I reckoned that I would probably be spared the fire and brimstone since I only used God's name because I really needed Him right then and there.

Chance was back at school the next day, sporting a full purple moon in the middle of his forehead. Everyone gathered around him like a veteran who was home from a long tour of duty. Chance was beaming. It was almost worth the whole doorknob incident to be held in such high regard by all. Him and me recounted the story to nearly everybody in Kelsey Elementary and that healed up scar of a moon is shining on Chance's forehead still.

Chapter 8

Chance's mom, Marny, had a seasonal job at the cannery, where she stood the line watching for rotting spots on the passing fruit, where she would quickly cut them off and lay the fruit back, unblemished, onto the line. She worked nights and slept during the day. We did a lot of tiptoeing around in the daylight hours. Chance's dad, and possibly mine, Joe Riley, was a tall, thin Indian. Cherokee, he said with pride. Half. His hair was long and black. He kept it mostly in a ponytail which he sometimes braided. His eyes were black, too, laying deep under his brow. His face looked older than his years, but his stature was youthfully strong. His mother, Miss Olive, was full-blood Cherokee. She had long black hair that she rolled up into a bun on the top of her head. Beautiful, she was. Even with the deep folds in her soft, leathery face. She had tender brown eyes. You couldn't help but stare. You know how you can just look someone in the eye and see clear inside? That was Miss Olive. Always full of kind words, with a good ear for listening.

She lived right next door to Chance. I liked to sit on the porch at Miss Olive's house, drinking sweet tea, and listening to her stories of the old days on the reservation back in Oklahoma. She always longed to go back, but she just didn't want to leave Joe Riley and Chance. I sometimes wondered if I should just go on and tell her that maybe, just maybe, I belonged to her too. I liked to dream that she was my grandmother. It made me feel all warm inside, knowing that her stories could also be of my people.

Joe Riley worked at the Black Hole. I always looked up to him, even before I started dreaming that he could be my dad. Any man who had a job and provided for his family held a high honor in my regard.

Now, Kelsey had a long history of racial exclusion, as the Klan had built a sturdy hold on the whiteness that still held tight to the town. I stayed way clear of those folks, who kept their capes hanging in the closets of their minds, as they held strong to their idea of the grand whiteness of things. They used their words and fists to sway their children and to force their ignorance on the fold. I would not fall into their false belonging, with something so frail as the thinness of our skin. They were villainous as they protected their stake, chasing down anyone who dared to be dark skinned, and venture too close in.

One day I watched in horror as the Dean brothers beat the shit out of a black man right in the middle of Main Street. The man had the nerve to think he could rent a little place on the far end of town while he worked the crops at nearby farms. He was just minding his own business trying to live his life. He was hurt real bad. An ambulance had to rush him to the hospital. It still pains me that I didn't come to his aid, nor did anyone else who was just standing around watching it all play out in vivid color. Some people were even cheering, like it was a heavyweight boxing match with the heavies picking on a featherweight. The Dean boys didn't even get a slap on the hand. Their father was proud. The farm worker got the message and was never seen again. Workers from Mexico had the same fate. I didn't see it firsthand, but I heard about the underground Klansmen chasing them down for just coming into town for a bite to eat after working all day on the farms. I heard a lot of *off-color* jokes in the school yard and when hanging out by the Hole. It was a serious affliction for our town and *word spread.*

Joe Riley and Miss Olive were the only *non-white* folks *allowed* to live in town. They were allowed a pass since Marny was white and was the daughter of the former mayor. The *Kelsey Klan* didn't cause the family any grief when they moved into town to raise their *mostly* white boy as was the wish of his grandfather, the mayor. That didn't keep folks from talking. Circling the edges, in wait, for just how "Indian" Chance might become. He was the spitting image of his father, to their chagrin.

There was talk of a forced extraction when the mayor died some years later, but by that time, there were enough good souls gathered to fight back on that fierce notion.

I was but eight years old when I watched Dr. Martin Luther King's supporters march from Montgomery to Selma on a newsflash on television, and was horrified when they were brutally beat down with clubs. It was hard to imagine that the color of a man's skin could cause someone to unleash their demons like that. Discrimination is ugly, no matter how it raises its head, by stick or word. I had been on the receiving end of some form of it for most of my life. Not from race, but from circumstances, like people thinking they are better just because they have more money. They place us in a space where they think we belong, in their own minds or in chains. I had a stance that kept me from befriending those that leaned toward the Klan. It wasn't a brave stance that took on the fight, but I kept an eye out for those who spewed hate. They were not my people, as I could not trust anyone who could hold so much evil spiritedness and then use it to lash out on the innocent. I learned hard lessons not to follow along with the crowd, but to walk away. Most times silent, but with steady steps toward my own common sensical right.

One day, a new kid in town, Johnny Brindle, took to making fun of Chance for being of Indian descent. We were out on the playground in a game of kickball when he started shooting off, tapping his hand over his open mouth in a native war cry whenever Chance kicked the ball. He kept chanting louder and louder as Chance went off to chase a ball way out of bounds. The guys all joined right in laughing and making fun of him. It embarrasses me to admit that it sounded funny, and I started to chuckle right along with them, until I looked at Chance. His face was turning red. It wasn't funny to him at all, us making him the butt of Johnny's joke. I felt awful, as Chance ran off. I had fallen right into Johnny's bigoted belittling of Chance. I had to right my wrong and yelled at Johnny to stop it and sneered at the rest of the guys.

"What's wrong you sissified Indian lover?" Johnny snorted.

I just stared my rage into him as my uninvited tears burst out. My fighting them back with all my might.

"Well, we have ourselves a little bitty baby Indian-lover here." Johnny continued to build up his voice to make himself seem all the bigger while pushing me to the ground. None of my *so-called* friends stepped in to help me. I was alone with my convictions and having quickly recognized my best friend's back. I was preparing to ball up my fists to sock him right in his kisser when the noon duty supervisor ran over and grabbed Johnny by the scruff of the neck, hauling him to principal's office. Luckily, all she saw was him push me down, and she couldn't hear the rage that was building up inside of me. I wanted to pummel him with all I had. And might have, had she not intervened. I was ready to take a serious pounding had we gone to blows, Johnny being much bigger than my scrawny self. The thought of his red faced belligerence still makes my blood boil.

I found Chance crying in a bathroom stall. He didn't see me disgrace him, thank God. I would never forget my moral lack and disrespect of my closest friend. I was grateful that he would never know the error of my ways, and to have learned the importance of standing up against folly that can easily disguise itself as fitting in.

Johnny was a constant pain in the side of Kelsey. He collected quite a following at school as kids wanted to find his favor, like a jailhouse bully. He was nothing but a bona fide bigot to me and Chance. We stayed well clear of him and his henchmen.

I would have surely fought for the Union Army had it been in my time. Though slavery was abolished way back when, I could still see the uphill climb through the racism that was alive and well in Kelsey. Being *unwhite* was still an issue, and it seemed that an overall indifference was just as powerful as clubs in keeping it that way.

Chapter 9

One weekend in September Joe Riley and Chance invited me to go deer hunting up in the Sierras. The Sierra Nevadas are a beautiful mountain range that we studied in geography class. It was our neighbor. The thick valley air kept it faded in the distance on most days. In winter, if you held your sight on the eastern view from atop of Red Harrington's barn, you could see the snowcapped mountaintops far across the miles. It is a jagged range of mountains that looks like a saw's edge. *Sierra.* Spanish for saw. It hugs the deep depression of the Central Valley of California on the west side and the Great Basin in Nevada on the east. This was an opportunity of a lifetime to see it in person and not just on the pages of a geography book. Not to mention, they were going to hunt deer.

Mom gave me some grief about going. She didn't much like the idea of me being so far away. I figured she would be happy to have me out of the house, leaving her free to meander on home as she pleased, me not peering from the darkness, assessing. I would have to work on her.

We were both feral in our ways, doing what we had to do to survive, and I spent most of my nights alone with my books, records, writing and my dreaming. I spent my long summer days working at Sydney's, hanging out with Chance, and running around the streets of Kelsey. I spent a lot of time right there in the free library doing my reading, as I was not very good when I scurried home with books on loan. They got lost in the rubble of our lives most usually. I had to spend hard-earned money to pay a couple of fines before I learned how to handle the responsibility of them, in the midst of the chaos of my life.

My record player was a well-worn Silvertone with four speeds: 16, 33, 45 and 78 RPMs. I stood around Mr. Jones' garage sale, loitering over it, wishing I had the money to buy it. When he got finished with his paying customers, he moseyed on over to ask me if I had found something that I wanted to buy. I think he knew full well that his record player had ensnared me. I told him that I was just looking around and didn't have any money. But if I did, that fancy record player is what I would buy. "How much is it?" I asked, as if it mattered.

"How 'bout you rake my leaves for the record player?"

My mouth flew open from the shock that I could be the proud owner of that fine machine.

"Deal?" he asked.

"That's a deal." My voice raised with glee.

He smiled and went over to get me a rake. There were a lot of leaves. I raked every square inch of that huge yard. There wasn't a single leaf to be seen after I finished putting them in the wheelbarrow and hauling them to Mr. Jones' burn pile.

"You did a mighty fine job, Levi. I'm gonna throw in a record for you too. If you come back in two weeks to rake up the leaves again, I'll give you a box of records I have hanging around here." I was all in. I hadn't yet pondered the need for records.

It could use a new needle, per Mr. Jones. He told me to tape a penny or two on top of the needle arm. That might give it a little more life. I could hardly wait to get home to listen to my new record. I taped a penny on top of the arm with some Scotch tape, just like Mr. Jones said, and pulled some lint from the needle, then placed the record on the turntable. I plugged it in, and switched it on, carefully placing the needle on the spinning vinyl, trying all of the speeds, then settling on 78 RPMs, which was actually written on the label. I started the record over. Hovering over it, my soul drew in *Frederic Chopin's Nocturne Op. 9 No. 2.* That day, it was imprinted on me. I listened fully and was spellbound by what I was hearing. The music played right into me, where I could feel it, like goose bumps on my arms. The sound got better as the tube warmed up. I restarted it and was transformed. I lay on my bed with my eyes closed, being carried off to a higher place, somewhere between here and heaven. I listened to that record so many times that I had to add another penny to the needle arm. I returned to Mr. Jones' house two weeks later to clean up the last of the leaves that had fallen from the now-bare trees in his yard. It was worth that hard work and I know I got the better end of the deal. Mr. Jones had forfeited a fabulous collection of records in exchange for my work, including one album, *The Freewheelin' Bob Dylan*. It was risqué to put it mildly. I was entranced by the idea that he could write whatever came across his mind and make a song. Dylan's words inspired my writing to float high above what was appropriate for a boy to spill. There was a kind of knowing that happened in the breach between accepted words and those that rise up to that place where no other word will do, but the ones that cause the ladies to faint. I could use all those words that floated from my imagination and put them to paper, hidden away for only me, an expression of thoughts that carried me high to the lofts of great expectations, then back down to work through the depths of my sadness. There is a sense of healing in the written words that I could twist and turn to my liking, sometimes erasing the most dastardly ones for fear that someone may find me out. Then, sometimes, I would put them back in. But most importantly, I was figuring things out. Asking any question that came to my mind. Nothing was off limits. I found that from the asking, my pencil would jot down answers in free flow. Like magic. I felt that God was reading my words with me, laughing with my jokes, and that He understood why I used such language. I had come to terms with the idea that He was not just hanging out at the

Assembly of Fire and Neighborly Love Church, where I came by my *God feared-ness*, and where my mother got sanctified when we first moved to Kelsey. God was in my room and in the heavens, and somewhere deep inside of me, all at the same time. I could just never believe that He would harm me. That notion tangled up my mind because God is Love and Love is good.

Life is a journey of so many moments of figuring things out from a place of unknowing ignorance. There is a gentleness to it if you start with honest reflection. I felt more of a comfort from my thoughts of God, as I took notice of the truth laid bare from my imagination. It was not to be feared or pressed with guilt. It was my prose, my inner voice of God, that I felt encouraged to write as I worked things out. It was clear that I should not use any expletives in public. I just kept them to myself and God, safe on the pages of my notebooks. I once dreamed that I was the long-lost son of Bob Dylan. It made sense, being that I was an honest poet and song writer, just like him. I had the notion to write him a letter once but changed my mind when I thought it would just get lost in the mix of his full mailbox. I was pretty sure there were a whole lot of other kids wishing they were a part of his fine repertoire.

The other records in my collection could equally curl your hair, including:

Wonderful World and *A Change is Gonna Come*, by Sam Cooke;
Le Vie en Rose and *Autumn Leaves*, by Edith Piaf;

Moonlight Sonata and *Silence* by Beethoven;
Somewhere Over the Rainbow, by Judy Garland;
The Great Pretender, by the Platters;
That's Amore and *Return to Me,* by Dean Martin;
In the Mood and *Moonlight Serenade,* by Glenn Miller;
The Last Farewell, by Roger Whittaker;
They Call the Wind Mariah, by Harve Presnell;
Ombra Mai Fu, from Handel by Enrico Caruso;
and *Ava Maria,* by Schubert.

I learned every word of those songs and felt each note, as I spent my once-lonely nights in the arms of a better God and the melodies. Music, writing and books changed my life, awakening my soul to the reaches outside of the turmoil that laid wait for me, as I meandered the difficulties of life lived in want.

Chapter 10

"Please, Mom. Please let me go with Chance." I was whining.

"It's so far away." She shook her head.

"I know! That's why it's so exciting." I smiled as big as I could, lifting my eyebrows for a more enthusiastic look. "Please, please, please. I wanna go so bad." Mom stared down at the floor, struggling.

"I'll get to see the mountains up close for the first time."

Mom's expression softened. "I'd like you to see those mountains."

I lit up. "I want to, so bad. Can I go . . . please?"

"They're only going for two days?" She was breaking down.

"Yep, Saturday and Sunday."

She hesitated, thinking deeply. I waited. She looked toward the window and gave out a heavy breath and finally gave in. "Okay, I guess. I guess it'll be alright. You can go." She looked worried.

I wrapped my arms around her neck. "Thank you! I love you so much."

She smiled an easier smile than I had seen in a while. "I love you too, Honey. I'm happy that you'll get to see those mountains. I'm sorry that I could never take you there myself."

"It's okay, Mom." I understood. "I can't wait to tell you all about it when I get back." Part of me felt bad that she had never gone either. Life wasn't quite fair.

I whooped and danced all the way to Chance's house to share the news that I could go on my first deer hunt.

Joe Riley made it quite clear that there would be no gun-handling by Chance and me. That was fine with me. I just wanted to head for the hills. One week until the big trip took about two-and-a-half months as near as I could tell. I had never seen days last so long until finally the big weekend arrived. After Chance and I got out of school that Friday we went straight to his house to get all the camping gear together. Joe Riley had to work until 2:00 a.m. the next morning and we would leave right when he got home. Eagle Meadow was the place. It sounded like a song.

Eagle Meadow, Eagle Meadow
Hues of yellow green
Standing tall in the midday sun
Pine trees and trickling stream

Chance and I pulled out the dusty old tent that Joe Riley had picked up about 20 years prior at an old army surplus store. It had a big box of poles and stakes to hold it to the ground. We killed about 10 black widows that were fixed to the wrinkled canvas. We finally decided to lay it out and sweep it with a broom to free the spiders. Then we made sure to stomp each one dead so we wouldn't have to imagine those giant black monsters lowering their fat bodies down to sink their venom-filled fangs in us as we slept. It took us quite a while to feel safe that there were no more live *widders* around. Then we rolled the canvas back up and laid it in the middle of the driveway along with the other camping gear. Joe Riley and Chance each had a sleeping bag, but I brought an old wool blanket from my bed and a sheet. That would have to do.

I could hardly wait to see the gun. I had never seen a real one before. I imagined taking that gun and having a big gun fight in the middle of Main Street. Everyone in Kelsey would be standing along the edge of the road hollering and making wagers. I was standing tall, wearing all black except for my white Stetson. A brand-new beaver-skin. I wore a turquoise bolo. I looked sharp. My boots were snakeskin. Black, of course. Under those boots were just an old pair of white tube socks with a hole in each big toe, but no one in Kelsey would ever guess. The man at the other end of the street was walking slowly toward me. He had a big stride and a slight limp, kind of like John Wayne, but he was a bad guy. He was tall and as near as I could tell, he was thick. He wore a long canvas duster with a hood. The hood was pulled clean over his head. Under that hood was . . . nothing. He had no face at all. This hollow of a man was standing ready for me. A cold chill ran down my neck. The goose bumps rose high, making me shiver. I blinked hard to bring myself back to reality and looked over at Chance who was tucking a towel into his duffle bag. I poked my jacket down into the duffle and an extra pair of socks, just in case my feet got wet. That was Mom's idea. She had huddled around me as I gathered my things to go. She was sad for missing me already, but happy that I was able to go see the beautiful mountains in the distance that called for me.

"I wish you had a better coat," Mom said while holding up my raggedy one.

"It's real warm, Mom. Don't worry. It'll be just fine."

"You got any better socks?" as she rummaged through my pile. Most had holes in them. The good thing was that they were all white, well, *dingy* white, so there was never any need for matching. Not that I would have bothered anyway. "I'll have to get you some new ones. These are all worn out." She looked disappointed as she rustled through the mess.

"I'm good, Mom. Don't worry."

She started to whimper, as she sat down on my mattress. It was a dreadful sound. It always troubled me when she folded up. "I love you so much and I've been a terrible mother." She bawled like a lost calf.

"No, you haven't. You done the best you could."

"I didn't!"

"Yes, you did. I love you, Mom. I'm really happy." I didn't want to settle in to the long and winding sadness that would rise to the surface sometimes. I felt sorry for her and put my arms around her neck. I wondered if she ever had anybody to hug her when she was little. She felt more like a child than a grown-up person. I stepped back and grabbed my bag. "Look, I get to go to the mountains, because you said so. That makes me happy, Mom." I meant it and I also knew I had to say something that would ease her so I could get going.

She got up and went to the bathroom to blow her snotty nose. I peaked in. "You okay Mom?"

"Yeah, I'm alright. You go and have yourself some fun. I love you."

"I love you too." I ran quickly out the door before the echo of her cries tried to lure me back to console her. I hoped that she would be okay as a swarm of guilt leaned heavy on me.

Joe Riley finally got home as Chance and I had drifted in and out of sleep for about the umpteenth time. We jumped up with excitement. Miss Olive had made us some tunafish sandwiches wrapped up in wax paper and fried up a mess of chicken gizzards and hearts. She put them in a paper sack that had soaked up most of the grease and placed all of the food into a small box and topped it with three big shiny apples. She had filled two milk jugs and a small canteen with water for our thirst. It would be a fine feast for a group of mountain men.

Joe Riley went to his room and came back with the gun. It was a Remington 30.06. The wood on the stock was dark from age and deer-killing. The bluing was scraped off all along the barrel. That gun had seen many a wild beast and at least one man in its crosshairs and the stories were written on every inch of it. Per Miss Olive, in its early days it had belonged to a Cherokee warrior named Light Deer Foot. It had been a noble gun, providing food for the Indian children of days past. There was a story of Light's best friend, Tho, who had killed a man. The Cherokee council sentenced Tho to be shot and allowed him to choose his own shooter. Tho chose Light to conduct the sentencing. It was told that Light stood fast taking his aim and shot Tho to death with a single bullet to the heart. No one knows if Light was a master marksman or such a bad shot that even his attempt to simply injure Tho completely missed the mark, thereby killing his best friend. That gun had killing history. You could almost see it billowing like smoke from the barrel. Joe Riley carefully placed the gun in the gun rack that stretched across the back window of the truck. Then he went back in and brought out his guitar and a large Buck knife in a holster with a stone for grinding the sharp back into the blade. He fed the holster belt through the belt loops of his jeans and fastened the long tie string around his right thigh to keep the holster secured to his leg. We loaded up the gear and were ready to hit the road. Joe Riley had gassed up at Mr. Bill's single pump before work and checked all the vital fluids. He even scrubbed on the windshield and squeegeed it slick for better deer-seeing odds.

It was nearing 4:00 a.m. when we finally hopped in the truck and headed east down Main Street. I sunk low in the seat as I peered out the window into the darkness, fearful of catching a glimpse of the *man with no face*. The old truck made it through town without so much as a belch. Me and Chance drifted in and out of restless sleep as we quickly put miles between us and Kelsey.

Before long we were winding through the hills approaching Lover's Leap. The leap is a high cliff where it is told that an Indian boy from one tribe and an Indian girl from another leapt to their death. They had fallen in love, but their tribes were enemies so they could not live in this life together. They held each other close and fell gently off wrapped in their forbidden embrace, away from the simple minds that forced their foolish fate. How deep their despair must have been. There is romance in the tale, but the truth of these two young lives lost, was senseless. They gave away any chance of hope. They killed it. All because they believed in the label of enemy, and there being different clans of humanity. How easily they became labeled, just because someone speaks of *a difference* of some sort, and then carries it steadfast for generations. Once a person gets labeled, it's like affixing the words onto their forehead. Some folks can never rip themselves free of some silly words. They sort of get branded on them. Clear to the bone. I never liked labels. People were already labeling Chance as stupid because he couldn't read. My worst fear was that he would start to believe it too. And I overheard one lady try to brand me when

I was within earshot, *that poor little bastard.* I had to be careful that that poor and pitiful notion didn't stick around so long that it would leave me there to expect nothing better for myself.

I had a lot in common with those lovers standing there on that leap when I was nearly pushed to my death by the banter of a crowd in pursuit of my end in the summer before kindergarten. It has haunted me for all these many years to recall the feelings from that day, as it was a near miss by the kiss of death. It pains me to remember . . .

On that day, my faithful dog, M'lady, died while trying to give birth to some very large pups, as was her fate after locking up with Grover, a large and likable Labrador Retriever, who had found her in the heated way. She was a terrier mix so it was a death sentence for her to be in the family way by Grover. M'lady was on my bed whimpering and in big trouble. I ran to Mom's room, but she was not there, as usual. I put M'lady on a blanket on the floor and laid down next to her throughout the night, as I worried and waited for her pups to arrive. None came. I laid there helplessly until she gave up and died. I was so distraught, as I shared this news with the Hole gang outside the gathering place at the Hole that morning, after burying my sweet M'Lady in a hole she had dug in the back yard. Without giving much thought to the words, I blurted out that I wished I was dead so I could be with M'Lady. Edger Watts, a kid that I always watched from the eye in the back of my head, said, "Why don't you go down to the canal and jump in?

Then you can go be with M'Lady." The pitiless words stunned me.

Everyone gathered around me saying, "Are you gonna do it? Are you really gonna jump in the canal?" Somehow, my five-year-old mind saw no other choice. I didn't want to do it, but there was quite a bit of pressure mounting, and I found myself being led to the canal by the procession. My guardian angel started flapping her wings wildly and the hair on the back of my neck started to bristle. I felt the shadowy fear of my impending death. I walked slowly, trying to figure out how to get out of it. It, having created a life of its own, my undoing. My innocent mind was racing, with few options that could save my life. I was on a runaway train of peer pressure and thought about saying, *I'm not gonna do it.* But I could see that the disappointment of the crowd would be insurmountable if I let loose my cowardice. I somehow had to save face. Nearly six-year-old kindergarten face, before the mob. They had grown excited with an infectious giddiness. After what seemed like a lifetime, my lifetime, we had all walked to the edge of the main canal. The water was high, as we were at the peak of summer. And it was swift. I did not know how to swim. I had only ever *swum* in the smaller canals that fed from this one. In those, I could touch bottom. Shoed, of course, since broken bottles and rusty nails were like land mines waiting for feet laid bare, I had learned. I was in a death trap, standing on that edge, against every warning of every parent of every kid there. As my mind raced to save myself, I wondered if I might be able to reach the other side if I jumped. I pondered it momentarily, as I assessed the swiftness of the water, and the thick amount of litter that was spinning around on the surface, unable to pass beneath the Water Street Bridge, the garbage sloshing up against the bottom of the bridge rail. I knew I would not make it across. Too risky. But did I have a choice? I was either going to jump to my death and save face, or walk away, a coward for life in the eyes of my peers. Both options would be grievous. My heart raced from the fear of the great unknown. I began to worry that someone may just push me, as their impatience waned. My guardian angel's wings must have flung me back with a swat, as I spun around to face the wild-eyed crowd and, with great relief, the words fell out, "Naw, I'm not gonna do it." I stared up to heaven and then lowered my head in despair and relief and walked slowly back toward home. I could feel the disappointment of the deathwatch with each step.

"I knew he wouldn't do it," I heard. I was a laughingstock but remained insufferably alive, no thanks to the Hole gang. From that day forward I *mentally* disavowed myself from them as a whole. Each was my friend, but something unworldly happened to them as a group. They could never be fully trusted with something so sacred as life itself. That fear of death, I would always remember. *Stand up tall, kid. Think for yourself, kid. Don't let anybody push you to the brink of anything.*

These thoughts laid heavy on my mind as we drove by Lover's Leap, and passed as the road opened up before us, settling back into the quiet place where my greatest lessons lie for safe keeping.

An American flag waved in the breeze as the headlights flashed long across the high rock face as we cornered the bend. The moon shone bright and glimmered upon the river below.

The radio in the old truck was blaring in and out as the crooked coat hanger that was used as an antenna would pull in a signal now and then. Joe Riley would just sing out whatever words were dropped by the airwaves. He tapped his fingers softly to complete the rhythm on the steering wheel and hummed the words that he didn't know. Chance and I rolled back and forth in the seat with the winding of the road and the gentle sway of the truck sputtering its way further and further away from Kelsey.

I was awakened by a lurch when we hit a big bump as we headed off the pavement and down onto the dusty road that led to Eagle Meadow. The sun was considering it's start of the new day as the darkness began to filter away. There was a strong scent of manzanita and pine. You could nearly smell the dew resting on the ground. "Are you boys awake?"

"Yeah," said a startled and just-awakened Chance and I in unison.

"Are you ready to hunt some deer?" That brought us both straight up tall in our seats.

"Where are they?" I asked as I rubbed the sleep from my eyes.

"They're anywhere and everywhere. You've got to keep a good look out."

We rolled slowly down the dirt road watchful for deer. We were craning our necks as we poured over every hillside. Finally, we reached a fork in the road and veered right as we inched over a rocky creek bed. After several more miles, we pulled up under a large pine tree. "How does this spot look for a campsite?" Joe Riley asked.

"Looks good to me," said Chance.

"Alrighty then, this is it."

It was a perfect spot. There was a nice flat place for the tent and a big rock that we could use as a table. Someone had nailed a long nail in a tree that we would use to hang our lantern. We were giddy as we unloaded the truck. Then we began to put the tent together. Joe Riley said that any idiot could put it up in about five minutes. It took us about an hour to match all the poles together and finally get the thing up. But once up, it was fancy. And there were no spiders to be seen. We laid out our bedding inside and zipped the tent closed so no mosquitoes could hang out in waiting for a late-night snack. We gathered some wood for a fire and prepared it so it would only require a quick match to light upon our return from the hunt. We each grabbed our tunafish breakfast sandwich, which was the best I had ever eaten. It had white onions, pickles, celery, and even boiled eggs in it, all swirled around with mayonnaise. I marveled at the flavors in every bite.

"Are you boys ready for a hike?"

"Yeah," shouted Chance.

I smiled with excitement. "I'm ready."

"Well then, let's go."

Joe Riley put the three apples in a knapsack along with the canteen. "The deer should be finished feeding by now and are probably all bedded down for a nice nap in the shade, but we'll take a scout around to see if we can find some sign."

"What kind of sign?" I asked.

"We'll look for some well-traveled trails and fresh deer shit," Joe Riley mused. He didn't curse in front of us kids much, but it was in fact . . . *shit*; that we would be looking for. "We call that a sign. Have you ever seen deer shit, Levi?"

I shook my head. "Nope."

"It looks like a pile of brown peas," said a tickled Chance.

"Brown peas?" I laughed.

"Um um good," sang Chance, "Um um good . . ."

". . . that's why Campbell's soup's are um um good," I chimed in.

"Let's go find us some sign and track us a buck," said Joe Riley.

I wondered if it would be alright to say *deer shit*. After all, it really was *shit*. What else would I call it? Deer poop? Deer crap? I decided to try and talk some *deer shit* a little later when I felt the time was right.

Joe Riley grabbed his gun out of the truck and pulled a little bag from out of a box behind the seat. "Come here, Levi. Chance has been around guns all his life, but I want to show you a little somethin' about this gun." He began to tell me things that a son should know. I imagined him being my dad, teaching me like I was his very own blood. He was a good teacher and a good dad. This I knew. I just didn't know for sure that he was my own. I hoped though. "First of all, you should always treat a gun as if it's loaded. There have been many a man shot by an *unloaded* gun. There can be a bullet stuck in where you can't even see it and that can get you into trouble if you don't know that. And sometimes people just plain forget to unload their guns if you can imagine that. It can be a very deadly mistake." Joe Riley took two bullets out of the little bag and shoved them one after the other into the bottom of the gun. "See there? You can't even see them now. And see this little button here by the trigger?"

"Uh huh."

"This is called the safety. Do you know what that's for?"

I thought, "Our safety?"

"Chance, can you tell Levi about the safety?"

Chance grinned with pride as he spoke veteran gun talk. "The safety is supposed to lock the trigger so that you can't pull it and make the gun shoot."

"Good. Now tell Levi what else you know about the safety."

"You should never trust the safety."

Joe Riley continued, "That's right. You should never trust anything about a gun. You must always be on guard when you or anyone else around you is handling a gun. Don't ever let the barrel point in any direction that you would not feel safe pulling the trigger. This means that you never let the barrel face in the direction of a person or a building. You never know when a gun, especially an old gun like this one, will just go off. When you handle a gun, you should point the barrel down toward the ground or up toward the sky. If you point it toward the ground while you're walking or climbing, you want to be very careful not to let dirt poke into the end of the barrel. This could be very dangerous when you went to shoot the gun. The bullet could be blocked, and the entire barrel could blow apart."

I imagined the gun barrel of Elmer Fudd when he was out hunting Bugs Bunny. It seemed he always blew out the end of his gun. I had no idea that it was probably dirt that had filled his barrel.

I could not help but feel the void that created my hunting ignorance. All because I didn't have a dad to teach me such necessities. It made me feel a little sorry for myself for being unfathered. I hoped that Joe Riley was trying to make up for that.

He continued, "If you point your gun toward the sky, you want to be careful when you're walking downhill. If I am in front of you with my gun over my shoulder pointed toward the sky, it could be pointing right at your head if you are following directly behind me going down a hill. So, let's watch out for this gun together. Everyone needs to watch out for each other too, okay?

"Okay," I said, feeling a little scared of that loaded gun. It must have shown.

"It's good to be extra careful boys. That's the respect you must have around a gun. Okay fellas, let's hit the trail." Joe Riley rechecked the safety, as if it mattered, and slung the rifle strap up over his shoulder with the barrel aimed straight toward the sky. I looked up, calculating my safety in regard to the gun barrel. I didn't need to worry as long as that barrel of that always-loaded gun was looking up. But I would keep my eye out, that's for sure.

The sun was well up into the mid-morning sky. "Where does the sun come up in the morning Chance?"

"In the East."

"Right. Levi, do you know where the sun sets?" He questioned fatherly.

"In the West?"

"That's right. The sun is your friend when you're in the wilderness. By watching the rising and setting of the sun you can always have a good idea where you are and about what time it is. Always pay attention to your friend, the sun. He's your compass and your guide."

We hunters headed north along the tree line next to a large expanse of meadow. The sun was looking down on us from the eastern sky, still morning. We were happy and excited and watchful for deer shit and the barrel of that loaded gun.

We then turned east into the trees and trudged uphill into the deep forest. Our steps were loud yet soft, as we crunched through the sea of pine needles and fallen twigs from centuries of their falling in the same place, untouched by man. The giant trees stood close together and shadowed the ground. We walked carefully and steadily into the thick trees that towered overhead. My senses were sharp as we made our way through the forest. The smell was so . . . *clean*. Like Pine Sol, but real, asking my lungs to breath it in deeply. Joe Riley spotted a deer trail and stopped to inspect the tracks. "This one here is a buck," he whispered. "You can tell by the long hoof prints pushed deep into the dust followed by the two dots behind the hooves. The weight of the buck will create a deeper track than a doe. This is what we've been looking for." He stepped over a fallen timber lying long on its side. Much of the wood had rotted away from years of weathering on the ground. There was a place next to the log where the pine needles and twigs had been smoothed away. "This is a deer bed," he said, "or that of a bear."

I looked quick at him. "A bear?" I imagined a big bear lying in wait for us. I was a little wide-eyed.

Joe Riley continued, "Don't you worry about any old bears. They can hear and smell us coming from a long way off and are more afraid of us than we are of them. They will ditch any scent of us quick."

I decided that I could trust that he was probably right, considering he had never been mauled by a bear after all the times that he had been in this territory hunting.

"This is just the kind of place where deer will lay in the heat of the day. We should just sit a spell and wait to see if a deer will come walking through." We each made a seat on the log and sat quietly waiting for a big buck to venture by.

We watched as a chipmunk climbed up to the top of a majestic Mariposa pine. It moved slowly out on a high branch and nibbled a pinecone free from the lofty limb. It tumbled, bouncing from branch to branch before it crashed to the ground. We giggled as we watched the chipmunk scamper back down to scope out its treasure. A cool breeze was blowing across our cheeks and through the flowing bows of the trees, making a soft whooshing sound. It was peaceful and quiet, yet full of the soft sounds of the forest.

We sat quietly, there on that log. The birds soared high from tree to tree singing to each other a repetitive song. It sounded as if they were having a conversation.

"Where are you?" asked one bird.

"I'm over here," answered the other.

The smell of real pine gave me a profound feeling of peace for the first time in my life, giving me a strong sense of wholeness. Me and the natural world were together at that very moment sharing each breath. It felt surreal. We sat long on that log just being there in the midst of all that makes sense in the world. Silent and still, just being there. I never wanted to leave.

Finally, Joe Riley whispered, pointing to the north, "Well, fellas, would you like to hike up to the top of that ridge?" We both nodded, as we rose to our feet and headed up. I looked back at my throne on that log. It was a snapshot that I would hold in my memory bank whenever the world was not so favorable.

It was a steep climb. We had to stop every once in a while, so that we could catch our breath. We didn't need to worry about the gun because it was pointed to the sky and Joe Riley was in the lead so that barrel was nowhere close to anyone's head as we trudged up. We had climbed up several yards when a deer crashed through a thicket of manzanita and ran straight up and over the top of the ridge. My heart threatened to beat out of my chest. "It's a doe," said Joe Riley in a half-whisper. He had already pulled his gun from his shoulder and was readying himself to shoot had it been a buck. That deer sprang so high and darted off so quickly that had it been a buck, I wondered how Joe Riley would have ever been able to pull his gun up in time to shoot before it went out of sight. Yet, after pondering for a moment, I realized that everything seemed to go into slow motion when the deer had jumped. Joe Riley was calm and on the ready. My heart was still galloping as we walked up to where the deer had been bedded down, not 40 yards from where we had sat on that log. We had all been together, in the same presence with our stillness. Us and the deer. Joe Riley knelt down to feel the warm earth that was left behind by the startled doe. Me and Chance reached down to feel it too. I felt the warmth, thinking about the deer just lying there, feeling so safe and content, until we tromped in. The speed of her getaway was incredible, as she sprung up and out of sight in a blink. We stood there silently listening to the gentle breeze and letting our hearts settle down enough to continue the climb up the ridge.

As we trekked up the final rocks onto the crest, I was in awe of the landscape. There were gently rolling waves of low-growing, leafy shrubs with tufts of yellow floating in the breeze. I turned to look back at where we had just hiked from and there above the trees was the view of a massive mountain range. They looked as if they wore a coat of pines and armor of rock. It was a magnificent site. "Whoa," said Chance as he took in the view. Joe Riley turned to have a look. We stood still, listening to the quiet rustle of the leaves as they flickered in unison with the breeze. Two hawks circled high in the deep blue sky. We hunters stood silent with the view and the delicate air that rustled through the trees. Our senses on high in perfect union with the wonders of the earth.

The sun was beginning to lay toward the west, as if resting atop the mountains. Joe Riley said he figured it to be about 4:30 pm. He pulled out the three shiny apples that Miss Olive had packed, throwing one to each of us and sinking his teeth deep into his, nearly pulling half of it into his mouth in one bite. I made quick work of mine and my hunger was begging for more. We each had a couple of swallows of water that helped to satisfy our pangs.

"Well, fellas, let's circle over the top of this ridge and head back around to camp. We've got a couple hours 'til twilight, so that should give us plenty of time to get back before dark." We headed off in single file, as I filled my senses with the sights and scents of that magical place, imprinting them firmly in my memory.

We walked quietly, as the sun lowered behind a great peak, casting its shadow over the entire hillside. As we carefully moved toward the valley floor, Joe Riley spotted some peas. He passed the toe of his boot gently over them to find that they were soft. Me and Chance bent down to take a good look at the peas. "Deer shit," I muttered under my breath. I looked over at Chance and smiled.

"Fresh deer shit," grinned Chance. We crept down, down, down the dry creek bed until we came to a small meadow before the final drop down toward camp. There were what looked like dried cabbage plants over the entire meadow. Each step echoed a loud crunch under our feet. As we prepared to drop the final decent, Joe Riley stopped cold in his tracks. There, to his right, was a lone buck standing, staring at us, ears wide, antlers high. "It's a buck!" said Chance in a broken whisper. Joe Riley, dropped slowly to one knee and laid his eye toward the sights along the weathered barrel. Chance put his fingers in his ears, and I followed his lead. Everything went into slow motion, as my heart began to beat in my ears. The deer just stood there, as if he had just been waiting for us. *Pow!* The sound echoed loudly between the mountain ranges. The buck stretched its neck out long and stumbled. Joe Riley put another sight on him and, *pow*, quickly drew the life from the stately creature. Its death was swift as it succumbed to its fate. I was literally shell-shocked, as I watched, wide-eyed, as its life was taken from him. My heart raced from the adrenaline that poured through my veins. I had mixed emotions between exhilaration and grief, as my mind was trying to make sense of it. Through all the talk of deer hunting, I had not thought through to the actual killing. It happened so fast, the stillness, the excitement, the gun, and then he was gone in a flash. Still. Lifeless. Gone. I tried to gather myself, not wanting to play the fool, as my emotions ran the length of their tether. I concentrated hard to regain my composure, biting my lips and then peering away, trying to find myself by looking out over the landscape around us, which was vivid green and yellow. The sky was a deep shadow blue. The air was soft and cool. I was very much alive. I slowly gathered myself, as we started walking toward the buck that lay some 50 yards away.

As we carefully approached, Joe Riley held his hand up to motion us to stop. "We need to be sure he's completed his journey." Joe Riley whispered, as he slowly crept up to the deer's motionless body and nudged it gently with the gun barrel. No response. He laid his hand softly upon the deer's tawny coat. He then motioned us to join him. Chance had experienced this before and ran quickly to his father's side. I felt a pang of uneasiness as they stood entwined. I took a long deep breath and moved in, trying to appear unscathed by the dead deer and unmoved by the deep connection between Chance and *our* dad. I walked closer and stood over the lifeless body of the deer. The warm steam from its life energy was still floating up and into the cool air. I started to tremble, as my mind raced. This was not the first time I had seen a dead body, and it was not the memory of M'Lady that was calling me back . . .

Chapter 11

I woke to Mom crying. It was nothing new, but these cries were different. I found her in the bathroom, in the bathtub, filled with bright red water. "Mom!" I gasped. "I'll get help!" As I ran for the door.

"No, Levi. I need you! Come back!" I stopped and turned to her.

"Levi, come here." Her voice was weak.

As I walked toward her, she unfolded a bloody towel that she held above the red sea. I jumped back. "This is Violet, your sister. Here, take her. Careful now. The cord is still attached." I reached down as she placed the baby in my arms. I could see the cord trailing off into the water. My head was spinning from the fright, as I was barely able to hold on. She was blue. Unmoving. I nearly dropped her, as I shuddered, but knew I must keep her from the water. She was so tiny and perfect, except that she was dead. I stared at her, shaking, as the realization set hold.

"Stand right there but turn around." Mom muttered.

I was confused but turned to face the wall, shaking. I heard the tub squeak as Mom pulled herself up, water dripping.

"Don't look Levi."

"Okay," I whimpered.

The shower curtain slid across the pole. "Okay, hand her to me." As I turned, Mom was behind the curtain, wrapped in a towel. She reached around to take the baby from my arms. "Go get my robe. It's at the foot of my bed."

I ran to her room without saying a word, my mind filled with trouble, then ran back with her robe and held it out to her.

She reached from behind the curtain and grabbed it. I stood still, trembling. She let out a gasp like she was in pain, bending slightly forward. "I gotta clean myself up." She looked like a girl who had just climbed out of a swamp. "Go to your room now." Her voice was weak.

"Mom?" My lips barely able to form the word.

"It's okay. Just go to your room. I'll be out in a little bit."

I turned to go.

"Close the door."

I gently pulled it closed and walked numbly to my room. I stood there not knowing what to do, so I just climbed into my bed and curled up into a little ball of sorrow unable to free my mind of Violet's little face.

As I was drifting off to sleep, Mom called to me, "Levi. I need you. Come here."

"Mom?" My voice tried to awaken.

"Come here." Her voice sounded far away.

I sprung out of bed realizing that I wasn't just having a bad dream. When I opened the bathroom door, Mom was standing in her robe holding the baby, that was wrapped in a clean towel, with the cord still dangling down into the tub around the shower curtain.

"I can't move until you get me the scissors."

My heart began to beat fear into me. "Mom?"

"I need to cut this cord to free her."

"What do you mean?"

"The cord is attached to the afterbirth. I have to cut it to free her from it. That's the way it's done."

A faint relief took me to the kitchen to get the scissors from the junk drawer. I gripped them tight and walked fast back to the bathroom. I knew better than to run with scissors.

"Put them on the counter."

I did as I was told.

"Come here and hold her."

I moved closer as she placed the baby into my arms. The arms that yearned for her to smile up at her brother.

Mom picked up the scissors and I jumped back instinctively with my back clutched tightly to the wall, as she moved in and started cutting her way through the cord that came out of Violet's belly and ran down into the tub behind the curtain. I kept my eyes peeled on the scissors, in case they slipped toward the baby's body or mine. Once the cord was cut, it oozed a dark goo. Mom placed the towel back up over the nub left from the scissors. "I've got to clean this all up.

Get me the dustpan and the burn barrel garbage." Mom snapped like a sergeant.

"Mom! We can't put her in the burn barrel!"

"Dear God, Levi, do you think I'm crazy?"

Yes! My mind screamed. *Yes, I'm afraid that you really are crazy.* Dread was dripping down my face at not knowing what was coming next.

"I would never hurt your sister!" She was angry and jerked Violet from me.

I ran to the kitchen and returned with the trashcan and dustpan.

"Set 'em here."

I did, looking questioningly at Mom, afraid to rile her with my questions.

She handed my sister back to me. "Turn around."

I did, but then turned my head slightly to see what Mom was up to. She pulled back the shower curtain and used the dustpan to dip out the god-awful stuff that would not go down the drain, and poured it into the can with the garbage. It felt like a crime scene. I was in a daze, just doing as I was told, like a soldier in battle. My mind questioning, but doing my duty at all costs, at my fearless leader's command. When she was finished with the grotesque task, she grabbed the can of madness. I followed her to the back door, and stood there, watching, as she went out back and made an inferno, inside the burn barrel, big enough to cook up all the evidence of Violet's birth. I was afraid that Mom might want to toss Violet in, so I stayed inside the back door with my dead sister.

I had figured I would run if she was in danger of the fire. Mom stared into the silence, as the smoke billowed high into the air. I will never forget that strange smell of burning paper with a mix of barbecue. Mom used the burning stick to mix around the contents of the barrel until it was burned beyond recognition, and only then, did she head back inside.

Mom wrapped Violet in a clean blue flowery towel. We didn't have a pink one, which she toiled over, but finally settled for the best that she could do. Mom held and rocked Violet for two days, until she started to smell. I stayed home from school those days, tormented about what would become of Violet, and us, if anyone found us with our dead baby. Finally, at dark, on that second night, peering through the slits of her swollen eyes, Mom told me that we needed to dig a grave for Violet. The ache in my stomach felt relief, as the charade would finally end. My sister was dead and, finally, we both knew it.

Mom searched for a makeshift coffin and pulled out an old overnight case that I had found for her on one of my escapades to the dump. It was orange-ish. Leather. Well-worn, with a broken handle, which was surely why it made its way to the heap.

"I want to write her a poem."

"That would be so nice, Levi." Mom's eyes were wet and rimmed in red.

I pulled a piece of paper from my notebook, and a pink crayon from my Crayola box. Then I went to the kitchen table to write my sister's poem. My mind went to that place where words flow in, looking up toward heaven, at the cobwebs that hung like lace from the corner of the ceiling. I figured out the words from my heart, before finally putting them to paper. I sent them to Violet, as I read them out loud to my mother:

Sweet dreams for you
Sweet Violet of mine
You leave us now
To heaven you climb

"Yes, she's in heaven now," Mom whispered. She placed Violet inside the case, wrapped in her flowery blue burial cloth.

I ran and got my favorite marble, a cat's eye, that I had won from a big game in the school yard. I placed it along with the poem, inside with Violet, then Mom clicked the case closed with its latch. She picked a spot out back, right up next to the house, and I started digging. Mom laid the case in. Then took it back out. "A little deeper." Then, "A little deeper. It needs to be deep enough, so the dogs won't dig it up."

The vision of my sister being drug right out of her grave, kept me digging much deeper than I thought I was able. Finally, Mom and I felt satisfied that it was deep enough to hold her safe from the dogs. Mom slowly poured a handful of dirt over the makeshift casket, then sat down and watched me quietly, as I put in one shovelful after another of dirt into the grave until Violet was safely buried in the ground. "We can never tell anyone about her, Levi."

"I know, Mom. I know," I whispered as my tears fell in silence over my sister's grave.

"Dust to dust," Mom whispered, as she wept, then rose up slowly from her pew on the ground and walked straight to her bed where she stayed for days and days. There were never any more babies, that I knew of, but I would always know that I had a sister, whose body was buried in the cold dark earth behind our house, whose spirit would somehow be waiting for me in heaven.

Chapter 12

Joe Riley grabbed his deer tag from his jean pocket, completed it and tied it onto the deer's antler with a piece of string. Then he knelt beside the deer and with a nod, both Chance and I knelt down beside him. Joe Riley bowed his head solemnly, placing his hand on the deer's body. He spoke slowly, "Lord, you have brought this humble spirit upon our path so that we may partake of its flesh for the nourishment of our bodies. We respect the great sacrifice of this animal for our own lives. Its life, it has given to us, and its soul will forever be a part of our very own. These offerings, we accept with humbleness of spirit and thanksgiving." I stood still, my head bowed, taking in each word, feeling somehow consoled and connected to God, the Great Spirit of things. There was a feeling in the air that was bigger than life itself. There was an understanding between the spirit of the animal, which had given its life, and us, who had taken it. We were now one. I was very moved by the sanctity of the moment.

I wished that I had given Violet a proper eulogy. The intensity of her memory was set free to circle around within me. I struggled as I did not want them to know of my secret that showed itself as weeping. *But they could not see my thoughts. How could they?*

After a few moments of silence, except for the choking back of my sniveling, Joe Riley walked over to me and laid his hand gently on the top of my head. "It's okay, Son, you've been witness to the miracle of life and death and you will never take either for granted." *He called me Son.* Oh, how I wanted to fall into his arms and tell him that I had already been consecrated. I wanted him to hug me and tell me that he was my dad and that he would make everything in my life okay from now on. He reached out his hand to give mine a shake and I flew into his arms, having lost all sense of myself. I held him tight and wept. I could not stop, nor escape the haunting memories of Violet, lying deep in the ground outside my bedroom window. Finally, I was able to pull myself away. I bowed my head, ashamed that I lost control of myself and embarrassed for acting like a fool in front of these seasoned hunters. Joe Riley grabbed my shoulder. "I respect you, Buddy. You have heart. So much heart." His eyes were wet. "What happened here today will change the course of your life. You've shown great understanding for the depth of your witness. I'm proud of you, Levi." *But he didn't really understand.* He turned to Chance, who offered his hand to his dad with a firm squeeze. He smiled a knowing smile at his son, who had been baptized with the glory of deer killing multiple times before. Chance came over and punched me in the arm, as he cocked his head slightly with a grin. I punched him back, as we both danced around each other in a mock wrestling match, as our laughter broke the silence of the forest and the pain in my soul. It helped me find my way back. I was gonna be okay and my best friend, Chance, didn't hold a grudge for me glomming on to his dad.

Joe Riley stood there smiling, as he watched our antics. It felt good to run and to feel my heart pounding the blood back through my body and away from my painful memories. When we finally exhausted ourselves and fell to the ground heaving, Joe Riley unsheathed his Buck knife and got to work on his kill. Chance and I got up and watched, as he carefully placed the razor-sharp tip of the blade under the hide on the lower belly of the deer. He was like a master surgeon as he skillfully pulled the knife up the belly, just under the hide, about 12 inches. There was no blood. He then pushed the tip of the blade through the skin on the belly and carefully followed the same line that he had just cut under the hide. This opened up the abdominal wall in which he reached to firmly pull the intestines out onto the ground. He then reached inside the abdominal cavity and released the entire intestines and the liver which rolled out gently. He inched up into the chest cavity and freed the heart and lungs. Chance and I watched quietly as Joe Riley continued our spiritual journey and respectfully removed the organs from the carcass and placed them in a white cotton flour sack. He handed them over to Chance, who rolled them up tightly and placed them inside Joe Riley's knapsack.

"You guys go find a couple of lodge poles for our sled." Chance and I quickly found two fallen limbs for creating the sled. Joe Riley untied a rope that was tethered to his pack and carefully tied the carcass to the poles with it, creating a sled. Night was upon us as we headed down toward camp. Joe Riley held the lead as we followed closely behind. We had only been about 300 yards from camp. I was amazed at how Joe Riley led us straight to camp pulling the deer behind him on the makeshift sled. Chance had pulled out the flashlight not 20 yards from the campsite. As we dragged in, Joe Riley stopped and handed Chance his Zippo lighter.

"Light the lantern Chance, and Levi, you light the campfire." I wasn't expecting to be honored with such a responsibility. It was something that a son would do. Chance grabbed the lantern and began to pump the kerosene tank. Once the resistance on the pump was just right, he clicked the Zippo to ignite a long thin flame. He held it up to the hole just under the bell of the lantern, turned the kerosene on and the mantel lit quickly with a flash of white light. He walked over and hung the handle over the long nail that was protruding from the pine tree, then handed the Zippo to me. He reached down to scoop up some dry pine needles and laid them under the fine kindling that we had set up before we left for the hunt. I stroked the lighter which drew, again, a flame. I held it up to eye level and watched it for a few moments, mesmerized by the fire. I then crouched down to set the fire to the pine needles which quickly licked the kindling to a full yellow flame. I stood up, pleased with the completion of my charge, breathing in the gentle smoke of the campfire, a scent that lingered on my clothes and will stay in my mind forever.

Joe Riley threw a rope up and over a high limb of a tree near the lantern. He tied one end to the deer's antlers and circled around the tree. He tugged on the rope as it gently lifted the carcass off the ground. He wrapped the end of the rope around the tree once more and tied it off, holding the deer up in state. Then he carefully and skillfully skinned the deer and prepared it well for his family. He explained every slice of the knife as he delicately removed the hide from the body. Chance and I watched, fascinated by the skill of our father's hands. Hours later the deer was wrapped in a cotton sack as it hung from the tree, prepared for severing into cutlets. Joe Riley washed up and sat exhausted by the fire that we kept well fueled. "Are you ready for some liver and onions?" he asked. Chance skipped over to the ice chest and pulled out the liver that had slowly cooled. Joe Riley cut off half of it and sliced it into several thin steaks. He placed a cast iron skillet steadily over some rocks that held it several inches above the flames of the campfire. He laid in six slices of bacon and stirred it carefully. He then sliced up a medium-sized white onion and sautéed it to just limp. He rolled the liver steaks in flour with a touch of salt and pepper and laid them in the hot bacon grease. The aroma was delectable. My stomach rolled with delight as I awaited the hunter's feast. Joe Riley gave thanks over the fine food and each of us *men* ate our fill of that well-earned meal. We told stories and recounted the events of the day. It was a day of days. Joe Riley grabbed his guitar from the truck while Chance and I washed up the dishes. He crooned and fingered smoothly along the long neck of the guitar. He had a deep, mellow voice. I almost felt like Glen Campbell was singing along with him. *I always thought my dad would be a singer.* His voice had a comforting sound in the quiet of the night. There were millions of stars shining bright in the mountain sky. I took a deep breath trying to take in all the wonder around me, never wanting it to end. I was happy and somehow grounded by the depth of the day. After a few songs, Joe Riley put his guitar back in its case and stood up tall, his arms stretched high, and let out a big yawn. "Let's hit the hay, fellas." We all washed up and rolled our tired bodies into our beds. I felt content and whole and, somehow, happy. Then I fell quickly to sleep in the sanctuary of our mountain home, right there with my brother and my dad.

I heard a noise. It pulled me from my sleep. As I lay there listening, my ears pulled out a growl. Then a grunt. *Was it a bear?!* I laid perfectly still as fear rose up, pounding in my chest. Was a bear going to slam through the tent and kill each hunter one-by-one? Out of character for these mountain bears? Should I wait in hopes that it would smell us and leave? Or would it smell our scent and charge into the tent for a tasty bite? Should I wake up Joe Riley? But it might hear me if I so much as twitch. I lay there motionless, listening to that bear pondering my next fateful move. Just as I was readying myself to wake up Joe Riley, I realized that this 9-foot-tall giant bear, with grimacing teeth and big ferocious growl, was actually Chance, who was snoring with a most bear-like rumble. He would bear growl long and then grunt short as the air sneaked back out of his lungs. I was so relieved that I wore a grateful grin as I snuggled down under my blanket. Then I let myself wonder what I would do if a real bear were to tear into our tent. That fear sat there at my wits end, hovering and keeping me on high alert. It was like a vicious circle, fear creating more fear out of thin air as it tormented me.

This time around, as the hobgoblin carried me off to sleep, it conjured up a monster of a bear as it came growling fiercely, scoping out the campsite. It raised up on its hind legs as it reached the door of our tent, knowing that there was warm blood inside. I slowly drew the 30.06 from the scabbard, raising the gun readying for the attack. Everything was in slow motion. The bear tore through the canvas tent as if it were made of paper. I held the gun on it and pulled the trigger as it opened its mouth to take me with one bite, but nothing happened. The gun didn't fire! Every gun is loaded! Why didn't it shoot?! The safety was stuck! I tried to yell, "Dad!" but my words could not escape. I tried to get away, but my legs wouldn't move. I was stuck in my own fear, unable to flee. God help me.

"Levi, are you okay Buddy?" I heard Joe Riley's voice as it pulled me awake.

I was startled and sat up quickly. "Dad, it's a bear!" I warned, with sweat beading on my brow.

"Did you hear a bear?" *He ignored the dad part.*

"Yeah, there's a bear! I mean . . . No, it was a bear . . . I mean, I thought it was a bear."

Chance sat up. "You heard a bear?"

Joe Riley sat there listening for a moment. All was quiet. "You were just dreaming, Big Guy. No need to worry. You boys just go back to sleep and don't you be worrying about no bear. Remember, they're more scared of us than we are of them. They're miles away from this old campsite. And just in case, I'll be on watch. You just get back to sleep and don't worry about a thing."

My heart was pounding like a drum. I was relieved that the bear was only a dream and laid there quietly listening to the sound of nothing but Chance's gentle bear-like rumble that began about as quick as Joe Riley saying he would be on watch. It was rhythmic and sang me right back to a relieved sleep. Joe Riley surely had no intention of lying awake listening for the rest of the night, but his words were a comfort against some old bear carousing into our tent. The night passed quickly, with no more bears.

The sun rose warm on our tent. It was Sunday morning. Joe Riley rose first and pulled himself from his warm sleeping bag. He slipped into a clean pair of jeans and a sweatshirt and unzipped the tent door, stepping into the crisp morning air. He started a fire and put on a pot of coffee. The smell of the coffee rolled gently into the air. Chance woke up with a snort and a yawn and gave me a nudge. "You awake?" he whispered.

"That coffee sure smells good," I yawned. We rolled from our make-shift beds and slipped into our shoes, laughing at each other's hair that was standing up tangled on our heads. We pulled on our jackets and stepped out of the tent and into the cool morning. Joe Riley had just laid several pieces of bacon in the cast iron skillet over the fire. It crackled fierce from the heat. The fatty aroma filled the air. He warmed some milk and made us some hot chocolate, with a marshmallow in each cup. We sat around the fire and giggled, as I told the whole story of how I was going to save us all from Chance, the bear. Joe Riley fixed some eggs with the bacon and we enjoyed our final meal of the trip. I had never felt so good.

We pulled up tent and packed everything, including the sacred deer meat, into the back of the truck, and left camp even cleaner than how we found it, which was Joe Riley's way. He said that no one should ever know that you were in the forest, except for your footprints. This was a sacred oath that I would always keep.

As we rumbled down Eagle Meadow Road toward home I thought in a song:

Homeward bound, homeward bound
I'll miss the days gone by
Take me back to the land I love
In Eagle Meadow, I have wings, I can fly

The ride home was quiet, as the music ebbed and flowed with the winding road, down from the mountains to the valley below. It was beautiful from up above, with patches of irrigated crops, orchards, and vineyards laying like puzzle pieces all along the valley floor. I had never seen it from that vantage point before. From high, it was a beautiful tapestry. From low, I could see only the fray.

Chapter 13

To my surprise, Mom was home when I walked through the door with my bag of stories. She was tired, but engaged, wide-eyed at my bear story, howling with laughter on finding that the bear was only Chance, in bear's clothing in my mind. I relished in the moments when me and Mom acted normal-like. I could hang on those times for long dry periods of meth-induced physical and mental disappearances by my mother. I worried. A lot. I wore it, and pained from it, but since I was the man of the house, it was my charge.

I have learned a lot about addiction and mental illness throughout my life. Most learned yet not understood, in my youth. There is a loneliness that sets in as you try to protect a person you love from the authorities and from themselves. I never told anyone when Mom would be gone for a few days. I had made that mistake once and all hell broke loose. I ended up in a holding room at the county social services department, as they awaited someone to agree to care for me while we awaited Mom's return. She had been gone for five days, which was long for her. Her usual outings never lasted more than three days. That was usually about as much food as we had stored in the fridge. But this time, both the food and my wits ran out. On that fifth day, I went to school as usual, carrying my deeper worry along with me.

My teacher, Mrs. Lewis, surely noticed that I wore the same clothes every day for weeks on end, so that would have never been a sign of something being out of sorts. I'm sure I smelled like an old dog most days. Baths were not my game. I once was testing how long I could wear a pair of socks. I was on the count of ten days when I finally took a bath for the first day of school the next day. I was disappointed in myself for not keeping it going as I was really working on something relevant. It was a test of commitment to wearing those socks. I had battled with my dignity which finally wore me down and I bathed, unable to complete a sock-wearing world record. This forced me to get acquainted with a little sense of pride from my lack of body odor on the first day of school.

On that fifth day of Mom being gone, Mrs. Lewis, must have noticed the worry that had crawled out of my head, as she pulled me aside and asked if I was okay. Her words were like a match that lit a candle, with my worry and tears pouring out like warm wax. I told her that my mom had not come home the night before. I lied about how long she had been gone. She called the office and principal Hurley came to get me from class. He was tall, had a nice face, but I stayed clear of him, as I heard about some boys who got his paddle.

I saw it hanging right there on the wall in his office. It, indeed, had holes in it for more pain from his lashings.

Mr. Hurley called social services, who came to rescue me from my predicament. I was on a runaway train, having been picked up, hauled in, and interviewed about the circumstances of my missing mother. I was mute, except for the part about my worry that Mom did not come home *last night*. I waited in the emergency shelter for several hours, wondering and worrying about my mother and my own misery.

I was told that they would find me a family to stay with. But I had questions. Were they looking for my mother? Did they have the police out looking for her? My mom was missing, and I needed to hit the streets to look for her. I felt a heaviness in the pit of my stomach as my mind was racing for answers. To my relief, before I was placed elsewhere, Mom arrived to free me from my anguish. I don't know what story she told the authorities, but we went on home.

That whole next week, Mom and I cleaned and scrubbed our little abode for fear that social services would be paying us a surprise visit at any time. "We've gotta get this place in shape. They'll be coming, Levi. They'll be coming now." She was scared and guilt pressed in on me for giving light to my mother's failings.

Sure enough, one week later, knocking at the front door on a perfectly good Monday afternoon, was a social worker from the county. Mom and I were both there, tidying, having been well prepared for the masquerade. Knowing full well that they would try as they might to rip our lives apart unless we pulled off our charade.

The social worker was young, well-dressed, and attractive. Mom invited her in, offering her a glass of water and settling into the living room to begin her theatrics. I was impressed. The social worker empathetic. Mom pretended that she had several jobs around town, cleaning houses. She fantasized how she made plenty of cash money to support us. She was clean and neatly dressed, as she pretended to be *normal*. There was food in the refrigerator and our clothes were all folded nicely in stacks in our rooms. Everything looked like any other poor, but functioning, household would. Being poor was no reason to meddle into our business unless there was evidence of child endangerment or neglect. There was none to be found. Mom explained away the *night* that she was *late* getting home, because her ride did not show up. She made up a believable story about having walked all the way home, through the darkness, from a new cleaning job that was out much further than she would have liked. When she got home, and I was not there so she ran to the school and then got a ride to the county to rescue me. She was believably remorseful. The social worker nodded as she listened to Mom's fable. It would never happen again, Mom said. In the end, we were off the hook. And I was safe from capture by the protectors of children.

Mom crumpled to the floor after the worker drove off. It had been all she could do to hold herself together for the visit, and then she succumbed to her fear when she had ultimately pulled it off. I knelt beside her and told her it was all gonna be okay. I just didn't know how. We were far from okay. Those words and "I love you," were all I had to give her. I did love her but it had become a more sorrowful and sympathetic feeling, filled with ache and the hope that she would somehow make it, but I could not see how to save her from herself.

"I love you too, Levi. I do. So much!" She wept uncontrollably as I sat with her in her misery, a place that I knew well.

I was relieved for her, yet worried, about how long she could continue to hold it together, *unnoticed,* by the world around us. She apologized to me over and over for being gone so long and said it would never happen again. Promises, I had learned, were easily broken. But I vowed to myself never to report my worry again. Until I did.

Chapter 14

What's the difference between a past vision and that of a dream? There is most times, no evidence to be found as to the matter of facts. Were the memories of wrong doings and misjudgments real, or were they just dreams of such things? It's like our mind starts spinning with an idea or a notion that evokes a memory that was lost or found in shreds. I do wonder if our young minds are not yet formed enough to hold on to the ignorance around us, for our own preservation. We can only call up certain memories, leaving the vast majority of them to lie still, a welcome silence to their madness. I am sure that there are some children who lose sweet remnants of coddling, affection and devotion. That is just collateral damage for those of us who have seen more trauma than tenderness, as we must slide into the comfort of more recent memories from which to begin our meaningful and productive existence, after having seen the face of the devil firsthand. My memories still clash with the dreaming, but I have found comfort from the visions that I created from the folly, as I reworked the stories for my own survival.

I continually worked on my dreams through the night. They took me to faraway places. Fantasy lands of giants and pygmies, sometimes finding myself flying through the air or sliding off mountains. Me, always the survivor, though I would sometimes awaken with a start if I had taken a dream to my sleep as I fell.

The dreams that I created were a blend of pain, mortal danger, and fantasy. They became stories that I recreated, to my liking, as thoughts moved through the stillness of many nights alone in the darkness of my room. I would rework them as I went along, as sleep arrived to carry them forward, in a flicker of time.

Chapter 15

The next morning, after returning home from Eagle Meadow, Mom cried out for me. I ran to her room and found her lying across the bed. She told me to go get Sydney. I ran out the door, across the alley in a flash, and into the back door of the shop. Sydney was there most days, which was always a gnawing comfort if things ever went completely south for us.

Sydney had taken care of me once, when Mom had run off on a trip with Jim Bob Davison. They stayed gone a whole month. Mom took me to the shop and asked Sydney if she could watch over me for a couple of days. Sydney was such a kind soul, she just said, "Of course." Her face was a little uncertain and I was sure that taking care of me was the last thing she wanted to do, but she took me in, and right on home with her. When Mom didn't come back for me in a couple of days, Sydney bought me some new clothes and blended me right into her life. I think we both pretty much figured that I might just be staying, after Mom didn't show up for a couple of weeks.

When I stayed with her, I had learned that Sydney was a widow, having married the love of her life, Bernard, when she was just twenty years old. He was much older than her, by nineteen years. Her parents were supportive of the marriage, since he had a successful job at his family's winery, them having brought their knowledge to the states from Portugal. Him being Portuguese was icing the cake for them, making him a shoe in. He was quite a catch, Sydney told me, bringing home flowers and taking her out for nice dinners on a regular basis. He was smart and witty, and made her life one of bliss. They had always wanted children, but it was not to be, so they decided to become foster parents. When they went for their first meeting about becoming fosters, they were told that it was much harder for the county to find homes for older children because most people wanted babies. So, Sydney and Bernard decided to make their home an emergency placement for teenagers who needed temporary care. Sometimes, they would get calls in the middle of the night, when a trauma would strike for a child and their family. Sydney was so proud to give children a loving home when theirs was in crisis. The Mellos fostered dozens of kids who just needed a soft place to land while they awaited the mitigation of whatever crisis had caused their displacement. Sydney was an advocate for families, never looking down on the parents, but always giving hope that they would rise up to get their children back. They got close to considering adoption a couple of times, but Bernard's advancing age made them think better of it. That was the most rewarding time of Sydney's life, being a foster parent to young people. Then one fateful day her dear Bernard died of a heart attack at work. Her whole world crumbled as she faced life without him and her devotion to fostering children, which was not an approved practice for single women. She was left to find a way to make a living and made the decision to get her cosmetology license and open up her own shop with the money they had saved so that she could support herself. She missed the children, but many of her past foster kids would stop by on a regular basis to visit and to thank her for all that she had done for them. Her life slowly began to make sense again and she was standing strong on her own two feet. She had found her way and was always a pillar for kids and families in need in the county.

After nearly a month with Sydney, Mom came walking up to get me. I had mixed emotions. I was beginning to settle into the order of things at Sydney's, but I felt relief when Mom finally arrived to pick me up. She loved me enough to come back. And she was okay. That felt like something real. Sydney did pull Mom aside and lit into her pretty good, with a threat. How dare she just drop her boy off without a care. Leaving Sydney to worry and wonder what the hell was going on, day after day. If she ever pulled a stunt like that again, social services would be involved. She would not involve them this one and only time. The hair on the back of my neck stood up, for both me and Mom. And she wasn't done. If

Mom didn't start trying to get her shit together, Sydney was not gonna just sit by and watch my life go into free fall from neglect. "You know I'm right, Kat. You had better start putting him first, or you're gonna lose him. One way or another."

Mom just stared into the words, seemingly unfazed, but I knew she was letting them swirl around in her head, trying to make sense of them. Her mind had trouble sorting through extensive thought toward the long haul. I felt considerable uneasiness from the confrontation, and guilt for having caused Sydney to lose her cool. And I felt sorry for Mom, who just didn't know how to raise a kid on her own. I really needed my dad. Where, on God's green earth, was my dad?

Instead of offering to help me find my dad, Mom's answer was to move Jim Bob in with us, which only lasted a few weeks. His heavy drinking and malicious mouth disgusted me. He and Mom fought incessantly. I would lie in bed at night and listen to their screaming and brawls, praying that God would come to me as a flame and set on the tips of each of my feet. I had heard that was possible once. With God's flame setting on my feet, I could kick Jim Bob clear across the alley, clean over Sydney's shop onto the highway that stretched across the oleanders. Cars would run over him but wouldn't know it. He would just blend right into the pavement where he belonged. I knew it was sinful to think like that. It threatened my compass, but a *man* has his limits.

I had tried to intervene one night, which left me with a fat lip, and Mom in worse shape for jumping in the middle.

Mom told me the next morning to stay in my room when Jim Bob was slinging his hateful self around the house. So, most nights I would pray for God to do my intervening for me. I guess he did, somehow, as the fighting would always end, most usually when both Jim Bob and Mom would pass out. Sometimes Jim Bob would storm out in the middle of a fight to my relief. But there he would be, the next morning, sitting at the table smoking his Camels and drinking coffee. I would peek into the room in disgust as I heard their muffled voices. There was no room for two men in that house! Mom finally ran him off on Thanksgiving Day when he had gone so far as to take the Thanksgiving turkey that Mom had sprung for and traded it for a carton of cigarettes. Mom walked up to Jim Bob as he was sitting in the recliner watching the Thanksgiving Day parade on TV and crumpled an entire pack of cigarettes over the top of his head. He was pissed and belted her one in the nose before he slammed out the door. I sat there consoling my mother, as I laid a bag of frozen vegetables on her bleeding nose. She cooked up a chicken for Thanksgiving and I was never so thankful as to have Jim Bob gone and my mother back to my single worry.

Chapter 16

Sydney ran back with me to find Mom crying and rolling to and fro on the bed. She was sweating and delirious.

"I'll go call an ambulance!"

"No," Mom howled, "We don't have no money for an ambulance!"

Sydney finally convinced Mom that she needed to go to the hospital, so she drove us. We limped into the waiting room, helping Mom walk between us. When they called her name, we cradled our arms around her and tried to help her to stand. "Can you get us a wheelchair? Sydney asked the nurse in disgust. "She can't even stand up!" The nurse went back inside the door and a few moments later arrived with a wheelchair. She and Sydney managed to get Mom into the chair, which the nurse wheeled into the examination room. I tried to follow, but the nurse told me to wait in the waiting room. Sydney followed Mom, winking back at me, as they disappeared around the corner.

Sydney came and went between me and Mom, taking me to the cafeteria for food and going back in to check on her. After several hours of testing and waiting, a doctor came out and told us that Mom had a blood infection. They would need to keep her. It sounded serious.

They took her to a room and while we were sitting with her, she awoke in a delirium, screaming, "I want my baby! They've killed my baby!" she sobbed.

I was petrified that she was going to blow the cover of her secretly dead baby. Oh my God, the fear.

"Kat, look at your beautiful boy, he's right here," Sydney said innocently.

Mom looked at me with eyes framed in red, like a zombie, but she did not appear to see me, as she ripped the needle of the intravenous tube from her arm and sent the side tray falling to the floor with a bang. Sydney grabbed me, as we ran to the nurse's station. I quickly turned to look at Mom, but it was not her face I saw, but that of the woman she had become, while I waited and worried and wondered where her life might lead us.

They gave Mom some morphine to calm her all the way down to a deep sleep. Sydney shared with the nurse that she had to go check on her shop, but would be back, in a flash, and could I please stay there, as I had begged, to sit with Mom while she slept. The nurse said she would watch out for me, and I was finally able to go back in to sit next to Mom. I was disheartened from fear and guilt for enjoying Eagle Meadow while she was getting so sick. I didn't want to come home and now Mom was in the hospital. She must have known how much I hated to come home. But I had always missed her. Not the current her, but the *her* I always wished for. It was my fault. I was an awful son of an ailing mother.

"Mom, can you hear me?" There was no suggestion that she could. Then I began to whimper as I tried to keep quiet. My eyes became a fountain, dripping into small puddles on the floor. I was being pummeled by my misery. No dad. A dead sister. A long disappearing mother. The death of the humble deer, and the near death of my very own ability to cope. Mom's skin was yellowish and chalky, and she looked like she was dead. Why not have a dying mother too?

What else could I be asked to bear? Life is not fair or easy and many times it is not good. No one is promised anything in this life. This was just another deep, dark moment that's to be expected sooner or later. Something that I did not ask for yet must endure. My sorrow ran deep.

Finally, after a long while, Mom rolled her head and struggled to open her eyes.

"Mom, it's me."

"Le-vi," slipped broken from her mouth. Her lips were so dry that they were wrinkled up and stuck together.

"Mom? I'm here."

"I. Thought. They. Killed. You."

"No, Mom, I'm right here. I just went with Joe Riley and Chance, camping, Mom. But now I'm right here."

"Don't. Let. Them. Get. You," she slurred.

"I won't." I said, as I appeased her and wiped the tears and snot from my face with my shirt sleeve.

"I. Love. You. Levi."

"I love you too, Mom."

Those words always rang out between us, whenever we parted, no matter where the days took us. Our *I love yous* were a comfort in between the hollow spaces of genuine neglect and the feeling that they could mean something. What is love really? It was a fearful respect for sure. The love that I read about was different. It was warm and fuzzy. A place in which you could rest from the softness of it. I had never felt that kind of love from or for my mother. For this, my guilt rose up fierce.

"I'm scared, Mom."

She was out again.

I was overwhelmed and sat there with my head in my hands. Mom's brain had gone into fog. I sat motionless, alone with my many questions, afraid of and for her life. I sat there quietly pondering when social services might swoop in to get me. I would be dodgy just in case. I needed to stay safely alone, with myself and my mother.

It's funny how, when someone's sick, you begin to see how much you care for them. Everything gets soft. Regret starts rising to the surface, for all that I didn't do to make her life better. I had never faced my feelings for Mom quite like that day. It hurt to sense the pity of it. She had always done the best she could with the emotional ability that she had at the time, which was not much, most days. I know she tried to love me. She just didn't know how and was incapable of such a real thing.

I sat with Mom for a long while. The nurse would come in and smile while she took Mom's blood pressure and pressed more medication into her IV. I would stroke her limp hand. A nurse came in and brought me some milk and a peanut butter and jelly sandwich. I was grateful, as I was nearly starving to death.

It was getting late when Sydney finally came back to take me home with her. I didn't want to leave Mom, but the visiting hours were over and there were no exceptions, so they told me. We stopped by our house to get me a few clothes, which I sorted out from the floor. The drive to Sydney's house was long. She tried to make small talk. I was thinking about how I was gonna keep social services at bay, and out of my perfectly miserable life.

I laid, staring into the darkness from Sydney's couch. My eyes swollen and burning from the heavy assault of my salty tears. God? I needed His help. It was like He was missing. "God, please help me." I always knew He was right there within me somewhere, but now I could not sense Him. Maybe I would need to plead. Maybe I had scared Him off with my inability to love enough. I felt broken, and my inner voice translated every ounce of my sorrow into the night. I was afraid. More afraid than I had ever been, which was really saying something. Life was not making any sense. It was just tolerable before, but now I felt myself falling into a pit of despair. I felt like the world was just going to turn over and spin me off. My heart raced from the fear that was overtaking me as I laid there with my own thoughts. My breathing got heavy, my face grew numb and my ears began to ring. I was dizzy from the falling and was afraid that I might be falling straight into hell, a sure death. I had never felt such an overwhelming feeling of hopelessness. I couldn't make my mind stop its racing. How do you stop thinking? I knew not how to stop it. I was growing desperate, at my wit's end, so I jumped up, opened the front door, and ran. I ran through the darkness as fast as I could. I was running from my whole life. I wanted to run back to Eagle Meadow where life made sense, even with the death of the deer. I wanted to run from every regret of my young life. I wanted to run to someone but didn't know who. I needed my dad. The air was cold on my face as it began to rain. My body was tingling, and I felt dizzy from my mind and body racing into the darkness. I turned along the canal bank and down through a towering orchard of trees. Large walnuts. The ground was growing wet, and the dense orchard was black as it stood guard over the moonlight. I pushed myself harder and harder as I ran . . . then and there a branch, mighty and strong, stood low as it bowed down to greet me. I saw it just before I ran right into it. Everything stopped, cold. All my thoughts, my wonders, and my fear, as the branch forced my head to a stop and my feet forward in slow motion, as I fell hard and flat onto my back, gasping for air, as it was knocked clean out of me. I rolled over and writhed with the excruciating pain of no air, even as I tried to call it back into my emptied lungs. I was sure to die. Until, finally, I was able to grab a breath, as I forced it deep. I laid on my back breathing the life back into myself, staring up to see the moon shining right down upon me through the darkness, as my body remembered how to breathe. I was relieved, and then, as I rolled my hand over my forehead, felt it wet with warm blood. I lifted my shirt up from the neck and laid it over my face to press on my bleeding head.

I laid there, still, and thankful to be alive. Complete calm had fallen over me. I could hear my breathing, steady and smooth. My heart had settled down to a normal beat and my senses were keen. My fear was gone. I had outrun it, or the tree branch had knocked it clear out of me. *Don't let anything beat you,"* I said to myself. *If you're beat, you're dead,* and I wasn't about to let myself fall into no soggy swamp of self-destruction. I lingered there, in silent reflection for a long while, listening to the raindrops as they sprinkled all around me. It was that beautiful sound of silence which brings with it a calm from the slowing down to hear it, from somewhere deep, yet from somewhere else. I could smell the wet earth and taste the wet on my lips. Finally, I rolled over and got up, holding my shirt firm against my forehead. Though my face was wet with blood, I was no longer afraid. I tracked my way back through the orchard along the canal bank. As I walked, I languished my newfound freedom from the very fear that had threatened me. I had beaten it. This time. I trudged up the front steps and quietly made my way in through the open door of Sydney's house. I went into the bathroom to see what malice that tree branch had planted on my forehead. My first glance in the mirror was frightful, as my entire face was covered with streaks of dried red blood. Even my ears were filled with it. I turned on the faucet and let the water turn warm into my hands and then filled them, cupped. I splashed the warm water onto my face and then held my head low over the sink as I washed it clean. I finally looked up at the mirror to find a single puncture about the circumference of a number two pencil. It was just seeping by then, but I had pretty much bled like a stuck pig. There were some feathery scrapes around the puncture, but I was relieved to see that I was not mortally wounded. It took quite a while to clear my face and ears of the blood. I carefully cleaned up the sink and found some mercurochrome in the medicine cabinet, courageously dabbing the glass bulb of red smarting onto the wound to clear it of bacteria. I then placed a single Band-Aid on the wound and stared at my clean face in the mirror. I grabbed a comb from the counter and tried to paste my hair straight over to the right, it springing up, as usual, from its strong effort to curl. I grinned at my disheveled self in the mirror and wondered if I would have a red and purple moon to match the likes of Chance's the next day. I retrieved my paper sack of clothes and changed into another pair of pants and a tee shirt. I wadded up my dirty clothes and placed them deep into the sack, then made my way back to the living room and laid down on the couch with my head elevated, which I had learned was the appropriate thing to do in the first aid series during health class. I stared up into the darkness and could feel my heart beating, alive, in my forehead. I had been saved.

I felt calm, as I soared in and out of that place where my dreams are made. I was speaking in my mind, like I was writing a story in my notebook. It felt like poetry. With my inner voice, I thoughtfully transcribed from somewhere in the Universe . . .

You have found the abyss. Do not be afraid, though you must make your way to its edge, many times, as you place one shovelful of earth at a time into the void until it is filled to level ground with fertile soil. Though each shovelful will take you dangerously close to the edge, you will go courageously, and sift the soil into the darkness of the hollow. One day you will have filled it to overflowing with good earth. The evil place will be no more. It will have vanished, under your feet, as you will then realize that it was never substance, just a space in need of filling by the toil toward the fullness and miracle of life itself. You will stand firm upon it and plant your own beautiful garden. It will be sacred ground, from which you will cultivate your life. The chasm, as with the fear, was never real, but was only a representation of the adversity that formed your life thus far. Fear does not truly exist in matter or form. It is created by the unknowing mind. Be not afraid, my Son, for you are now acquainted with the Truth that will set you free.

I hoped that mine and Mom's saving was strong enough to get us all the way through this time, when we really needed to lean on it. I begged God's forgiveness for all of the blaspheming that I had ever done, even in my writing, just in case He had changed His mind about my reflecting in such a way. I begged for his mercy and drifted in and out of my healing dreams.

Sydney noticed the Band-Aid and reddish bruise on my head first thing. I told her everything. "Why didn't you come and get me?" she questioned.

"I don't know. I just ran."

She sat down next to me and hugged me tight. "You were just overwhelmed with everything, Honey, and that's understandable."

"Whatever it was, it scared the daylights out of me!"

"I bet it did. We all have to learn how to deal with the difficulties that come our way, and sometimes it just feels like an overload. I understand that sensation that you felt. And I learned a trick to keeping that runaway feeling at bay. You're gonna be alright."

I listened, hopeful, for an answer that would save me from my overwhelm. She taught me how to stop, take a slow deep breath. Hold it. Breath it out slowly. Then repeat this deep breathing four more times, all the while focusing my attention on the air that is drawn in through my nose and then released through my mouth. "Keep your attention right there. Now let's try it together," she said.

We sat there breathing in, hold, out, in, hold, out, until I got it right. It felt so good to breathe. Somehow, clarity comes with the calm. It was like magic, and I have used this simple exercise throughout my life, whenever the world went stupid crazy before me or within me. I have extended it to ten minutes of meditation daily, having read a book about the miracle of the mind. I learned to draw myself back into the simplicity of stillness, as the world spins out of control around me. I truly believe that this very *trick* has saved me from all the madness that threatened to set up shop within me.

I've seen a lot of things, that I have let disappear, but this day was marked in dark red ink. It was my preparation, for the marching orders, of the next miserable chapter of my mother's life. A time when my own strength would be all that could carry me through, along with the desperate leaning on my go-to people on the worst of my days.

I stayed with Sydney and Mom stayed in the hospital for four days, until she walked out of her own accord, and against the wishes of the doctor. She had spent three full days in restraints just to hold her there as they pumped her with antibiotics to clear the heavy infection. Each time she would ebb out from the effects of the morphine, she would set out to pull herself free of the lifesaving IV. Hence, the restraints and no more visits from me. The doctor had also diagnosed her with cirrhosis of the liver, which he said, *was advanced*. She was suffering from the DTs . . . Delirium Tremens. That was why they had to use restraints. Her body was raging with fury, crying out for the chemical enlightenment that kept her in state, hovering just above the grave. The doctor ordered new medications to alleviate her distress, her mental confusion and her failing liver. She finally settled down long enough for them to remove the restraints. That is when she put on her jeans and walked, barefoot, clear on home to her faithful gloss, thus confirming her death sentence, and my lifelong fear.

Chapter 17

I was in middle school the year my mother disappeared again. It happened quite matter-of-factly, as she ventured in and out of my daily life. One day, she just never came back. I waited the allotted days I had allowed until the worry stormed in. It had lengthened from five to seven to ten days. I had been forcing myself through each day, keeping the ache to myself. On the fourteenth day, it had risen, and stared me down.

Sydney had told me, the week prior, that she was going on a vacation to visit her aunt in Nevada for a couple of weeks, and that if I needed anything to tell Wanda, one of the beauticians at the shop, to give me an advance from the drawer or whatever I needed.

I had considered asking Sydney if I could go with her on her trip, but I had that issue with wetting my pants that still threatened me on car trips. When I was in the fourth grade, I had come in from a great recess of kick ball, not having time to use the bathroom before going back to class. Mrs. Holt was a stickler when it came to me. I was quiet. Preferring to stay along the edges of things. She hated that part of me. The very first day of class I found a chair in the back, but Mrs. Holt brought me to a chair right in front of her later that week, staring me down in my unwashed shame. She liked to use me as a whipping boy of sorts to show the other kids how not to be. She expressed to all that I needed to wash my clothes and not wear the same ones every day. One day she noticed me scraping my unbrushed teeth with my pencil right before we were to chew on the red tablets provided by the dental foundation to establish how well we all were brushing our teeth. I seldom brushed mine, hence the act of trying to save some face with my pencil. She called me to the front of the class to explain to all of God's children that you always need to brush your teeth before school. She handed me the bright red tablet, as everyone watched. "Come on, chew it up!" She waited, watching every move of my mouth. "Good. Now show your teeth." I knew it would be bad but had no choice. Everyone laughed and giggled as I shined my bright red mouth, the proof of a no-brusher, hardly ever. Humiliation became the norm in that year. It pushed me deeper into the dark corners of my life. Mrs. Holt didn't like my disheveled-ness, nor did society as a whole, I had learned, and all made it clear with their words, taunts, rolling eyes or total neglect. I tried to do a little better with my personal hygiene, having been shamed beyond measure, but I had bigger fish to fry on most days. Mrs. Holt came with many warnings from her former students. We all knew that to draw her as your teacher meant a year lost to the possibility of any kind of joy in the classroom. And two rules were written in red on the chalkboard: Always be on time and use the restroom, *only at recess.*

I sat in my chair before Mrs. Holt, completely miserable, agonizing in the pain of my situation. I had to go so bad! Finally, I gathered myself, having no option, and went up to ask her to go to the fateful restroom. She said, "Absolutely not! You should have gone at recess!"

"I know, and I'm sorry, but I really need to go."

"Get back to your seat, Levi!"

I was a rule follower, so I obeyed, and struggled, and ached, and finally after holding all that my bulging bladder could bear, my urine flowed free on its own, against my will. Out. As it seeped through my pants, and dripped from my chair, I moved my feet around in slow circles, mixing it with the dirt from the floor, in hopes that no one would notice. I would be humiliated, again, if anyone figured me out. Class lasted what seemed like days, as I stayed in my own head and in my seat, worrying about how to hide my disgusting wetness and the smell that wafted up free from my saturated pants. Finally, at long last, the bell rang. I waited for everyone to get up and start mingling toward their coats that hung near the door. I slipped out of my chair, grabbed my coat, and ran as fast as I could toward home. Mrs. Holt was yelling that there was no running in the corridor. I could not have cared less.

I made it home with a newfound obsessive-compulsive focus on urination. The rest of my fourth-grade year was filled with the grievances of Mrs. Holt and hitting the restroom twice during each recess. Once in the beginning and once before going back to class. I was in the bathroom more than I was out playing. I didn't go on field trips for fear that I may wet my pants along the way. I was always sick on those days. My bladder could not be trusted. I accepted no car rides. I became a bit manic, until that next summer, when I lost focus of the act of holding and freeing my bladder. Just sometimes, the pants wetting worry would sneak back up on me.

Sydney would be gone for at least ten more days according to my calculation. I checked all of Mom's usual hangouts one last time and had a sense that there was no more time to wait. I ran over to the Hole and told Joe Riley about Mom being gone. He dropped his head, and said, "Aww, Buddy, I'm sorry man. I'll go looking for her when I get off work." My mind raced as I wanted to jump into his arms again and profess that he was my dad, but now was not the time.

"I've been looking! No one has seen her for over week!"

"We better tell Sheriff Bender. Don't worry, Buddy, he'll help us find her."

The days turned even darker as my world tipped over.

I was sent to the county home once again. Joe Riley had gone down to the county to try to get me but explained that there was something in his past that he was not proud of, that kept me from staying with him. I wondered if he was beginning to believe that he was my dad too.

This time, on the afternoon soon after I arrived at the county home, a real family, in a neighboring town, took me in. They were well-to-do from my standards. Everything was so clean. There was only one problem, their family of four had a long-planned vacation, in two days, that did not include me. They apologized to me, fed me, provided me with clean clothes, and sent me back to the county home the next day, where I sat, until Sydney flew into the room to rescue me. I leapt into her arms and hung on for dear life. She apologized for not being there when I needed her. When she got home, Wanda told her the news and she rushed right in. She told me that she talked to the social worker about having me go home with her. It was not quite that easy, as the judge would have to decide if that plan was best for me first. *Dear God! They just needed to ask me!* I needed to be with Sydney. I sobbed in disbelief that I could not go with her straight away. It was going to be a long two days, before the judge would hear my case, and I would sit alone with myself to wait and worry about my mother's whereabouts. I was one of many kids there, and the caregiver of the home, Miss Thompson, stayed close, but had her hands full with many unraveling lives.

I stayed clear of the others, holding close to my bunk. From a bookshelf, I grabbed the book, "The Adventures of Robinson Crusoe," and spent the next two days with Robinson on that island. We shared a similar life of dodging cannibals and mutineers. As usual, when reading, I asked Miss Thompson for some paper and a pencil to write down the parts of the book that I wanted to remember, which she obliged. I wrote in long hand.

Robinson Crusoe:

"It is never too late to be wise."

"Fear of danger is ten thousand times more terrifying than danger itself." Though I questioned that.

"All evils are to be considered with the good that is in them, and with what worse attends them."

I had to study that last one a bit but got the gist. If you ever did something bad because of a potential good, there is probably something worse that will happen. I had already learned that one, pondering the summer of the pickles. Well, sort of. Luckily, we were spared the worse part. I didn't even realize that I was stealing those pickles, until Miss Olive asked us where we had gotten those fine dills that day. She went through a very long and winding story about how we had stolen those pickles and how they belonged to the pickle company, and we could actually go to jail for theft if we were found out. So, we would have to lay low. Chance and I were aghast that we were thieves. We kinda prided ourselves in being the good guys. Miss Olive said that she would not turn us in, *this time,* and would cover for us just this once. If we ever stole again, she would have to turn us in since we now understood the error of our ways. We did not tell her about the battle helmets that we stole. We kept them hidden in our fort and decided that our thieving days had better be left behind us, lest we end up jailbirds like so many of the other *men* in our town.

I skipped through a lot of the story, as my mind would leave my side, and run for my mother. In the end, Robinson Crusoe was rescued, as was I, when Sydney was finally able to free me from my protective captors. It had been more difficult that she had hoped. Though it was not a surprise that the judge had a problem with her being a working woman, and a single one at that. Even though she was a former foster parent, she had to jump through a lot of hoops and make some strong promises about her work hours. She gave several references, even some from social workers, who wrote letters and shared their high regard for her character. One came from the current mayor of Kelsey, who had worked side-by-side with Sydney during several charitable events that she had spirited. She was a pillar in the community. She was my person, my hope, and I needed her. When the judge asked to speak with me, I told him so. He finally agreed to make an exception to his general rules for fosters. It was an emergency declaration. It helped that there was a shortage of foster homes, with the caseloads growing at an astronomical pace, which I witnessed as the care home kept filling with more and more injured souls with each passing day. I was one of the lucky ones, with someone there to fight for me. Sydney finally took me home. She was a mortal angel, with wings that she must have held just out of sight.

Mom had gone and done it now. Where could she be? It had been my greatest fear, besides her impending death, that she would just wander off for good.

Chapter 18

Sydney took me to my house to gather some clothes and see if there were any new signs of Mom. I left a note in big letters on the kitchen table,

Mom, I'm with Sydney. Come to the shop so I can come home. I love you,
Levi.

Then we went and talked to Mr. Cooper about our rent, which I was sure was already late. I'm pretty sure he had been forgiving some for a while. Sydney did not say what she paid but told me it was all taken care of. We still had our house for me and Mom to go back to.

Sydney took me to school each day. Afterward, I would run home, in hopes that Mom was lying there on her bed. I wandered through Mom's regular hangouts, talking to anyone who crossed my path, on whether and when they last saw my mother. Chance's house was a solid place for an after-school snack from Miss Olive. And the library took me out into the world. I was always drawn to the poets, after attending a little workshop given by Miss Charlotte, the librarian. Many were over my head, but some spoke to me. One of the first ones was by Katharine Tynan. I was drawn to it because the author spelled her name just like my mother did. I read her words from Mom to me, should I die, somehow a hero:

A Hero, by "Katharine Tynan" *(or maybe Katharine Strong, if she were able)*

He was so foolish, the poor lad,
He made superior people smile
Who knew not of the wings he had
Budding and growing all the while;
Nor that the laurel wreath was made
Already for his curly head.

Silly and childish in his ways;
They said: 'His future comes to naught.'
His future! In the dreadful days
When in a toil his feet were caught
He hacked his way to glory bright
Before his day went down in night.

He fretted wiser folk—small blame!
Such futile, feeble brains were his.

Now we doff hats to hear his name,
Ask pardon where his spirit is,
Because we never guessed him for
A hero in the disguise he wore.

It matters little how we live
So long as we may greatly die.
Fashioned for great things, O forgive
Our dullness in the days gone by!
Now glory wraps you like a cloak
From us, and all such common folk.

I always ended up at the shop, doing my homework or sweeping up, while waiting for Sydney to finish her workdays. We were both spent each night as we headed back to her cozy home for supper, and what sleep there was to be found, amid the awakenings of worry. Though anxiety and uncertainty were my constant companions, I was beginning to find a newfound competency in the art of daily living. Routine was becoming solid ground. One shovelful at a time.

One day, Sydney asked if I had ever seen my birth certificate. Social services needed a copy, and they had no idea where to begin looking, not knowing where I was born and all. I had no idea and had never seen it, nor had I ever even thought of having one. I began to wonder if just maybe my dad's name might be listed on it. It would be some kind of miracle, but I knew that miracles could happen. It was not likely that one would happen to me, but it could. I confessed to Sydney that I had always hoped to find my dad someday. She gave me a firm hug and told me that she would do her best to help me find him if it were at all possible. My greatest hope ignited, as it might possibly be within reach since I had finally shared it. *A lesson . . . sometimes you've just got to ask for what you want. How else is anybody gonna know how to make your dreams come true if you don't even tell them what they are.*

Sydney explained to me that I should not get my hopes up about my birth certificate holding the name of my father. When a young unmarried woman had a baby, the father would not be listed. This luxury was only given to a child if their mother was married. Sydney had learned this while fostering children in the past. It seemed so wrong to leave off something so important to the very life of a child. It made me angry to think of it. How dare the documenters of births purposely withhold such information if it were known. She said that if Mom was married, a father's name would be listed, as a child would be legally his because of the marriage. She was preparing me for all the possibilities whenever my birth certificate might be found. She didn't want me to have any false hopes so my disappointment would not grow out of reach for my ability to cope.

We went to my house the next evening and started looking through things. It was chilly and a mess, the smell dank from the lack of body heat and outside air for so many days. It made me feel sad that me and Mom had to live that way. I had already begun to take for granted the warm comfort of Sydney's house. I felt a deep ache in my belly knowing that

Mom was *not* just out there somewhere doing what she had always done, but she was missing. Gone. It is a terrible word, gone. I had looked it up. *Gone; no longer present; departed.* And I realized that it perfectly described my mother, even when she was home.

Sydney and I stayed together, looked around on shelves, in drawers, and in closets. I didn't want to leave the warmth of her side. In Mom's room, Sydney crouched down to look under her bed. And there, hiding among a large swirl of dust bunnies, was a box titled, *My Papers.* Sydney pulled it out and set it on the bed. As she opened the flap and began rustling through the papers, there, sitting right near the top, was an envelope with the words *Leviticus's BC* written on the front. Sydney grabbed it and smiled widely. "Oh my God, Levi! This may be it!" She handed it over for me to open, as a splinter of hope gripped our common desire to see the name of my dad written clearly for all to see. The questions roared through my mind. Could Mom have been married at such a young age, me knowing that she was only sixteen at my birth? My hands were trembling uncontrollably as I reached inside and pulled out my birth certificate. We both leaned in as I opened it up. I immediately scrolled down to the line for my name and then, *Father of Child.* It was blank.

I knew in my gut that my dad wouldn't be listed. I felt Sydney's hand touch my shoulder. "I'm sorry, Honey. I was so hopeful that your father's name would be there." She knew I was disappointed. But it was just another reminder that

Mom could show no remorse or consideration for my lack of a father.

After gathering myself from the evidence of no dad, I read through the entirety of the birth certificate. It read:

Certificate of Live Birth
Los Angeles County

Name of Child: Leviticus David Strong

I always had to remind my teachers to call me Levi instead. The kids laughed their heads off when they would spit out my full name.

Sex: Male

Date of Birth: **November 12, 1957**

A Scorpio, which is known for outward shyness and inner determination. I had proven this to be true.

Time of Birth: 2:04 pm

Mom had said that she labored all night long and into the next day with me.

Birth City: Santa Monica, California *This I did not know.*

Mother of Child: Katharine Mary Strong

I never knew her middle name.

Age: 16 *So young!*

Father of Child: *Blank*

We put the box back under Mom's bed and took my birth certificate with us. As I looked it over again and again, I couldn't keep from dreaming. Maybe my dad was an actor, being that I was born down so close to Hollywood, and Santa

Monica being such a highfalutin town, from what little that I knew of it. There was a big pier that stretched way out into the ocean, with rich people's homes dotting all along the coastline. Wouldn't it be something if my dad lived right there in one of those houses? It gave me butterflies, as I imagined running out the back door of his house, out onto the beach, where I would surf along the shore, bask in the sun, and build sandcastles at my leisure. I would wear Hawaiian shorts, from our many trips off the mainland. I liked that dream. Then my hope burst in. *Dad, whoever and wherever you are, please come for me.*

Chapter 19

The next day, Sydney took my birth certificate to social services, where they were well pleased that it had an official county stamp, making it acceptable for my file. Sydney asked them if they could help me to find my father. They didn't have any reason to believe that they could, unless someone came forward for me. I thought of Joe Riley. Hadn't he already come forward to get me when social services scooped me up? Maybe he was my dad after all, and not just some kind of childish whim. My mind raced with the possibilities again, as I continued my hope for the finding of my mother while still longing for my dad.

We checked in with Sheriff Bender about Mom every few days. The answers were always the same . . . . "No new leads." We all knew that there wasn't going to be anyone from the underbelly of Kelsey who was gonna be sharing what they might know with the cops. Nobody, unless there was some kind of reward, which was highly unlikely. I wondered if anyone was even looking for her, knowing that they didn't really care if they found her or not. Her worth was less than nothing, to society as a whole. The distinctness of our social class caste us low even in the hierarchy of Kelsey, and that was saying something. Hope had been lost on us long ago. Even amongst ourselves, really. We lived in that lack, considered draws on the system. Mom trudging to stay above the grave. I, dangling from a tiny hook that she held from the end of her pole that kept some form of purpose in her existence. She could see me there, hanging like a carrot before a horse, drawing her toward me, but never allowing her to reach me. She would shake me up and down, and hold me high above the abyss, as I dangled, then drop me down to hit the bottom. I could never set my feet firmly on the ground, until, finally, she dropped the pole and ran. There I stood, at the edge of the chasm, looking for a shovel.

I busied myself at the library on weekends, keeping my mind buried deep in the fiction of storybook tales. The non-fiction of my life was viscous if I dared to open the pages too wide. I stood at the edge of the abyss daily. One shovelful in, one shovelful out, hanging in the balance of the unknown. One day I dared take a book from a shelf about mental illness. I skimmed the pages, feeling squeamish, as I recognized my mother's behaviors, having always known, though not understanding. The desire to medicate herself however she could, I always understood. But I had no idea that there could be so much hope and help for her: counseling, therapy, medication, support, and if absolutely necessary, even shock treatments. She was completely disconnected, having no support system whatsoever, the very opposite of what she needed for a chance to build a happy life—connecting to people and resources. Maybe there could have been a way out for her. It hurt to know. Why did she have to stay suspended in her own misery when help was out there? It was like a secret. I wished she could have known this early on. I felt deeply sorry for our ignorance. It had defined us, and left my mother tangled in her illness to battle it alone, with her gloss. *Oh Mom, please come back. We can find the help you need. There's hope now.* Oh my God, there had always been hope, hidden from us, just out of sight. Maybe it wasn't too late for her life to get better.

The next month after Mom went missing, Sydney talked to me about moving all my things to her house. I stared at her and saw the pain this conversation brought to her, so I did not fight back, even though this was the first step toward giving up on my mother. The only question that had to be asked was, "What if Mom comes back to our house, finds me gone, and then leaves forever?"

Sydney's eyes dripped, as her face grew red, with the breaking of my heart. "She'll know that you're with me, right across the alley at the shop. She'll always be able to find you when she is ready and able."

That *able* part struck me. Was she not able to get back to me or was she out living her own life on her own accord, having decided I was too big a burden to bear any longer? I drew up a vision of her lying at the bottom of a cold dark hole, unable to free herself. I started to weep for fear of that vision.

Sydney held me close. "I know this is so hard, Honey. You're having to face some bitter truths that are highly unfair for a boy your age. You always have. We don't know if your mom will ever come back, and I hate it. I wish I could fix it, but I can't. All I can do is promise you that I'll always be here for you. We'll march down this road together."

I was grateful in a way, that she didn't rosy it all up with false hopes of Mom coming back soon. I would have known, as hope was seeping out with each passing day.

I sat there for a while gently rocking back and forth in the comfort of Sydney's arms.

"She'll know I'm with you. When she comes back, she'll know," I whimpered, giving my own self the rosy.

Sydney held me even tighter as I nestled there in her arms, safe from the world that raged outside, breathing in the warmth of her embrace, and breathing out from the bank of fear that I held deep for my mother.

At the time, I didn't think to thank her for all she was doing for me. I didn't understand the depth of love and compassion it took for her to completely alter her perfectly good life in trade for the turmoil of my daily existence. For this, I am ever grateful.

We spent the next Sunday, with several empty boxes that we got from behind Mr. Bill's store, filling each with mine and Mom's baggage and taping them closed when they were full. Sydney asked for my opinion on every piece of trash that went into the garbage sack. We remembered to grab the *My Papers* box from underneath Mom's bed and placed it in the *keep* stack. It was a long and dreary day of emotional sorting.

Sydney decided that we should lock all of Mom's things in the shed behind the shop. They would be safe there until Mom came back. We put all of my things in my new bedroom, which was Sydney's former sewing room. We had already changed it over to my room with a new *used* twin bed and a blue bedspread with curtains to match that Sydney made for me. We also found a small dresser with four drawers at the thrift shop. We moved her sewing machine and things to the storage shed, making the room strictly for me. I busied myself the whole next week after school with lining up my few trucks, looking through my notebooks, playing my records, sorting through my baseball cards, and tucking my clothes into the dresser drawers. Sydney had washed and folded them neatly, which was a new normal for me. I generally just pulled my clothes from a pile on the floor, never really caring if they were dirty or clean. Sydney had a washing machine right outside the back door and a clothesline along the side of the house. Now, my clothes were always clean. I quickly appreciated the difference.

Chapter 20

I had been thinking a lot about Delano. He was mine and Mom's secret. He was surely responsible for Mom's disappearance. I, alone, knew that. Hopefully, he brought some comfort if she found herself alone, but knowing him, I knew better than that.

He had moved in on us slowly. Shy at first, only making small talk, in a whisper. Mom hid him from me for a time, until his brazenness left no room for him to hide. His verbal attacks kept her all shook up much of the time. He finally sashayed on in to set up camp right in the middle of Mom's head and became a regular caller.

"Put your ear to mine Levi. It's Delano. Can you hear him?"

I listened carefully. Nothing. "No, I don't hear anything."

"You must be able to hear him! He's screaming! So loud!"

I could not. I could have lied, but I did not go down that road. I did find a way to follow along, always calling him by name. It helped Mom, somehow, that I recognized his existence. He told Mom that he was named after Franklin Delano Roosevelt, which gave him great authority over her. Mom wrestled with him endlessly, as his intent grew only to keep her riled up. She grew weary from his antagonizing, until she found a way to flee his grasp, sometimes. Alcohol and drugs helped to keep him at bay. Sometimes she had regular conversations with him, as I listened. She would pause as he spoke, answer his questions, even shaking and nodding her head in response. If I didn't know better, I would have thought she were reading the lines of a play. She was a really good actor.

Mom spent most of her time trying to quiet Delano when he came calling. Alcohol would simply shove her down to the ground to sleep him away, and the drugs seemed to quiet her hapless mind as she spun in circles, keeping him hovering close but just out of earshot for days on end. Each drop of her elixirs was an attempt to bury him deep into the quiet of her mind, at all costs. It was a critical matter, as his intent was to steadily weaken his host until only he would be left as the emperor of the palace. With each attempt to free herself, Mom grew more weary, having sacrificed her consciousness for a chance at freedom that would never come. She was held hostage with no ransom. I would have paid anything. She was held by her captor, as the only vessel for reaching out of the darkness from which he came. He mutilated her from the inside out with every verbal attack, as I stood by and watched the malaise, being the brunt of it, too, on the worst of days. I felt shame and guilt for not helping people to understand that it was Delano's fault, not hers. I let her show the outward evidence of living this nightmare alone, while the judge and jury of Kelsey labeled her a lesser person, as if she made her decisions from a desire to be such as she was. She made her decisions in an effort to be. Simply to be let be. They judged her and I knew it. And worst of all, I did too, even knowing of the battle that raged inside her.

Sometimes, I would try putting on a record to see if it would quiet Delano. I would start with the volume low and slowly increase it so as not to startle them. And there were times when Mom would stop the conversation and listen to the calming fluctuations of the music. One day, she came to my room and stood at the door, as she listened, then pulled me up to dance with her, as if at a ball. She smiled, with her head raised up listening, with her eyes closing gently with each blink. At the end, she curtsied, and I took a deep bow. It is a moment that I shall forever hold dear, our time to dance.

Delano made Mom do things. She fought him, and sometimes she could win. But other times she bought into his madness. On one of her weakest days, she called me into the kitchen. I had been playing solitaire, which I had recently learned from Miss Charlotte at the library. I purchased the deck of cards myself, at the thrift store from money I made at Sydney's. They had an official sticker from Harrah's Casino in Lake Tahoe, having reached their working life expectancy on the card tables. The sensation of beating the deck of cards kept my mind in gleeful silence on many dark nights. And even if I lost, there was always another game, as I was in charge.

I ran in to the kitchen. Mom was sitting at the kitchen table with a lighted cigarette in her hand. That wasn't unusual, but the way in which she held it gave me pause. She was holding it between her thumb and forefinger like a dart. *Why was she holding it backward?* "Come here, Son," she said, as I looked back and forth between her eyes and the smoldering dart, searching. I inched closer, as if balancing on a tight rope. My hesitation grew bones, as she quickly grabbed my arm and held the cigarette to my skin. I screamed and jerked to try and free myself. She held me tight, as I fell to the floor. "Just two more Levi!" Her voice was quavering. She quickly dabbed my arm twice more before letting me free to skirmish all the way back against the wall, under the table.

"I'm sorry! I'm sorry! I didn't want to do it! But it was our only chance! Delano saw the devil! We had to protect you! He said this was the only way."

I gazed at her, seeing her distorted fervor, my arm on fire.

"You needed a sacrament, Levi! Divine grace to protect you! Baptism by fire! This was the only way! It had to be done and it had to be three! Three points of light!"

The pain did not release me. "You hurt me bad, Mom!" I howled. "So bad!" My mind raced in search for an escape.

Mom crawled under the table, as I shrunk further into the wall. She started to sob, trying to hold me, rolling us up in a ball, repeating the mantra as I squirmed, "It had to be done.

It had to be done," through her wails. "It's over now and it'll never happen again. I'm so sorry that it hurt you."

My body shuttered from the pain that would not let me go, my arm screaming, my mind stunned that Mom would succumb to Delano's conniving at that level. They could never be trusted again. That is when the eyes in the back of my head grew even stronger, as the hair would stand high on my neck when things didn't seem quite right. Those eyes kept watch, even in my sleep.

Mom grew frustrated as she clambered out from under the table, trying to pull me out with her, as I tried to squirm away. "No Mom! No!" I was like a wounded animal, trying to claw my way free.

"Stop it!" she screeched. "You know it had to be done! You know it! Stop it now!"

I took notice of the fear in her eyes and the red that was flowing into her face, as she drug me out from under the table. I didn't want a spanking too.

"No, Mom!" I wailed as I tried to get free of her grasp. I fell to the floor, crying uncontrollably, as she pulled me up to my feet. She did not spank me. I was spared Delano's lashing. He was always the one who made her lose her temper. I despised him. Mom was still fuming, though.

She led me over to the sink. "Just be still!" Her frustration mounting. I did not move, but for my uncontrollable shivering with a stream of tears that rolled steadily down my face. She turned on the hot water and held her jittery fingers in the stream until it warmed. Then added some cold until the temperature was just to her liking, all the while grasping my injured arm in her other hand, assessing the damage. One of the burns was deep, the other two, more on the surface. She stared with approval that my fate had been sealed, then tried to wash them, while I jerked and yelped out in pain. "Levi, stop!" she yelled. I tried to. She haphazardly cleaned my arm. I held my breath, trying to hold back a wail, then let it out carefully, as a long shuddering sigh. When she finished, she shut off the tap and pressed a dish towel to my arm. "There now. See? You're gonna be fine." She led me to the bathroom where she placed a Band-Aid over each spot. "Good, we're done. I'm so relieved. We have to keep this clean, now," she said, as if innocent. Then she curled her lips to a smile, pleased with the overall outcome, having saved me from the devil himself.

I stared at her and then at the floor, gathering my courage. *Maybe I should keep my mouth shut and just fly on out of here.* "Mom?" I looked right into her eyes as the words crept out warily. "If you ever hurt me like that again, I'll run, and never come back." My eyes slowly lifted to see if I was finished.

She stared silently at my words, as they hovered, then seemed to sink in. She placed her hand over her heart. "I could never live without you, Levi," she said pitiably. "It'll never happen again. It's over. Delano said it's done, okay?"

"Mom! You have to be stronger than Delano!"

Her face wore her anguish as she started to sob.

I saw her frailty and felt pity for her, even though the burning on my arm felt like a real fire. I knew that her inevitable guilt would deepen her suffering, which was all that Delano wanted as he slid back into the abyss to gloat. But I meant every word, knowing that giving her and Delano the slip may be required if there was ever such a threat again. I decided right then and there that if there were a next time, I would run.

Chapter 21

I suffered through the pain in my arm and my soul, as each got to the work of healing. I figured that if anyone at school noticed my arm, I would make up a good story about falling on a burning stick that I pulled from the burn barrel. *Protect and defend.* And there on my arm for eternity, are the three points of light, the visible scars of my mother's insanity. Mom was remorseful and my only hope was that the crazy devil thing was a one-off. My soul found some footing, as I stayed strong, watching and somehow wishing for that opportunity to run.

His Footstep, by "Katharine Tynan" *(or maybe Katharine Strong, if I run)*

The boy will come no more
Although I listen and long;
The sound of his foot on the floor
Was like an old song.

His foot had the music in it,
And now the music's dumb
Like the song of the lark or linnet
Glad that Spring's come.

There's nothing stirring at all,
'Tis quiet all by yourself,
But a wee mouse in the wall, (and Delano)
The clock ticks on the shelf.

Like the song of the lark or linnet,
That's singing early and soon,
His foot had the music in it
Like an old tune.

Chapter 22

There is some relief in that Mom ran first. It saved me from the guilt that would have haunted me had I gone and left her. Even if it had been warranted. I hung on, and on, and did my best to be a good son. There is comfort in that.

My life was starting to make sense, even with Mom being a big question mark. I felt safe with Sydney, who kept my mother alive, as we thought of her, and talked about her often. Sydney had a way of giving me hope. She believed in me, and helped me to know that if and when Mom returned, she could get the help she needed to find some hope in herself. She was teaching me to not hang my hat on Mom's life story, as it was hers, not mine. I had the ability to create a better one for myself, all the while still feeling love and compassion for my mother. I worked hard at school and around the shop, seeing some promise in myself and my ability to become more *normal.*

Sydney applied for and was issued temporary guardianship over me. I appreciated my place in her world.

After a year, Mom and Delano were still gone. Peace tried to find space in that place that I held open for their return. One day when Sydney and I were talking at the end of a long day, I decided to tell her about Delano. I had never wanted anyone to know the depth of his madness, as he spurned on my mother with his rage. That secret kept me free from social services for all of those years, as I knew they would have swept me up quickly, leaving Mom alone to deal with the terror. We had managed his existence, which was morbidly wrapped inside of my mother's addiction, except when it wasn't.

I told Sydney everything, including the night before Mom disappeared when Delano was chattering away, getting Mom all riled up.

* * *

I opened my bedroom door and swiftly closed it behind me, leaning back to face the darkness. The moonlight glanced through the curtains, along with the wind that murmured through the crack beneath the slightly open window. I lodged a chair beneath the door knob, giving the leg a solid nudge with my foot to secure the hold. I tested the knob for reassurance. This measure was swift, well-practiced, and a solid recipe for a chance at sleep on nights like those. I yawned wide, sighing it all the way out as I pushed the curtain aside to see the tree limbs swaying back and forth in their rhythmic dance with the breeze. I placed my fingertips on the window and hung with all of my weight to pull it shut, then slid into bed. Suddenly, there was a loud bang at the door that woke me. I sat up, startled, my heart fluttering from the added beats. I could see Mom's shadow moving with the light that crept in from the crack underneath the door. I got up and leaned into it with one hand, as I sidestepped the chair. I felt the coolness of the door on my cheek and closed my eyes in defeat to the illogical system of things when it came to Delano and my mother. Mom was ranting and arguing with her nemesis. I crawled back into my bed and slid down under the covers, sticking my fingers in my ears to silence her voice. She just couldn't keep Delano at bay. I did not risk showing my face on nights like those for fear that Delano may be up for a fight which might have me brawling with him, while trying to protect my mother, an impossibility that held me tight to the confines of my room. I thought of running for help so many times, but I just couldn't risk it. So this was our silent contract, Mom's and mine. We were just doing what we had to do to survive. The torture of dealing with him was far less than that of losing me if anyone found out about him. That's what Mom told me anyway, and somehow, I let myself believe it.

When I roused again, it was daybreak. I could hear muffled voices as footsteps tapped across the floor of the living room. As her voice got closer, I realized that Mom was having a conversation with the television set. Delano had taken flight and we were free of him once again. Little did I know that both he and my mother would be gone without a trace before the day was done. If I had known, I would have given Mom a much bigger hug when I left for school, and made her pancakes for breakfast, with real syrup and fresh orange juice. And I would have written her a poem, telling her how much I loved her, because it was the truth.

* * *

Sydney cried at learning of Delano. She had a tenderness that felt like being wrapped in a soft warm blanket in front of a fireplace in the middle of winter. I wanted her to know the truth. It inched out a little at a time. She was always square with me, and I was learning how to be the same. Freedom came with the relinquishment of my secrets. Somehow, talking them out lifted them right off my shoulders, as they floated away and almost out of existence. Sydney encouraged my sharing, whenever I felt the need. Once, she asked if I wanted to talk to a therapist. "Can't I just talk to you?" I questioned.

She smiled, "Oh Levi, of course you can." My heart began to heal slowly, as the anxiety would rise up, land in her lap, and then fade out of my life. The truth was like a truce with the devil. No more secrets, so he could no longer badger on me.

I stayed busy, and finally finished up my eighth-grade year, having barely graduated. I am pretty sure pity was the party that handed over my diploma, as learning took a backseat to the blur of waiting for my mother. Life had given me greater lessons that surely bridged the gap of my intellectual learning that year.

Kelsey did not have a high school. I had a couple of choices; Valley High, which most of the kids from Kelsey went to, or Mission High, which was closer to Sydney's house. We decided on Mission, so I could walk to and from school, instead of having Sydney drive over to Valley to drop me off and pick me up each day. I really wanted to go to Valley, along with Chance, but my selfish side collaborated with Sydney's goodness. Valley was twenty minutes from the shop. I calculated that she would spend an extra forty minutes in the morning (twenty each way) and forty minutes in the afternoon, driving me to and fro. That was eighty minutes a day, five days a week. Four hundred minutes! According to my math, that was over six-and-one-half hours per week. What's crazy is, I think she would have done it for me, but I figured it was asking way too much, after her giving me everything else she had to give. I got signed up at Mission and set out to spend a nice long summer running around Kelsey with my best buddy Chance.

Chance and I signed up for the summer baseball league. We hadn't intended to until there was a big happening down at the baseball field the day of signups. The whole town of Kelsey was gathering there to pay tribute to Rollen Barton, a boy who had been killed in Vietnam. He was a great baseball player, with hopes of playing professionally, but he stepped right out of high school, having been drafted straight into the war, and was killed before he could send a single letter home to his parents. He arrived home in a box, draped in an American flag. His parents held onto that flag for a while, until they decided to donate it to the baseball league, to be raised up the flagpole and honored during the *Star-Spangled Banner* that was played before each and every game. Chance and I were so moved that we wanted to be a part that. Weren't neither of us any good at baseball, but we wore our hats proud, in honor of our fallen soldier.

Some of the guys were great ballplayers, even spending the end of the summers on traveling ball teams. I learned a lot from them. They were really dedicated to the game. In another life, I may have been too. One thing in my favor is that I was fast. I had a lot of practice with my running. And those eyes in the back of my head gave me an advantage too. My peripheral vision and senses were keen, as I could judge the trajectory of the ball, whenever it flew out to my position in right field. Not that I could catch it very often. My glove was a bit awkward, but boy did I run for it. Coach Kendall would drop his head when I came up to bat though. "Come on Levi. Keep your eyes on the ball, Buddy." It was glamour talk, as I had no skill. I felt more sorry for Coach than myself when I would strike out for the third out of an inning, ending any chance of scoring a needed run. It was usually a hopeless effort, until that one time when I actually hit the ball. I didn't even realize it when everyone started yelling for me to run. I took off, as fast as I could, making it to first base, then on to second when the short stop threw the ball over the first baseman's head. As I was standing out there, taller than normal, the umpire had to call time-out, as a white dove flew right out there across the infield, nearly landing on my head, then circling around onto the ground not six feet from me in the baseline toward third. We stared each other down, as everyone laughed at its antics. "Scare it off Levi," Coach yelled. Luckily, it heard his words and flew off on its own accord. I watched it fly up and onto the roof of the dugout. I thought of Rollen. Maybe just maybe, he sent that dove to cheer me on. *Job well done, Levi.*

I got thrown out while slap-dashing into third. I looked up, and the dove was gone. We won the game, and Coach said I was instrumental! That feeling of boastful pride was new, and I realized that a single success can make up for many a failed effort or lack of trying.

After each game, either home or away, all of us guys would climb into the back of Coach Kendall's truck, as he drove us straight to the Jolly Cone, and treated us to a frosty. I always chose the chocolate dipped vanilla cone, with nuts. Oh man, there are no words.

Chapter 23

The summer was winding down, as the trees began to turn to the orange and gold of autumn. The air smelled of its sweet molasses and leaf piles. I particularly remember the dew that morning, as Sydney and I were out in the yard, early, hanging laundry, my sneakers soaked on the toes from the wet grass. It was another welcome sign that the heavy heat was likely behind us.

We saw the car pull up to the house, from our vantage point in the side yard. Sydney walked out to greet the visitor. I was finishing up the last pieces of laundry, as I could hear the low voices out by the car. I pinned up my favorite shirt that Sydney bought me for my first day of the eighth grade. It was green, which she said matched my eyes. It had been handy on St. Patrick's Day, too, so as not to get pinched.

As I walked out, there, standing with Sydney, was Sheriff Bender. My mind raced to the fear that my new life was over. Had he found my mother? It quickly switched gears, as I searched the car, and his eyes for her as I approached them.

My fear fell to sorrow, as she was nowhere in sight. Sheriff Bender's body language was like a wilting weed.

I held my lips between my teeth as I forced my way to Sydney, as through a blizzard. Head down and leaning forward. She pulled me close. I didn't want to know . . .

"Thank you, Sheriff. I'll come down in a bit."

Sheriff Bender nodded his head solemnly to us both, as he turned toward the car. I caught a glimpse of his sadness that lay there in the furrow of his brow.

They had found my mother's body down at Dewey Creek. It appeared that she had been there all along, alone, hidden in the weeds, not more than a hundred yards down the embankment from a main road. She was fully clothed, the only physical harassment appeared to be that of small animals, trying to get at a food source. Somebody had stumbled upon her remains three days prior, and the detectives set out to identify her. They found her purse nearby which solidified their inkling and, luckily, Mom had a bad tooth pulled a couple of years ago, making her full dental X-ray a perfect match, and making it not necessary for any other person to try and identify her decayed body.

They did not know the cause of her death, but overdose was likely, as a needle was found near her body, though foul play could not be ruled out. I knew that she had been using heroin. Yes, another secret I had not yet told. She had added it to her arsenal of tricks to keep Delano at bay. She never gave up trying. When I caught her shooting up one day, I was angry. But she told me that this gloss felt like a gentle hug that held her close while she sat and listened to Delano's voice slowly disappear. I was grateful when the lab ruled her death a heroin overdose and prayed that she felt safe and warm in its gentle embrace to the very end.

Why is The Rose So Pale, by "Heinrich Heine" (Why Mom? Why did it have to be this way?)

O Dearest, canst thou tell me why
The Rose should be so pale?
And why the azure Violet
Should wither in the vale?

And why the Lark should, in the cloud,
So sorrowfully sing?
And why from loveliest balsam-buds
A scent of death should spring?

And why the Sun upon the mead
So chillingly should frown?
And why the Earth should, like a grave,
Be moldering and brown?

And why is it that I, myself,
So languishing should be?
And why is it, my Heart of Hearts,
That thou forsakest me?

Chapter 24

The day that the coroner called with the cause of death, he asked Sydney if we had Mom's birthdate and family information, as he needed it to complete the death certificate. I told her that Mom's birthday was July 4th, Independence Day. That's all I knew, and it wasn't near enough information for the legal documents. Sydney thought about the box of Mom's papers in her shed behind the shop. She was hopeful that Mom's birth certificate was buried somewhere inside.

After lunch, we drove over to the shed, to go through Mom's things. Sydney asked me if I would rather stay at home, but I wanted to go. I wanted to search. After pulling down the box marked *My Papers*, and seeing all that was left of Mom's life, I felt a deeper sadness for its futility, and nervous to see what we might find. It would have felt like a treasure hunt, if it wasn't for us looking at the only physical proof that my mother even existed, except for me, of course.

We carried the *My Papers* box into the shop, and Sydney sat it on a chair. As we pulled the flaps open, we started going through the papers. There were lots of receipts, old coupons, my report cards, an old magazine and a rolled-up newspaper. While Sydney sorted through the box, I pulled out a perfectly good pencil with a full eraser, some crayons, two sticks of chalk, a box of tacks, a tiny silver key to who knows what, playing cards (how could I have known), and some dice. I would add them to my collection box of *things*. Then Sydney reached in and pulled out an envelope. On the front was marked, *Katharine's BC*. It was Mom's birth certificate.

"Thank goodness," she said as she pulled out the document. We sat down to inspect it.

Mom's birth certificate looked just like mine:

Certificate of Live Birth
Los Angeles County

Name of Child: **Katharine Mary Strong**

Sex: **Female**

Date of Birth: **July 4th, 1941**

Independence Day

Time: **1:36 am**

City: **Santa Monica, California**

We were born in the same town. I didn't know.

Mother of Child: **Mary Margaret Strong, Age: 35**

I stared at the name. Sydney looked down and smiled warmly, "Levi, this is your grandmother's name."

Wait! No! "Mom was an orphan. She ran away from the orphanage when she was fifteen!" My mind raced through the stories. "She said the nuns gave her the name, 'Strong,' because she had a strong spirit from the very start." My mind twisted like a pretzel, just before unraveling, just like Mom's story.

Sydney wrapped her arms around me. "Levi, we'll figure it all out. Just breathe with me. Take a deep breath. It's all gonna be okay." I could always look to her for calm, as she talked me back to my senses, whenever my mind tried to run down a rabbit hole. She had a way of making me feel so much better. I was her perfect boy, no matter what. I liked the feeling of maybe being perfect, and her calling me her boy.

I opened my mouth to breathe in as much air as I could, and let it out slowly, closing my eyes.

"One more time," she said in a whisper. *It helped.*

There was no father listed on Mom's birth certificate either. Like mother like son.

Father of Child: *Blank*

Inside the envelope, Sydney found a little piece of paper with a note scribbled on it.

If you need anything else, just let me know. Signed, *Peter.*

Sydney stuffed the birth certificate and note back into the envelope, and we hurriedly put the box back into the shed, as we roared off to the coroner's office before they closed. The clerk led us to the office of Mr. Lampley, coroner, as it said on the nameplate on the door.

Sydney handed Mr. Lampley Mom's birth certificates, as we sat down in front of his giant desk.

"I see that there may be some relatives to notify," he said.

I stared at his mouth as he said the empty words. "My mom was an orphan. We don't have relatives," I said as the all-knowing.

Without even acknowledging me, he carried on with his business. "We'll have to send for the official state copy before moving forward."

"Can you send for Levi's state copy too?" Sydney asked. I loved her for just taking care of things. "He was born in the same county."

"I think we can do that."

"His full name is Leviticus David Strong." He wrote it down, as I watched for a smirk. "He goes by Levi," Sydney explained. I loved her for telling him, even though he didn't seem to care. "About how long will it take to get them back?"

"Two weeks or so."

Sydney shook his hand as we stood up to leave. I thought about offering mine too, but he did not even look my way. I was invisible.

It seems I was always waiting. I read once that time was just an illusion. Could be true, especially when you are in the midst of turmoil, where everything spins around in circles, while you are left standing right there in the middle, unmoving, waiting, watching it swirl like the tornado in the Wizard of Oz. There are chairs and cows and witches on bicycles storming around in that space. Then it will blur to a stop. Still. Everything falling to the ground. Then silence. There is only my breathing there. And time, if it exists, stands still, too.

I laid in bed, dreaming about my grandmother, Mary Margaret. I imagined her walking barefoot in the night, her baby girl in her arms, wrapped in a pink flowery towel, as she made her way to the orphanage steps. I could see her holding her baby up toward God and asking Him to protect her. She stood there crying, one last kiss, and then laid her baby gently on the stoop. Things must have been really bad for her. I mean, Mom's life was in the gutter, and she was still able to hang on to me. At least Mary Margaret found a safe place for her baby. I heard stories of babies being left in dumpsters to die and knew they could be buried in back yards to be consumed by the earth. I wondered if Violet was there to grab hold of Mom's hand, as she rose up to heaven. I could not imagine that God would have sent Mom to hell. She had already lived through hell, right here on earth. She needed to step through those pearly gates and live out eternity in the arms of the angels. I tried to imagine my grandmother's face. I'm sure she was pretty, like my mother once was. I hoped she would be happy to know about me, if she were ever able to be found, but I dreaded her knowing of Mom's miserable life. l felt sorry for her, and I felt sorry for me, as I cried myself to sleep.

Mom's funeral was postponed until the details of her life could be confirmed. That didn't stop the Kelsey Kourier from writing a little story about the death of my mother. My home room teacher, Miss Rosewood, was asking for donations to be sent to a bank account that she and Sydney set up for me. Sydney handed me the newspaper so that I could read all about it. I was surprised, but then, not really, to see that my family in Kelsey would stand by me. They were the ones who gave me some kind of normalcy, as they were really the ones who raised me. Mom loved me and early on taught me right from wrong. But that was before her mind wandered off to another place. There wasn't much direction after that. I was all she had though, and our house was the place that I would go at the end of each day, to watch over her. My daily life was lived in the arms of Kelsey, with Sydney being my constant.

About three weeks after we dropped off the birth certificates, Mr. Lampley called Sydney. They had hit a snag. Neither of our birth certificates were valid. Forgeries. He had picked up my copy at social services to confirm. They were looking into the note that was in the envelope by the *Peter* character, though it was doubtful that it would lead anywhere. Detective Sherwood from the Sheriff's office had been assigned to investigate the identification of my mother.

Things were going more sideways. I thought Mom's death was an end to all the madness that I would have to endure.

But since she was found, it kept growing legs. I had a grandmother for a minute, and now she was dead, too.

Detective Sherwood called to introduce himself to Sydney and made an appointment to pay us a visit. It would be Tuesday evening at 6:00, after Sydney got off work. He wanted to talk to me especially. That made me nervous. My stomach ached with the formulating of what I might have to spill.

The next day is a blur until 6:00 p.m. sharp, when the doorbell rang.

"Detective Sherwood?" Sydney said, in a higher voice than normal when she opened the door.

"Yes, but you can call me Jake," he said with a polite smile, and a tip of his hat. He was short and stocky. Fifty-ish, with dark black hair, which was greying heavily at his long sideburns. His hair was a little long and curling out from under his grey fedora. His face well shaven, though you could see the dark blue stubble that had forced its escape from a long workday. His eyes were grey, the same color as his hat. His kind demeanor didn't help my uneasiness. I had a strong feeling of dread.

"Please come in, Jake. This is Levi." I was practically standing on her heels.

"It's nice to meet you, Levi." I reached my hand to his, as he reached out. I didn't think to grab on but let him shake it firmly without my help.

"Shall we sit at the kitchen table?" Sydney asked.

"Yes, that'll be fine."

"Would you like something to drink?"

"No thank you, Ma'am, I'm fine."

I felt dizzy from the dread, as we all took our places for the interrogation. Jake removed his hat and placed it on his knee under the table. "On second thought, I'd like a soda if you have one."

"I do." Sydney got up to grab him a Fresca from the refrigerator. "Would you like one Levi?"

I nodded, "Yes, thanks." She grabbed three. One for each of us, and grabbed the bottle opener, that was shaped like a mermaid, and popped them open. It broke the ice.

"Levi, I'm really sorry about your losing your mom."

I looked down at the floor. I didn't want to cry, as the tears tried to burn their way free. I felt heavy.

"So, I hear you'll be going to high school soon. It seems like yesterday that my kids were in high school. They're all grown up now." I knew he was making small talk to try and rescue me from myself.

"How long have you lived here in Kelsey, Levi?" The questions began.

"Since I was about four, I think."

"How old are you now?"

"Fourteen."

"Wow, that's a long time. What's your birthdate? "

"November 12th, 1957."

"And your full name?"

"I go by Levi." I looked up at Sydney, who was smiling at me. "But my full name is Leviticus David Strong."

"What a big name! Did your mom ever tell you why she gave you your great name?"

"It was biblical. That's all."

"Do you remember where you lived before you came to Kelsey? He scribbled as he talked, without looking down at the paper.

I thought deeply, trying to pull it out, "No, I just remember a few things."

"What things *can* you remember?" he asked, waiting patiently for the answer.

"We lived in … I think it was a motel … next to a highway. And there was a big field out back."

"Do you remember what color the motel was painted?"

I remembered, "It was green."

"Green like grass or green like an olive, on the dingier side?"

"Green like grass, and the doors were all red." That image just popped up out of nowhere.

"Do you remember any signs out in front of the motel?"

I saw the vision, "Yeah, there *was* a sign."

"Do you remember what it said?"

"I couldn't read, but it was white with black letters. The kind that you can change around."

"Okay," he kept writing.

"Do you remember any other places that you lived?"

I shook my head, "No."

"Did your mom have friends there?"

"She would talk to people, but I don't know if they were her friends."

"Did you have friends there?"

"I played with kids, but I didn't really know them."

"Is there anything else you can remember about the motel?"

I shook my head, "No."

"Okay. When you came to Kelsey, did your mom drive you here?"

"No, we rode the bus."

"How did you get to the bus station?"

I thought, "We walked."

"How long did you walk?"

My eyes stared up, as I tried to recall. "I don't think it was far."

"Did you take the same bus all the way to Kelsey?"

"No, the first one was a regular bus, with no bathroom. Like a city bus. We took that bus to another place where we took the bigger bus."

"Aw, okay. Do you know how long you were on that bigger bus?'

I pondered, "I think we got to Kelsey in one day."

"Okay. In like a whole day, from morning to night or like a 24-hour day?

"From morning to before dark, it was still light when we got there."

"Did you stay on that same bigger bus all day?"

"Yeah, I think so."

"Do you remember which direction you were traveling on the bus, when you got to town?"

"Yes." Jake looked surprised. "We were on the highway, in the lane closest to the feed mill when we got here. We got dropped off right there by the mill and had to run across all the lanes to get to Kelsey."

"So, you came from the north."

"Yeah, we would have been heading south."

Jake nodded, "Okay. Did your mom ever drive, Levi?"

"Nope, she never drove a car. She walked everywhere."

"Do you remember any family or her talking about any family?"

"No, Mom was raised in an orphanage. She didn't have any family."

"Oh, yes, I had heard that." I think he had heard lots of things. "Did your mom ever talk about any family?"

"No, never."

"Did she ever talk about your father?"

I wiggled my feet on the floor. He was all I ever thought of. "She told me she didn't know who he was." I knew that sounded silly, as it was nearly impossible not to know.

"Okay. Did she talk about where she was from?"

"Just about being raised in an orphanage and then running away when she was fifteen, and then having me."

Did she say what town the orphanage was in or mention the name of the orphanage?

"No."

"Did she say that you were born in a hospital?"

I pondered, "No, she never said. I just assumed, I guess."

"Did you ever feel like your mom was trying to keep anything from you?"

I hesitated, "She pretty much kept things to herself. That was just the way she was." I thought of Delano. She shared lots a crazy things with him, and he with her. Most just secrets between them.

"Levi, did your mom have any close friends?"

I thought about Delano again and started fidgeting in my chair. I felt sweat beading up on my nose. It was hot. "I don't know if you can call them friends, but I know she would hang out with people." I took a long drink of my Fresca.

"Did people hang out with her at your house?"

"No, she never had anyone come over. She would, sometimes, hang out at the old blue house next to the canal over on Magnolia Street and under the new overpass on Second Street. I went to those places to look for her when she went missing."

"Did you talk to anyone while you were there at those places?"

"I yelled out at the people under the bridge, on if they had seen Kat lately. Some just stared; a couple of others said that she hadn't been there in a while. I kept my distance. I also knocked on the door at the blue house. A man came to the door. He hadn't seen her in a few weeks either. I checked back often. Always the same answers."

Jake stared at me, his face soft, tilting his head slightly, and continued to write. He turned to Sydney. "You have some papers that belonged to Katharine?"

"Yes, but they're at my shop in Kelsey."

"I'd like to see them."

"All of Kat's things are in my shed at the shop."

"May I come by there tomorrow?"

"Yes, that'll be fine. I'll be there all day. My shop is on Main Street, *Sydney's Beauty Parlor*. Can you come by around noon? I have lunch slotted out then."

"Yes, I'll be there. Thanks. I think that's enough questions for today." My shoulders dropped down to their normal position in relief, having been pinned tightly to my ears. We all stood up and walked toward the door. "Thank you, Levi. You've been a trooper. And again, I'm so sorry about your mom."

I tried to grin, awkwardly, and nodded my head, like an adult.

"Sydney?" He tipped his hat, "I'll see you tomorrow."

Chapter 25

I went to work with Sydney the next day, as usual. "You don't have to be here today when Jake comes by." She was trying to protect me.

"I know, but I want to." I didn't tell her that my intentions were to watch over my mother's things to make sure that Jake didn't make away with anything. Those things were all I had left of her.

He arrived promptly at noon. He asked if they had good burgers over at the Jolly Cone that he passed by on the way. Sydney told him that they were the best! Especially, the Big Bang Burger.

"How about I go pick us up some?" Jake offered.

"Sounds like a great idea," agreed Sydney. We would save the sandwiches she made for later.

"I'll spring for the shakes," Sydney smiled.

"No way, I've got it. Come on Levi, I'm starving!" I hesitated and looked at Sydney. She smiled, and I followed Jake out the door. He didn't mention my mother. I was grateful. He talked mostly about his boys, John and Jacob Jr., who were both off at college. John wanted to go into law enforcement like his dad, and Jacob was an English major. As different as they could be, he said of his boys. I wondered what Violet may have done, if she had made it. She would have been an artist, I think. I liked the sound of that.

We returned to the shop with armloads of food. That Big Bang was delicious, as usual. It had a quarter pound of beef, cheddar cheese, bacon, avocado, lettuce, grilled onions, tomatoes, dill pickles, and chopped jalapenos, all on a giant, and toasted, sesame seed bun. Our eyes and noses leaked from the heat of the peppers, as our taste buds stood up and cheered. We giggled at the mess we were making, dripping clean down our arms and over our napkins. We got fries and the onion rings that Jake could not pass up. Mine and Sydney's shakes were vanilla, and Jake's, chocolate. They helped to put out the fires.

We finished up eating, singing the praises of our burgers, while cleaning off the break table. I was stuffed! The ice was breaking, and I was, cautiously, warming up to Jake. He seemed to be a nice enough guy. Normal-like. Whatever that means. But the jury was still out. The bell on the front door chimed. It was Sydney's next client. "Excuse me. You gonna be alright here Levi?" she said, a little nervously.

"Sure." I grinned to give her comfort.

"Okay, if you need me, I'm right here," she smiled as she turned to greet her patron, Mrs. Harrison, and quickly got to work on her head.

Sydney and I had already brought Mom's things in from the shed. My inheritance. All in a few boxes, mostly clothes. How can such a big life take up so little room in the end? I showed Jake the boxes and he got right to work, slitting the tape on the first one with his pocketknife.

I sat down at the table, while he stood reaching into the box. "I don't want you to take my mom's things," I said bravely.

Jake stopped his work, pulled out a chair and sat facing me. "Levi, I can't promise you that I won't need to take some things today. If I find something that I think will be helpful, I may have to take it for a little while. But I promise you that I will return it to you as soon as I can."

"What exactly are you looking for," I asked, curious.

"I'm looking for anything that might be a clue, as to where your mother came from before moving to Kelsey."

"Why does it even matter?" I wondered out loud.

He took a deep breath and spoke softly, keeping his eyes steady on mine. "I know how hard this is for you. I talked to Sydney about whether or not you should've been here when I went through your mother's things today. I knew it might be hard, but Sydney said she's always straight with you. You're smart and you have a voice that she wants to honor."

I sat up taller in my seat, a more honorable posture.

"I want to be straight with you too, Levi. We'll go through this together, even if it's hard." He sat back a little, and continued, "When someone dies . . ." he seemed to hesitate at the harshness of the words, ". . . it's my job to ensure that we have accurate information regarding the identity of the deceased. It's my responsibility to not only obtain that accurate information, but to also do my due diligence to notify the deceased person's family members. Since we don't yet have an official birth certificate for your mom, I must do my best to find it."

"What if Mom doesn't have a birth certificate?"

"It could be possible, if she were not born in a hospital, and if no one ever notified the city or county of her birth, which they are supposed to do. If that's the case, I will still try to find out where she came from, in hopes of finding someone who may know of her. If she was raised in an orphanage, I want to find that orphanage. I want to do my very best for your mom. She deserves my very best, as do you. You understand?"

I scanned his eyes. There was hurt in there. "Yeah, I do." I wanted to know more about my mother too. I wanted to know all about the orphanage, the nuns, how they found her on the front steps, and the time when she was a little kid. And, most of all, I needed to know if she had ever been happy, or had Delano always been there to antagonize her.

I could see my mother walking away in each piece of clothing that Jake held up to examine. He made sure to neatly fold each piece and lay it in a tidy pile on the table, as I stood guard. He held her underclothes down inside the box, as he examined them, only setting them out after fully looking them over. He held up a cream-colored sun dress with a big sunflower on the front. I always liked that one. Mom looked young and kind of childlike in it. It was made for the hippie in her, one of the flower children that never came to be. Her flowers had wilted, and could not grow, as Delano blew his hot dry air over them and then cut them to the ground.

Jake wrote some notes about what he found and placed all the clothes neatly back inside each box. He pulled a new roll of packing tape from his briefcase, taped each lid back to closed, and sat them on the floor by the door.

"Are you taking those?" I questioned.

"No, I won't need to take them," he grinned, in confirmation.

He grabbed the box of papers that he sat on a chair in front of him so he could stay seated as he looked for something that might be evidence. Somehow, I was finding peace with the process. Even seeing Mom's clothes was some kind of comfort. She liked them mostly pastel, as they screamed for attention only from the gods. Now she wore her dress of glory, singing her songs to the angels.

Jake opened the box, the flaps not taped. I sat, watching with interest, as he carefully began considering each piece of paper. Lifting each one, scanning it fully, and placing it in one of several piles that he made on the table. One-by-one, he scoured over each tiny paper.

He pulled out the magazine and rolled up newspaper. He drug up the turquoise-blue rubber band that held the paper, as it broke from its age. He laid the newspaper on the table, folding it open in an attempt to lay it flat. It did not cooperate, so he held it smooth, as he looked down at it. I got up to take a better look. The headline in bold black print yelled from the pages: **"RUSSIA LAUNCHES SATELLITE INTO SPACE; U.S. FALLS BEHIND."** The newspaper was the *Wintonville Weekender*, dated Saturday, October 5, 1957. I was deathly afraid of the Russians. They kept us hitting our knees under our desks, during bomb drills, that prepared us for that fateful day when the blitz would begin. After the initial blast, if we were still alive, we were to run, single file, to the bomb shelter, following the black and yellow signs, as we dodged the radioactive fallout from the blast. Those were frightening days dreaming of the possibility of dying right there at Kelsey Elementary when Kelsey was blown clear off the map.

"There's a lot to read here. I'm gonna set it aside for now."

"Can I read it?"

"Sure. Just be careful with it. I'll want to read through it later." He handed me the paper. I read the Sputnik article, with a side eye keeping watch over Jake's chore.

Jake continued through the box, as I lost focus, dreaming of myself flying through space with my trusty dog, as we rocketed toward Mars. The article mentioned that, in addition to fruit flies, the Russians were keen on sending dogs up to space. Sadly, they never returned, but me and my partner would make it all the way to the Red Planet.

I heard Jake sigh.

"Did you find something?" as I sat up to attention. He had everything placed back in the box, except the magazine.

"I've looked through everything and, if it's alright, I'd like to take the magazine and the newspaper with me. I closed the newspaper and handed it over.

He busied himself folding and taping up the box. "Shall we put these back in the shed? He asked.

I jumped up, grabbed a box and headed out the back door. Jake followed and we made quick work of it.

We went back inside where Jake gathered his notes and briefcase, then peaked in at Sydney, who was busily back combing Mrs. Harrison's wiry grey hair. "I'm gonna head out now. I'll be in touch."

Sydney waved, "Okay. Thanks." I wondered what she would say to Mrs. Harrison about the goings on. It's nearly impossible to keep secrets in a beauty parlor. Everybody talks.

"Hey, thanks for standing by me today," Jake said, as he put his hand on my shoulder.

"You're welcome. Thanks for the lunch," I said politely.

"You're welcome. I might just be making the Jolly Cone one of my regular dinner spots. Hard to beat! I'll check back in a couple of days." Jake walked to his car.

"Do you really think you'll find anything?"

He stopped before getting in. "I won't give up trying, Levi. It's not in me." He got in his car, quickly waved, and drove off.

I held my hand up in the dusty air until he pulled out of the alley and off to find a lead into the start of my mother's life. I put the padlock back on the shed, placing the key back in the drawer of Sydney's desk. I thought about the key I found in Mom's box of papers early on. It was smaller than the padlock key. Maybe I should have told Jake about it.

When we got back home that night, I went to check out that key in my collections box. I pulled it out to see if there were any markings on it. I felt like a sleuth, and decided the next day, to go to Kelsey with Sydney and take it down to Mr. Bill's. He had a key making machine. Maybe he would know what kind of key it was.

"It appears to be a jewelry box key. That would be my guess anyway. Or maybe a diary key," Mr. Bill explained.

"Hmm," I wondered out loud. I'd never seen any jewelry boxes around our house or any jewelry at all for that matter. Mom didn't have a diary that I knew of. "Thanks, Mr. Bill." I turned to go, my mind searching my memory for the sight of a keyhole.

"You take good care of yourself, Levi. Hey, I'm real sorry about your mom."

I kept heading toward the door. "Yeah. I'll see you later, Mr. Bill." I bolted before the sniveling started, as it always did when someone reminded me of my grief.

I went back to the shop and told Sydney what Mr. Bill thought about the key. "I think we better call Jake," Sydney said. She pulled out his business card that she had placed in her collection and called him up. He picked up after the secretary rang her through. She told him about the key. He wanted to stop by that night to take a look at it. It might be something. She asked him if there was any news from the papers he had taken. He told her that he got pulled away, so he hadn't been able to look them over completely yet. He would take his time with them, so as not to miss a single word that may be a lead.

Jake arrived promptly at 7:15 pm. He was proving to be punctual. "Here's the key." I reached into the front pocket of my jeans and pulled out a small matchbox that I had placed it in for safekeeping. I opened the box and handed the key to Jake. He took it, turning it all around, looking for a clue.

"Can I see that matchbox?"

"Sure." I handed it over.

"Do you remember ever seeing any little jewelry boxes or diaries around the house?"

"No, I never saw anything like that."

"Where did you get this matchbox?"

I had to think. "I don't remember. I've always had it in my collection box."

Jake studied it, squinting his eyes, trying to read the tiny print on its side. He then placed the key back inside.

"Have a seat, Jake." Sydney waved toward the couch.

"Levi, I'd like to take the key to study it a little more, if that's okay."

I hesitated as I wondered why. "Okay."

Jake took off his hat and placed it on the coffee table, placing the matchbox next to his hat, as he took a seat.

"Who wants a soda?"

"I'd love one. Thanks, Sydney."

"Me, too. Thanks."

She went into the kitchen to get our drinks.

"Could I take a look at your collection box?" Jake asked.

I thought about the other little things I had taken from Mom's box, feeling like I was guilty of withholding evidence. "Sure. I have a couple of other things from Mom's box in there too," I confessed straight away so no guilt could build up on me. I learned that this was the best way to handle most wrongs, well before they grew out of proportion to their aim.

One time a couple of kids from the River Dale trailer park, came running over to the Hole with pockets full of gum balls from the machine that had gone on the blink by the park meeting hall. We all ran over and filled our pockets. The next day, I was moseying on by, just to check on the health of the coin operation, when Miss Opal, one of the ladies who I helped with her gutters sometimes, told me about how the gum ball machine had been burgled just that day before. I acted surprised. She said, "I'm sure glad you don't take to any stealing." Somehow, just by the way she said it, with a side eyed glance, I thought she might well have seen me running from the crime scene that day of the gum ball snatching. I went on home and kept thinking about my guilt. Thieving just kind of happened on me sometimes. I didn't plan on it. I was just in the wrong place at the right time, and luckily, never got caught or apprehended anyway. I ached all night with the worry that I had been had. I went back the next day and placed an anonymous envelope in the mail drop at the trailer park office, where I put in a quarter to pay for my offense. The relief was immediate. I would just have to stop my thieving ways. They had caused me grief and then hard-earned cash, which made an even bigger impact.

Jake was sipping his Fresca, and Sydney set mine on the coffee table, when I returned with the box. I sat down close to Jake so he could see inside it. I placed it on my lap and lifted off the lid, reaching in for Mom's things that I had taken. It was not an impressive collection, more of a junk box.

"What a nice collection," Jake smiled. "How long have you been collecting things?"

"Forever, I guess." He lost me with *a nice collection*.

One by one, I handed him Mom's things. He looked over each item carefully. None of them seemed to spark his curiosity.

"Levi, can I look at more of the items in your box?"

"Sure," I said hesitantly. I was a little embarrassed by some of the silly stuff I had gathered, but I handed him the box. There was an old cigarette box, filled with lipstick-laced filters with a few smokes left in them, from my gathering days at the Hole. They had that stale smokey smell, like from a heavy smoker who never washed their coat. I hadn't smoked in a while. They were pretty gross looking, as I remembered sucking air through the nasty things.

There were old coins, used birthday candles, a stale almost-empty bag of sunflower seeds, some chewing gum foils formed into little origami characters. I had learned this art form from Suzy Masterson, who was in my 5th grade class. She had a book on origami that she shared with the class one day. Our teacher, Mrs. Sampson gave us each a pack of Juicy

Fruit gum, which to enjoy and create our masterpieces. I thought mine were pretty good. Thus, saving them all.

Jake picked up the deck of playing cards, noticing the Harrah's seal on it. I explained that I purchased them at the thrift shop.

"Aw, okay." He quickly lost interest in them, then picked up a clear box, the kind that generally holds straight pins. He opened it up and inside were 5 matchbooks. The little cardboard kind, with a flap that tucks under the striker flap. They were all old, and mostly used. I had used them to light my smokes back in the day. Jake held each up, looking for clues. Each was the same, bearing the name of the matchmaker, except the largest one on the bottom, which was really a small sewing kit, that resembled a larger book of matches. I took in a quick breath. It was green, the color of grass, and on the front was a red logo and in the same red fluorescent letters it read, *The Medallion Motel*. Under that, *Grixley, California.*

Jakes hands began to shake ever so slightly. He flipped open the book to find a little plastic wrapper that held a single white button, a small sewing needle, several inches of white thread, and a small gold colored safety pin. The kit had never been used, but lay in wait. A small clue from somewhere in my past.

"Levi, could this be from the motel that you lived in?"

"I'm trying to remember. I haven't seen it in a long time. It could be."

He sat the kit on the table and continued poking through each item in my collection of things. After considering every item, he placed the lid back on the box. "I'd like to take the motel sewing kit and the key with me. I'll do some checking on this motel."

I hesitated. "Okay." I felt ache hit my stomach. Why did the room feel so hot? Mom's life was like a can of worms. Once we pried it open, we could not go back. I drank most of my Fresca in one long swig.

"It's getting late." Jake stood, placing one hand on my shoulder, tipping his hat toward Sydney with the other. "Thanks for letting me look through your things, Levi, and thanks for the soda. I'll take my time, looking over everything, and will be in touch." He stepped out the door and more into the mystery that was my mother's life.

Chapter 26

Waiting, still. Worry changed. It was replaced with learning to live with the old wounds from all my yesterdays, making the best of today, and preparing for my future. Sydney was my greatest fan, cheering me on at every turn, as always.

I no longer had to worry about my mother. Her thick armor of troubles fell from her shoulders, and mine. Though I felt guilty for feeling the comfort of that. Sydney helped me through my grief. It was not my job to protect my mother. My job was to survive. "You carried yourself through," she said. "May you always know that there's nothing you can't endure. As much as I wish I could have intervened sooner, there's something powerful in knowing that you can find your way through no matter what comes your way, with your own inner strength. That's a powerful reckoning for the rest of your life."

I did hold on through it all. Standing on my calloused soles, atop the graves of my saddest days. They taught me their hard lessons. I could now see the trees, for I was lifted from the forest floor. Most importantly, my mother's death was her own doing. There was nothing I could have done to save her from herself. Now, I was learning to live my own life. I would find peace with my memories of my mother if I could turn my feelings of grief to a greater sense of hope for my future. Breathe out grief, breathe in hope. Soon, there would only be hope left. Mom was no longer in pain. I was grateful for that, though, sometimes I felt guilty that my life was finding some meaning since she had gone and died.

I found myself dreaming more of finding my dad again. As Mom's memory began to fade into the background of my life, a new vision of my dad was trying to fight its way free. I wondered how he would feel if he found out about me. I only allowed myself to believe that he would be glad to know of my existence. Or what if he was looking for me? Mom having kept us buried in the rubble of our lives, leaving him unable to find us. I started talking about it to Sydney a lot. Once Jake could find Mom's birth certificate, and mine, maybe he could help me find my dad. She had called and talked to him about that. He said that he would be happy to help. I grew more and more anxious about that possibility. I stopped my obsession with Joe Riley, having heaped a giant pile of hope on him being my dad. But things had changed, as I would be leaning on a detective who would pay no mind to my nonsensical fixation and only look to real evidence in search of my father.

That space that was once overwhelmed with grief, was beginning to fill with the search for truth and girls. Well, at least one girl. I spotted her that first day in home room at Mission High. She, like me, knew no one. She did not float to any group of girls in the hallway but walked straight out the door at the end of the day and disappeared. My eyes followed until I lost sight of her. I liked the way she walked, her shoulders back, a smooth grace in her steps, like a dancer. Her salmon-colored dress flowed in a perfect rhythm with her stride. Her hair was short, and curly, and dark. Her eyes light blue. Her skin, a warm bronze, like a Coppertone ad. And she knew nothing of me. She was . . . perfection.

I got nerve on our second day and paced my steps to be walking in sync, right next to her on our way out to break. "Hi." My heart sped up as she turned, piercing me with those eyes. I was nearly stunned, feeling so seen.

"Hi," she said with a slight smile.

"My name's Levi."

"Yeah, I know, from home room. "Short for Leviticus," she grinned.

"Yeah." Maybe she liked my big name. "You're Izabella."

"You can call me Izzy, for short." Another smile.

This was my first communication with a girl who did not know of my unkempt past. I could present my new persona with no shouts from the crowd that it was all a lie.

I called Chance that night to see how his first day of school went. His was the same as mine regarding the girls. He had his eye on several around campus. That next week he called to let me know that he had some kind of reading disorder called dyslexia. He had to go to a special class for reading still, but at least he knew why he had such a hard time. He sounded good. We visited mostly on the phone since we didn't go to the same school anymore. I missed seeing him most days, but I did not miss my old life.

Izzy and I became quick friends, waiting for each other at break, and sitting together at lunch. I was a good listener, asking lots of questions to avoid the counter strike of any pushed back toward me. Izzy and her family had recently moved from San Francisco, where her father worked at Treasure Island. He was an avionics technician for the Navy and had been stationed there prior to being shipped out to sea. He specialized in radio and flight control systems on an aircraft carrier. I was impressed. Izzy's mom had relatives here, so they decided to move the family this direction during her father's deployment. She missed him, hence the sadness in her eyes some days. I wondered if I wore the missing of my own dad in that way. Mine would be more of a far-off look, as I could only imagine the unknown voice of my father.

Izzy had an older sister and two younger brothers. She told me that her father was black and her mother, white. No wonder her skin was so warm and beautiful. Not pasty white like mine. Her family had to move once, in the last year, due to some neighbors who found fault with the mixed race of her and her siblings. I understood that ache in her voice, as I knew of people who would do just that. I was upset about that kind of behavior before, but I felt it even deeper when it landed on the people I cared about. This time, Izzy and her family had been the brunt of their ignorance. I took hold of her hand gently and told her how sorry I was that there was such meanness in the world. She held onto my hand and leaned onto my shoulder. Her hair smelled of fresh coconut and vanilla. I had never wanted to be so close to anyone before.

I only told Izzy that we lived close to the school, and I didn't lie when I told her that I never saw my dad.

Chapter 27

Jake had been touching base regularly, as he had promised, even joining us for dinner a lot. He and Sydney were becoming . . . close. Jake had shared that he and his wife were divorced, so that twinkle in Sydney's eye began soon after. I liked Jake okay. He made us both laugh. And I had hope that he was gonna someday find my dad for me and the true identity of my mother. But I had a twang of discomfort that he was moving in a little too close and a lot too fast. I would have to keep my eye on things. I felt a bit protective of Sydney, not wanting her to get sucked in by a smooth-talking detective, who may just push me right out of the picture, as he moved on in. I was trying to think of a way to push him back a few paces. It was a conflict with the fact that I needed him on my team. I decided to lay low with my concerns, yet to stay sharp-eyed for any unseemly conduct or signs of upheaval. It was a difficult predicament, like letting a fox circle the henhouse. He had to be sly to be a detective; I just wasn't sure if he was gonna consume us chickens if he came on in.

The Medallion Motel was a dead end. Jake drove all the way up to Grixley to interview the original owners, who had sold it five years prior. They looked through their boxes of old records and found nothing from the years 1960 through 1962 when he estimated that we may have stayed at the motel. They had destroyed most of the older records, as the IRS could not go back that far should they ever request an audit. They had no recall of me or my mother when Jake described us to them. Jake looked around the motel, which had been painted a deep blue. He left his card with both the old and new proprietors in case they thought of anything later on. He drove through town and checked out the bus stop. Nothing to report. Nothing to help our case. No real leads, but if he happened on anything relevant, we would be the first to know.

Chapter 28

One night at dinner, Jake told us that he was looking through the old magazine that Mom had saved. He was reading it through carefully but had not found any new clues. Then he sprang it on me. As he started speaking, his voice got further and further away, as the blood drained completely from my face and ears. He had spoken to Mr. Cooper about going over to our old house, which was now vacant, having been condemned by the county. Though the Sheriff's department had looked around right after Mom's body was found, he wanted to go over the next day to "dig around."

I excused myself and went to the bathroom. I stared in the mirror at my face, which had been reduced to a chalky looking white mask staring back. I barely recognized myself and turned on the warm water to wash my face and induce the blood to return. I stared into the mirror and began to shudder. I was petrified.

"Levi, are you okay?" Sydney's voice broke through the noise from outside the door.

"Just a minute." I tried to steady myself, but it was of no use. My fear had its own mind.

"Levi, open the door."

"Just a minute!"

She waited. "Open the door, Levi." Her voice was monotone.

I finally steadied myself, wiped my face with a towel and gave in.

Her eyes were dripping. "Oh Levi." She bear-hugged me. "I'm so sorry that you have to keep going through this!"

I could not yet speak but knew that I had a confession to make. Could I trust Jake with it? I felt that I had to, or risk being found out and left to explain my way out of it after he found the evidence. I finally gathered myself, "I need to tell Jake . . . you both . . . something bad. Really bad . . . and I don't know . . . Maybe I might even have to go to jail." I broke down again, at the disappointment or anger they would feel when I told them and at the thought of Izzy who flashed across my mind. She would never speak to me again. A no-good jail bird, just like many of the men from my hometown. She would learn the truth about the real me.

We walked into the living room, where we found Jake pacing. He looked up, alarmed. "I'm sorry Levi. I keep asking you to be so grown up."

"Jake!" Sydney was serious. "Can we be off the record here?"

He looked disappointed and spoke slowly and deliberately. "Sydney, for God's sake, we've already been off the record here. You know how I feel about you."

My antenna went up.

She was undeterred. "Levi has something that he needs to tell us. He thinks he could be in big trouble. If there is any reason why he should not be telling you and me both right now, you need to tell me," she said harshly.

"I care about you both, personally." He stared at her, then looked at me solemnly. "You can tell me anything, Levi. There is nothing we can't handle. Nothing! On the record, off the record. I'll protect you." He stepped over and hugged me, then grabbed me by both shoulders, looking into my eyes. "I mean it!" I had never felt the strong grasp of a man's hug before. It was unlike my desperate clutch to Joe Riley. Jake seemed ready to slay a dragon for me if he had to. He was winning me over.

I sat down on the couch. Jake sat on one side, and Sydney on the other, holding my hand, as I broke their hearts for the telling, and mine for the remembering, everything about the life, death and days leading up to the burial of my baby sister, Violet.

Tears dripped from my chin with every word that flowed in remembrance. I completely broke down several times, as I tugged that fateful time from my memory.

"Honey, it's gonna be okay." Sydney wrapped her arms around me tight. "I'm so sorry you had to go through that." She wiped her nose on a Kleenex that she pulled from under her sleeve. Jake assured me that I had done nothing wrong. I was but a child, being asked to do the only thing I could do for my sister.

I looked at Jake. "You have to tell, don't you?"

He looked square at me. "It does put me in a predicament. We could hold this secret, tending to it for the rest of our lives, or release it from its hold on you."

"So, you think you should tell."

"I do, Buddy. This is a very big secret that you've held. To continue to keep it, would be detrimental to your healing from it. You were so brave to tell me. You did the right thing. I don't want you to carry it anymore. If you can trust me, I'll take care of everything."

Trust . . . the fox who had gotten all the way in.

Sydney spoke up. "The truth matters, Honey. We have to release it completely or it'll eat you alive. It's the right thing to do."

Could the secret have been the real fox? Eating me alive from the inside out? I didn't want it chasing me anymore, so I took the leap and told Jake exactly where Violet was buried. Mom had placed a rock right there on top of the grave. She would sit there sometimes, rocking back and forth, humming with the birds. I closed my eyes to see her there.

I was exhausted from pulling the memories of Violet from where I had kept them hidden for so long. Jake stayed long after I went to bed, as my grief continued its vigil on me. I could hear the low tones of their voices as he and Sydney talked well into the night. Sydney kept checking in on me, walking over and laying her hand on my forehead. I wanted to feel free from my burden, but the heaviness of Violet's grave pressed in on me deeper. I remembered to follow my breath, gently tossing away any thoughts that arose, as I followed it into an exhausted and deep sleep.

Chapter 29

The next day, Jake went to confront the reality of my dead sister. I didn't go to school, and Sydney cancelled all her appointments. She said it was a perfect day to drive over to San Francisco to get away for the day. It was my very first trip to the city that was less than one hundred miles away. Going over the San Francisco Bay Bridge, I saw the exit for Treasure Island. I stared back at the man-made isle as we drove high above it. I could hardly wait to tell Izzy that I saw where her father had been stationed. I wondered where she had lived within the beauty of the bay. The sky was bright blue with soft billowy clouds hovering close as we continued across the water. We found parking near the Embarcadero under the shadow of the bridge, on the city side. When I opened the car door I breathed in the briny smell of the bay, tasting the salt on my lips. Seagulls were soaring on the breeze crooning and calling as they fluttered about overhead. There was a distant call of a seal as it echoed below a pier as we held to the rail and leaned over to catch a view. There were several of them laying along the wooden structure just out of reach of the water. The stench of dead fish wafted up as pieces of their unfinished meals had stuck to the wooden platform rotting easily under the sun. We walked all day venturing into shops and watching musicians playing along the street. I even got a photo of a monkey sitting on my shoulder. Sydney wanted to have lunch at Fisherman's Wharf where we found a vendor serving up French bread bowls of fresh clam chowder. We found a bench and sat, enjoying our meal and listening to a three-string quartet playing right there on the street corner, the most beautiful live music I had ever heard. It was as if I was floating among the notes as they played. Everything left my mind but the music, my breathing and the contentment that found its way gently within me.

After lunch, we took a tour through the *Ripley's Believe It or Not* exhibit, which was highly entertaining. And then the Wax Museum, where we saw the likes of Abraham Lincoln, Sitting Bull, Winston Churchill and Greta Garbo, to name a few. I stared in amazement at how lifelike they were. It felt like they might start a conversation right there. I was particularly interested in Sitting Bull and spent some time reading through the sad history of his fight for survival of the Lakota Sioux and his tragic death. He fought so hard for his people. He was their great spiritual leader. Fourteen years before his death, he had a vision in the form of a dream, which foreshadowed the victory of the Indian Nations over Custer at *Little Big Horn*. I got to see the Hollywood rendition of it,

Little Big Man, with Dustin Hoffman. I watched it my very first time at a movie theater with Chance and Joe Riley. I cried as Custer's men slaughtered the Indian people—women and children included. The visual rose up again as I read the tragic story of the waxed hero. I stared at his face, imagining him sitting peacefully in his teepee in 1890, before being gunned down by government agents attempting to arrest him. There was a quote written on a stand in front of Sitting Bull. It read: "*I am a red man. If the Great Spirit had desired me to be a white man, he would have made me so in the first place. He put in your heart certain wishes and plans, in my heart he put other and different desires. Each man is good in his sight. It is not necessary for Eagles to be Crows.*" I asked Sydney for a piece of paper and a pen from her purse to write it down. It spoke to me.

Sitting Bull's story and the exhilaration of the day carried me completely away from Jake's gruesome work, though the thought of the Sioux children left me with the same kind of gnawing ache. I did my best at steering my mind away from Jake's task of rescuing my sister's body from the ground that day. Before leaving the city, we bought a full bag of saltwater taffy to take home to Jake, after plenty of taste-testing. It felt like a peace offering for the difficult challenge he had to face for me.

On the way home, I began to worry if some old neighborhood dog might have gotten to Violet after Mom and I had moved on. I tried to pull my mind off that vision, as I let the magic of San Francisco dance back into my head.

When we got back home it was dusk. There was a note pinned to the screen door. *Call me when you get home.* Signed, *Jake.*

Sydney called him straight away. "We're back . . . Yes, I think he had a great day . . . Oh, okay. Is everything okay?"

"What?" I asked, worried.

She held her hand up smiling and listened. "Yes, that would be great. I was just beginning to wonder what to fix for dinner. Okay, we'll see you soon." Sydney hung up the phone.

"What's wrong?" I asked.

"Nothing's wrong. He just wants to come by to tell us about his day."

"Is it about Violet?"

Sydney grabbed my hands. "Yes, he wants to tell us about Violet."

Sydney had explained to me and Jake from the beginning that she would always share the truth with me. Even if it hurt. "We can deal with anything, as long as it is the truth," she said. "And by learning little-by-little, you don't have to fall from a very high limb someday, as you will learn the facts all along as they come to you. No more secrets. You can prepare yourself and then reconcile with the fullness of what is true." She was wise that way. Something told me that she learned this the hard way.

Chapter 30

I was in the middle of the Carol Burnett Show, where Tim Conway was trying to help me unravel the knots in my stomach, when Jake knocked on the door. I was filled with dread, as Jake was a no-nonsense guy, and I was sure he had gotten right to the business of Violet.

"Hey Buddy, I hope you like Jack in the Box. I can hardly wait to hear all about your trip. Did you have a good time?"

"Yeah, it was great."

Sydney joined us, giving Jake a warm embrace, then we followed her into the kitchen where she doled out the bags of tacos and grabbed each of us a drink.

We told Jake all about our trip and showed him the polaroid picture of me and the monkey that was sitting on the table. He seemed to force a chuckle, which usually came easy for him.

"How was your day?" Sydney asked, innocently.

"It was busy." He looked strained and took a quick breath. "Levi, I've agreed with Sydney, that we should share everything with you, bit-by-bit, as we move forward. Even if it's hard."

Then he began to tell us the events of the day.

He had asked the coroner to join him at the grave of Violet, which the chief agreed would be protocol. They rode in Jake's personal car, so as not to pique the curiosity of any neighbors, as Jake did not want any news media poking around. They were able to easily find the grave, as the rock that Mom had placed there was just as I described. They made quick work of retrieving the case from the ground, and looking around the gravesite, before closing the hole. Back at the coroner's office, they examined the case and its contents. Inside, as they expected, there were remains of a baby that had been wrapped in a towel. It had been placed inside a blue newborn t-shirt type onesie with the words, *Baby Boy*, appliquéd in black letters on the front.

I frowned, puzzled. "I don't remember a blue t-shirt. *Baby Boy*?" I stared at Jake, trying to think back on that horrific day. My eyes grew wide as my thoughts raced. "Oh my God! You found another baby?!" *How many other babies may be buried in little suitcases in the ground?!*

"No, Buddy, we don't think it's a different baby. We found the poem you wrote for Violet, in pink crayon, in the case, and the marble, just as you said.

My mind raced back to relief. *Thank God, but then, how do we really know that there are no more babies out there?* I fretted.

"So, have you ever seen a t-shirt with *Baby Boy* written on the front?

"No, I don't remember ever seeing any baby clothes."

"Okay. We found something else."

Sydney and I both stared at Jake, making him squirm in his seat. Sydney grabbed my hand from across the table.

"Levi, in the case that held Violet, there was a zippered section up inside the lid where we found a small wooden box, locked, with a tiny padlock."

"The key!" My eyes stared off.

"Yes, your little silver key fit the lock." Jake pulled the box from his briefcase. The key was in the tiny lock. He turned it and pulled the padlock from the latch, then reached into the box and handed me a photograph of a girl and a little boy. I could tell that the girl was my mother, in her youth. She was wearing a light-colored dress and a big smile. She looked to be in a curtsy. Her hair was done part up and part down. The up part was in a bow on the side of her head, the down part laying long around her shoulders. She was so pretty. So young. I smiled seeing the innocence of her. The little boy was looking up at her admiringly. His hair looked dark, neatly trimmed around his ears and he was wearing a light-colored shirt and a tie. They were all dressed up. My heart grew heavy as I stared at Mom, the girl in the photo, who had so much promise, but the deception of mind and drugs had ripped her soul right out of her beautiful young life.

"Turn it over, Levi." Jake said softly.

On the back, it read, "Easter Sunday 1955. Elizabeth, age 14, Lars, age 8." I looked up at Jake, then back at the photo. "Wait. Mom's real name was Elizabeth?"

"If the photo is of Kat, it would appear to be."

"It looks like her. I can see the same beauty mark on her cheek." My nose began to sting, as I squinted my eyes to hold back the torrent that threatened a squall.

Jake hesitated, giving me a moment to regain myself. "Okay. I thought it may be but wanted to be sure."

"This is the only picture I've ever seen of her."

Jake smiled. "I'm so glad that we found it." He squeezed my shoulder.

"Me too." I kept staring at it. "Maybe the boy is her brother?"

"It could be. I'll try to find out Buddy." He squeezed my shoulder again. "We found one more thing in the box." I looked up. He handed me a tiny string of blue and white beads with a metal crimp at one end and a knot at the other. The white beads had black letters on them and were strung, *L*, blue bead, *A*, blue bead, *B O U D R E A U X*.

"Have you ever seen this before?" Jake asked.

I held it up close, twirling it with my finger in my palm. "Never. What is it?"

"We think it's a hospital baby bracelet. For a baby boy, because of the blue beads."

I looked up. "What baby boy? Do you think Mom had another baby boy?" *More babies in the ground?*

"We've got more questions than answers right now so I don't want to speculate, but we will do our best to find out."

Jake went searching for more answers. I was struggling with it all. Trying to come to terms with the fact that my mother may not be who she said she was. My mind stretched and wondered, trying to make sense of it, which was impossible. I really needed Jake now that the door of Mom's past had cracked open. He was becoming one of my people, as a detective and as a friend, and I was learning to trust him. Sydney had fallen hard for him, and I would be on watch to make sure he didn't go and break her heart while he was trying to save mine.

Chapter 31

The days were long, and school was hard. Izzy was the only reason for my going. That first day back at school after Violet's unearthing, she nudged me. "Are you okay?"

I told her that there was a lot going on at home.

"Do you want to talk about it?"

"Not really. I mean. I would, but it's a really long story."

"I'm a very good listener." She smiled and grabbed my hand.

I stared at her face, her sweet smile, and into the warmth of her eyes. I didn't want her to know more awful things that can happen in a life. She was dealing with her own stuff.

"I really do want to know, Levi."

I hesitated. It was risky to let her in, but her smile drew me to the comfort of her. "Okay. After school. I'll walk you home if that's okay?"

At first, I was pretty quiet, but then, my words felt so safe I told her about my mother dying, not knowing who my father was, and now, not really knowing who my mother was, but that Jake was trying to help us figure it all out. Then I told her about Violet. Izzy's eyes floated with sorrow, as I shared the horribleness of it all. At one point she just stopped me, put her arms around me and held me, for a long time. I rested my face in the sweet coconut of her hair. Every molecule in my body was ready to explode. We were both shaking. We held each other there and she held my story. I didn't ever want to let her go.

That night, I called to touch base with Chance. I felt like a traitor, not filling in my best friend about all that was going on. It had been more than a week since we spoke, and he was shocked to hear all that had been happening in my life. He kept saying, "I can't believe it, Levi. I can't believe it." Neither could I.

Jake and us were sharing most of our evenings together. He no longer felt like a threat. He was more of a comfort to have around, making our lives fuller in some way. My days were filled with school and Izzy, my evenings with a steady flow of homework, and long conversations on the phone with Izzy, and dreams at night of Izzy. She and Sydney and Jake helped to ease my sorrow from all the unknowns.

Chapter 32

Jake called early one morning to tell us that someone was fishing for information about Mom and the baby that was found buried in Kelsey. He warned us that it would only be a matter of time before the media got a hold of the story. The department did not provide details but did not deny it. Hence, a major fishing expedition would ensue. Jake apologized for the *leak*. I did not tell him that the *leaker* could have been me, unknowingly trusting the allegiance of my closest friends. I prayed that the *traitor* was in the department.

The following day, Jake called early again. The Kelsey Kourier broke the story. The front-page headline read:

Baby found buried in back yard of local woman who died under suspicious circumstances.

"Since it is such a small newspaper, the story may not get a lot of traction." Jake said, with hope.

"Jake, did Mom die under suspicious circumstances?" I asked, concern beating me up.

"Yes, it was suspicious that she went missing, then was found . . . dead." The word eked out, as the harshness of it struck him, his eyes looking forlorn from the reality of saying it out loud to me about my own mother.

"But was her death suspicious?"

"At first, it was. But after investigating it, there was no evidence of any foul play."

"But could there have been foul play, even if there was no evidence?"

"Look, Buddy, we know for certain that Kat died of a heroin overdose. We found the syringe and paraphernalia next to her, and more of the drug in her purse. The toxicology report confirmed it. There were no signs that she had been harmed by another person. Buddy, I'm so sorry that you even have to think about this again." He gave a forceful breath out, frustration pummeling his face.

Jake's low-traction hope was quickly crushed. The story grew and hit the Tapton Telegraph, that joined in on the frenzy. My life situation had become a neighborhood thriller, having summoned up the interest of the evil-minded, as well as the curious. The tabloids nabbed the story, and they were like vultures. Reporters came to our house and to Sydney's shop. They even tried to catch me walking home from school. "Hey, Levi, why do you think your mother wanted to change her name?" asked a balding man in a crumpled suit. I ran.

"Say nothing, except to ask for their card." Jake said. Then he would contact their papers with threat of a lawsuit for their pursuit of a minor.

This period became another blur of running and hiding, much like the life of my mother, as I was unable to function fully for fear of the evil doers. But, unlike Mom, I didn't have Delano, eagerly beating me down all the more. And I was not alone. I had a powerful support group at my side, ready to pounce. Sydney and Jake were on the offense, watchful for scoundrels who peered around the edges of our existence during those weeks. Izzy was a bulldog, ready to scrap if anyone said one word about me. The eyes in the back of my head became more alert, as the dismal antics of the tabloids pushed the envelope of propriety, tracking me like a hyena. They would jump out of nowhere, looking for clues. The final straw was an article from the Big News Weekly that read:

Woman buries her own baby in back yard, after killing her, or did she? Could her son have killed his own sister?!

I became a notorious suspect in their rag, as they tried to tip the scales of their sales. I was being beaten to a pulp by the press. The one that people bought for its hair-raising headlines which were presented as facts and believed by those who didn't know any better. It was gobbledygook disguised as *breaking news*. The torment of the written rubbish threatened to push me right over the edge. What if someone believed them? I could hardly bear the thought. I had always understood that Mom's problems were hers, and there was nothing I could do about that. I learned to live with it. Now, her improprieties had been pushed onto me, a reality that took on a life of its own. People can be cruel, for no reason but their own egos and sales quotas. I became another whipping boy, a feeling I had almost forgotten.

A couple of days after the article ran the district attorney contacted Sydney about interviewing me regarding Violet's death. Jake was livid, as he had been blind-sided. I was scared, and Sydney tried to console us both. Jake had no power to change the DA's mind, and his job was threatened if he did not back off. An interview was set up for November 6th. The Monday before my fifteenth birthday.

I felt like David, standing in the middle of a coliseum, facing Goliath. When you are on the bottom rung of life, the outside world can seem predatory, as the *giants* try to push you into dark corners, and out of sight. There was nothing to fight with. I was at their mercy. I was being judged for my circumstances. They, not caring that I had already done my sentence for the crime of being born to a mother who could not protect me from herself. My innocence was robbed from me so long ago, way before I was handed my dead sister. To be questioned as to my blame for it was unfathomable.

Chapter 33

Jake was removed from my mother's case, as he had gotten *too personally involved*.

"You're damned right, it's personal," he slurred, as Jake poured another jigger of whiskey into his glass. I had not seen him drink before. I watched in dismay as my blood began to boil, and the alcohol continued to flow. The fox had finally arrived. *I knew it.*

Sydney sat, looking sympathetically at him. It made me angry that she didn't understand the danger. I knew all about it. Alcohol was a cover. Fear was squeezing in on me. I would have to protect Sydney from him.

Jake continued, "I will always take care of my own, thank you very much. I have no interest in participating in the department's sloppy handling of this case, and if that means I investigate your best interest on my own time, then shall be it." He gave me a drunken grin. "Don't you worry about a thing." I couldn't take him seriously. My disenchantment growing with each word. "Too personally involved. Haw!

They have no idea. This is for the best. I love you guys, and we'll get through this together, I promise." He blinked slowly as his head wobbled in an effort to hold itself upright. *He loves us guys. Haw!*

I took the longest breath possible and stood up, grabbing my courage. I had to say something. I had to return my truth to him. His words made it impossible for me to yell at him. I was starting to feel sorry for him, just like I did for my mother when she would drunk cry. But I was not willing to go down that road with him or anybody else ever again. "Jake, I'm not gonna let Sydney be hanging around with a drunk. I'm not." I stood my ground, ready to fight if I had to.

"Levi!" Sydney jumped to her feet. "Oh, Honey, he's not a drunk." Her voice was shaky.

"Then what is this?" I asked, confident in what I knew, floating my hands out toward him.

Jake stared at me, licking his lips slowly, pulling the last of the whiskey from them, blinking in an attempt to sober himself. I knew the drill. He bit his lips and took a big breath to speak, but before he could, Sydney spoke up again. "Honey, Jake doesn't drink."

"Well, he certainly is drinking right now," I said, condescendingly.

"I'm sorry Levi." The words eked out of Jake's whiskey-laced lips. "I don't usually drink." *Usually?* "But today, I did. And I drank too much. I'm sorry. All I can say is I'm sorry. I should not have gone and done this in front of you."

Aha, a secret drunk. I knew it!

Jake started stammering, his brain unable to handle the words, "I - I - I've made a terrible mistake." His chin bunched up under his pursed lips as he hung his head.

Sydney stepped over to Jake to console him. *She chose him over me.*

I stormed off to my room and slammed the door as I flew myself across the bed, sobbing. I was heaving so hard that I didn't hear Sydney enter my room. I felt her hand lay lightly on my shoulder, as she sat down beside me. Having her there made me cry all the more. She sat there patting my back until I finally found myself able to suck back my tears, though still sniveling like a baby. Her voice gently rolled into my ears. "Honey?" I laid still, sniffling back the water in my stuffed-up nose, listening. "I know you're disappointed in Jake. And you have every right to be. He made a mistake today. Now, it is my opinion that it is perfectly okay for an adult to have a drink or two."

"Not me!" I yelled, sounding like a spoiled teenager.

"I know, Honey. We should have been more considerate of you tonight, understanding that drinking might make you feel uneasy. Jake had no business sitting there drinking at our table, feeling sorry for himself. It was wrong. He made a mistake. He feels so bad that he upset you. You didn't deserve to deal with any of it. I'm so sorry that he disappointed you, and that I let him do it. I just want you to know that I believe he is telling us the truth about him not being a drinker. That's why it hit him so hard, the drunkenness. It's no excuse, but he wanted you to know that he is not a drunk, though he knows his actions showed you otherwise. You had every right to stand up to all of it." She spoke in a whimper, which tore deeper into me. "I appreciate you standing up for me." She could barely get the words out. I sat up and hugged her. I would have fought a circle saw for her.

Jake had a friend pick him up outside. His friend's wife drove Jake's car to his house so there would be no impression of impropriety at Sydney's house, though a lot of unseemly behavior occurred at our kitchen table.

Jake was at our door at ten a.m. the next morning with a large box of fresh donuts from the Donut Hut. Sydney let him in, and I listened to their voices from my room as dread sat there keeping me from going in to see him face to face. It was Saturday morning. I was still laying in my bed suffering from the night before.

"Levi?" Jake knocked on my door. *Oh no.* I didn't want to face him. He tapped the door again.

"Yeah, I'll be a minute." I held him off.

"Okay, I'll wait."

"Yeah, okay. I'm coming." I threw on my clothes and took a couple of long breaths, steeling up, and opened the door. We stood face to face.

"Can I come in?"

"Sure." I stepped aside to let him in.

He walked over and pulled out the chair at my desk and sat down facing me. I just stood there, not wanting to lower myself to sitting down. He waited for me to sit, but I didn't.

"Levi, I owe you an apology."

"Uh huh," is all I had to say, with my arms folded across my chest.

"I don't blame you for being upset with me."

"I don't care if you blame me or not."

"Okay, I deserve that," he said calmly.

I got right to it. "If you ever lay one hand on Sydney, I'll fight you with all I've got," I snarled.

He looked surprised at my aggression. "Levi, I would never hurt Sydney," he said slowly.

"How am I supposed to believe you now? Now that you've shown your other side, your drunken side. It's only a matter of time. That's how it works. I know all about it."

His eyes poured over me, finally beginning to understand where I was coming from. "I know I hurt you, and I'm so sorry about that."

"Sydney can't be in a relationship with a drunk. She can't. I won't let her," I said emphatically. "You'll hurt her someday. You will. That's the way it works. Did you beat your wife? Is that why she left you?" I was being mean now.

"You're out of line, Levi." He still held his calm under my attack.

"Oh, I see, now *I'm* out of line." I was being a punk.

"Levi, sit down."

"Why, should I?"

He was calm. Not up for a fight. "Because I want to talk to you. I need you to listen to me. Please, sit down Levi." His demeanor was unchanging, just calm. I was beginning to feel bad for being so mean. He had done so much for me. *Wait.*

It was all his fault. I had another come back but I bit my tongue and sat down.

"I did an awful thing last night. I was being selfish, sitting there feeling sorry for myself when you've been through so much." His voice broke. "I know how much your mother's substance abuse hurt you. And I had the gall to open that bottle, which was the worst thing I could have done to you. I don't drink, Levi. I don't. My wife drank, a lot."

I slowly looked up at him. His jaw tightened. He was trying to remain calm, but I could see that he was ready to explode.

"She left me and the boys. It hurt them so much. Her drinking and her leaving. I vowed that I would never drink again. I never had a problem, but just didn't want the boys to worry about it. And then I went and pulled that stunt on you. I don't know what got into me. I wasn't even thinking about how much pain it might have caused you or the wounds it may have opened up. It's kind of unforgivable when I think about what I did. I understand that. I just hope that you can find a way to forgive me. I'm having trouble forgiving myself, Buddy."

Me too. Why should I let you off the hook just because you've found yourself some kind of excuse? I didn't say it out loud. It seemed as sharp as a sword. But I wondered if it would be a matter of time before he showed his true self again.

"I hope you can find a way to give me another chance. Maybe not today, but I hope you will, eventually, because I want to be here in your life, with you and Sydney. I'm so happy to have you in mine."

His eyes wore a sign of ache. I wanted to believe him. Was he telling the truth or was he really that fox sitting there in sheep's clothing, trying to trick me? Like Delano.

Sydney tapped on the door. "Can I come in?"

I looked up, "Yeah." It was almost a whisper. I hung my head, pondering my predicament.

Sydney came and sat down next to me and laid the big box of donuts on her lap. She placed a large stack of napkins on the top. The scent of warm maple wafted from the box and began to work on me. Should I give Jake one more chance? Selfishly, it might be in my best interest. Heck, he might even find my dad for me. But what about Sydney? I had to look out for her. My mind was racing through the facts. I glanced over at Jake. I had turned on him and was beginning to feel bad for not giving him the same grace I had always given to my mother. Could it really have been just a one-time mistake? Only time would tell, and I needed his time to maneuver through the maze that Mom made for me. I could keep watch to protect Sydney and keep Jake on my team. My anger was melting like the icing on those warm donuts.

Without a word, Sydney opened the large pink box and handed me a maple bar, my favorite. She flashed me a knowing smile.

"Thanks." I grinned and accepted her peace offering.

"What would you like, Mr. Sherwood?" So formal. Maybe she had taken a step back herself.

"Regular glazed, please."

"Here you go, kind sir." She smiled at him and bowed her head, as if they were just meeting for the first time. Starting over. We were trying to start over.

I took a large bite of my donut, the sweet taste of the warm pastry started to work on my senses. The pleasure of it, twisted my mind to consider all that I should be grateful for. The imperfect person sitting there in my room with my imperfect self was trying to make amends. It was an important moment in my life, to face our demons together, them showing their ugly faces, us realizing that they were only a mask. They were not our best selves. We could both do better.

After a few bites I felt ready. "I want to be able to forgive you, Jake, but it's hard. I wish the whole thing hadn't happened. I'm feeling kinda bad for talking so mean to you, especially after you've been trying to help me. I tried to hurt you as much as I could with my words, and that doesn't feel very good right now."

"I kind of deserved it Buddy. I'm just glad to hear that you might be able to accept my apology. We could have both seen better sides of ourselves, but we're just not perfect yet." He smiled. "Relationships take our best effort, and we're doing that right now. We've got to fight for what we've got here and for one another. I promise I'll do better."

His words touched me. "Me too. I'll try anyway." I gave him a nodding grin. He stood up, as did I, as he grabbed me tight, hanging on. I hugged him back. We both had shown each other some of the worst of ourselves. But we hit it head on, instead of letting it mull around. It was ugly, but somehow, I felt a little stronger for working my way through it.

"Okay, it's over. Good riddance drunken me." We all laughed at his remark. It helped.

Sydney came over and grabbed us both. "Hot chocolate coming up," she said cheerily as she danced off to the kitchen. Jake and I followed her. She was the center of our universe.

Sydney warmed up the milk to make us our beverages as Jake and I sat across from each other at the kitchen table. We were okay. Emotionally exhausted, but okay.

"Before I sloshed myself around in here last night," he shook his head and lifted one side of his mouth, "I had wanted to let you know that I hired an attorney to accompany us to the interview with the DA. Just to make sure they don't try to pull anything on us."

"Do you really think I need one?" Worry gathered around me.

"With these crack pots, I wouldn't want to risk walking in there without one."

"Do they really think that I hurt Violet?" The words hit me like a mallet.

"Of course not. They're just interested in their own careers and their preposterous ideas of notoriety. They want to see their names sensationalized in the press, even if they have to try and drag you down to do so. They are the scum of the earth and are not going to get away with it."

He was angry now. He said that this was not my problem, but theirs. They were evil doers who would be dealt with, as they had stepped over the line. "They're just parasites, Levi. I'm sorry that you must learn of them, as I would have wished to protect you from this sort, but here we are. They will pay for what they've tried to do to you."

There was a lion inside Jake. He was facing the hyenas for me, as if I were his cub. My worry began to waver with a feeling of strength, from my renewing trust in him and for all he had done for me.

Jake was serious. My new lawyer, Edward H. Madison, Esquire, threatened a lawsuit on the Big News Weekly if they did not call back the hounds. Jake spent a lot of time talking to me about standing up proud. I had nothing to hide. We started laughing again, as we pushed our quarrel behind us and our worry right into the lap of Madison.

Chapter 34

Sydney, Madison and I walked into the office of Harold Crump, an assistant to the District Attorney. The D.A. had gotten pulled away on some bigger matter. Jake waited outside. Madison thought it best for him and his job if he just stayed clear. Madison also told me that he was gonna be tough on Crump if need be and to not worry about any riling up that may occur. It was all gonna be a stage where they would be performing whatever was called for. I was shaking from the anxiety that took hold the night before, which threatened to bring up my breakfast. I had told Madison all about the day of and days following Violet's birth and I felt weak from the telling. He told me there was nothing to worry about and to just be truthful. My stomach told me otherwise.

Before we went in, Madison reminded me, "Just tell the truth. We have nothing to hide. If Crump gets out of line, I'll stop him, so you have nothing to worry about. Remember, I'm gonna be on stage." He gave me a wink.

I told the whole story again, as I pulled the vision of those dark days back into my psyche, where I had forced them out so many times before.

"When your mother handed you the baby, was the towel that she was wrapped in wet or dry?" Crump asked.

I stared off, trying to bring my senses back to that moment, my body trembling from the memory. Tears welled up. "I think it was dry." I lied. I looked at Sydney. She smiled and nodded. I wanted to say the right thing, whatever that was. I wanted to make up a totally different story, one that didn't dig so deep into the tragedy of it all. I wanted to run just like Mom, away, away from all of it. Why was it always following me? I wanted nothing more than to outrun it. It had fists, clambering around, trying to find a weak spot to break me down. Maybe I was going mad, just like my mother. Maybe my future would be the same, spent running from the crazy that continues to try and beat down my door. I was sick. Sick. Sick of all of it. So, I ran, out the door of Crump's office and out to the curb, to vomit.

"Levi, Honey!" Sydney's voice trembled, as she had followed me. I hate that I was hurting her, just like Mom hurt me. Dragging her and Jake right into the middle of Mom's mess, and mine. She moved like a ballet dancer to me, handing me a Kleenex, and placed her hand on my back, as I heaved to dryness, my eyes pouring from the lurch. Sydney was weeping, as she twirled me to her, holding me, laying her head on my shoulder. Somehow, I was much taller than her. I had not noticed before. She had seen me grow into whatever this was that I was becoming. Standing there, in her strength, holding us both up. I could never repay her for loving me, through it all. From the very first day that we met. She scooped me up, gave me hope, a reason to try. I wanted nothing more than to make all the madness end. She did not deserve it. "Oh, Honey. I wish I could take you away from all of this," she said with her eyes closed, shaking her head.

I had no words. They were stuck, blocked by the lump in my throat. My anguish was unyielding. I felt Jake place us both in his big bear hug. He had found us. We stood in silence, him holding us both, swaying back and forth as if slowly lulling a baby to sleep.

"We're almost done here, and we'll put it all behind us, Buddy," Jake said, as I wanted so to believe.

"I don't think I can do it." The words broke free.

"There is nothing you can't do, Levi. We'll get through this. I promise." Jake's words tried to sink in.

"Jake?" I whispered.

"Yes?"

"I thought that Violet was born dead but I'm so afraid that she may have drowned." The words forced their way out, from where I had held them from that day, buried, unwilling to give them credence, until now.

He grabbed me and held on tight. "You had no control over any of this . . ." His voice was trembling. "I've a mind to march back in there with you."

"No, no you can't!" My mind switched to the protector.

"I know, Buddy. It's best I stay right here. Let's just get this thing done so we can finally put Violet to rest."

My mind kept telling me to run, but my good sense told me that Jake was right, and my running would only prolong the agony for me, and them, and the memory of Violet, in the end. Bad things catch up to you if you run, like Delano chasing down my mother. I was trembling in my effort not to take flight.

Madison came over to us. I felt certain that he had watched the whole dreadful scene.

Jake spoke first. "Madison, Levi's afraid that the baby may have drowned."

Madison steadied his voice to a soft tone. "Son, that concern that you may have, is not a fact, and it has nothing to do with the truth. It's just a fear that you have carried for way too long. You never should have had to carry it. I want you to hand that fear right on over to me. It's much too big a thing for a boy to carry around. I've got it, you hear? It's in my hands now, not yours. Okay?" He looked deep into my eyes. "Levi? Let's get in there and get this thing done. You have suffered enough, young man."

We all poured back into Crump's office, except for Jake, who could barely let go of my hand. Crump was impatiently tapping his pen on the desktop, looking snide. "Are we ready to continue?" he asked, condescendingly.

If looks could kill, Crump was already dead from Madison's sneer.

"Yes, we're ready." Madison tried to hold himself, looking at me with a forced smile.

"So, you mean to tell me that the baby came from the bathtub dry?" Crump's question was like another cannonball to my stomach.

"Wait a damn minute." Madison yelled. "Your condescending attitude it not necessary, *sir*."

Crump shot darts at Madison with his eyes. Madison was standing up over him, "This young man has been through hell and he deserves a hell of a lot of respect here, and if you don't have the ability to show some, we are marching out of this office right now."

Crump's face grew red, but Madison's was on fire. Sydney was shuffling in her seat. I had to save us from a brawl.

"Mom was sitting in a tub full of bloody water, holding Violet . . . the baby . . . above it, when I came into the bathroom. When Mom handed her to me, the towel was bloody and wet."

"Was the baby breathing when she handed her to you?"

"No. I understood that she was dead."

"Did you think your mother may have drowned her?"

"You ignorant son-of-a-bitch." Madison jumped up again and lost it, slamming his hands on the desk. "You're out of line. What the hell difference does it make what he *thought* may have happened. We're done here you no good dirty rotten son-of-a-bitch. I'd like to . . ." Madison pressed his lips together hard, staring down at Crump, breathing fast through his nose like a bull in a bullfight, his face as red as a cape. Crump's face looked the same. His nose flared and his lips were pursed, holding back whatever he really wanted to blurt out.

Madison lowered his voice, still staring at Crump. "This young man is done here." He looked over at Sydney and motioned his head toward the door. "Sydney, you can take this fine young man on home now."

My mouth was still standing open and my eyes were like saucers as Sydney scooped me up, and moved us quickly out the door. Madison stayed behind, yelling curse words that I had never even heard before.

As distressed as I was from the whole ordeal, there was something exhilarating about someone standing up so strong for me. Something that maybe a boy would feel if he had a dad watching out for him when things got rough. It felt like a mountain began to grow under my feet, as these incredible people held me up that day, when I unveiled the biggest worry of my life.

With the help of Sydney, Jake and Madison, it was no longer a secret burden that was eating me alive. That monster was dead. I had learned that my fear was not a real thing, just my imagination carrying me away to a very sad place, and for the first time since the day of Violet's birth, I felt that I could put her and my own mind to rest.

Chapter 35

Madison came by to report that the debacle with the D.A. was over. There was no case. I overheard him telling Jake that he nearly got himself fined, and suspended, for landing into Crump so hard, but everyone up the ladder knew what an ass he was. *Those were Madison's choice words.* And it didn't hurt that Madison had a good reputation in the county, even though I felt sure his mouth had probably gotten him into trouble before. He was honored to stand up for me and for right. He said it made him proud to be a lawyer when right was on his side. He became our friend. Our dirty mouthed, hilariously funny, amazing friend.

Relief tried to take hold. It is an interesting phenomenon though, how your mind will jump from the worst thing to the next worst thing so quickly. My mother's history was still an open case. I wanted to know more about Elizabeth and Lars. I had family somewhere, though my need for them had diminished, with my growing connection to Sydney, and

Jake. Sydney made it clear that as soon as Mom's situation was figured out, she might be able to pursue a more permanent legal parentage of me. Though she was careful not to make any promises, as there was still the possibility that Mom's unknown family members might have an interest in me. I doubted that very much. But the law was clear, that Sydney could do nothing about my legal permanency with her, until Mom's family was identified, and notified.

Chapter 36

Sydney and Jake surprised me for my birthday by inviting Izzy, Chance, his new girlfriend, Amy, Joe Riley, Marny, Miss Olive, Madison, and his wife, Julie, to meet us at Brookview Park, where they had reserved a large table under the shade of an enormous black walnut tree. As we walked up, I could hardly believe that all of my dearest ones were sitting at the table to greet us, jumping and yelling *surprise* as we walked up. They all ran up to hug me, Izzy kissing me square on the lips, which sent me reeling. The table was loaded with food: fried chicken, potato salad, fruit salad, chips and dips, and Izzy had made a giant chocolate cake with *Happy Birthday Levi* written in long hand on the top, in yellow icing. Fifteen orange candles were lit, for my wish, which was to keep my life, just like this. Happiness written on the faces of all of my people. I never wanted it to end, this day of magic. Madison keeping us all in stitches with his stories, Izzy and I holding hands, as we walked around the pond, throwing bread to the ducks, catching up with those who had always been there for me. I was celebrating so much more than my birthday. I felt free for the first time that I could remember. I laid down my worry for a while, as I basked in the glow of feeling loved and supported by the people who cared for me the most.

Later that evening Jake took Sydney and I to a fancy Japanese restaurant, called the *Mikado*. I tried some sushi which would have to grow on me. The chopsticks made us all chuckle, as Sydney and I tried to get the hang of it. Sydney grabbed one in each hand, as she tried to pick up a single grain of rice. She was determined. Jake placed his napkin to his mouth to hold back his snicker. I watched her with a feeling of utter joy. Then we all busted up when Sydney finally looked up with a smile as she slipped a piece of fish and some rice into her mouth with her fingers. It felt so good to make light of things. Laughter had been shy for a little while. It was nice to have it back.

When we got back home that night I was in the clouds. Jake stayed late, which had become the new norm.

"I have another gift for you." Sydney handed me a present.

I opened it to find a brand-new harmonica and a book on how to play it.

"Thank you, Sydney." I ran a few breaths into it.

"I thought you might enjoy playing along with Dylan."

"I will."

"I'm glad you told me that you were interested in getting one." She said.

"Yeah, I hope I can learn it."

"Of course, you can. There's nothing you can't do if you set your mind to it."

"It'll sound pretty awful until I get the hang of it."

"You just close your door, and we'll plug our ears for as long as it takes," she said cheerily.

We all laughed, and Sydney walked out of the room as Jake gave me his gift. It was a wallet with a twenty-dollar bill inside.

"You'll need this when you get your driver's permit in this next year and a man should always have a twenty-dollar bill in his wallet. That's what my dad always told me. You have to always be prepared."

"Thanks, Jake." It was a nice leather wallet.

He then commenced to telling me about the birds and the bees. I tried to stop him by telling him that I already saw the film along with all the other boys in the sixth grade as we marched into the cafeteria that year. The girls had seen it right before us and giggled their way back to their seats before we headed out. We didn't know what we were in for and couldn't look the girls square in the eye after that. It answered a whole lot of life's questions, that's for sure.

Jake went into more detail, much more than the boys in gym with all their condescending and boastful remarks about their conquests with the *easy* girls. Jake said that since I had a girlfriend, it was important for me to know a few things. I should always be a gentleman and he told me about mutual respect, mutual permissions, mutual protection and all that sort of thing. I was red-faced. I didn't much want to face it, him knowing the truth about where my thoughts were spinning around with Izzy. I told him that she was a *good* girl and that she already told me that she wouldn't have sex until she was married.

"Good." Jake gave a relieved sigh. "It is your responsibility to honor that, young man. And some day, when you are contemplating having sex, it is your responsibility to think it through, discuss it carefully and make damn sure that it is a mutual decision and that you're both protected." He was damn serious.

"Yeah, I know." As much as it toiled with me not to touch Izzy in that way, I knew.

When I went off to bed, I thought a lot about Izzy and all that Jake told me. I respected him for caring enough to make sure I understood. It was a big deal. As I laid there listening to their voices in the other room, I cracked the door to eavesdrop and overheard Jake and Sydney talking affectionately and dreaming about the possibilities of their lives. They talked of getting married some day and making me their son, as I could soon be legally free for adoption, which Sydney had already been thinking about. We could be a family, living a full life together. I fell asleep with a more clear understanding of life and a warm sense of belonging, as good fortune was shining right down on me.

Chapter 37

I was coming to terms with the death of Violet, as I believe in my heart that Mom did all she could for her. I had to believe that, for my own sanity. She did the best she could with the emotional ability that she had at the time, which was not much. Maybe Violet did drown. It breaks my heart to think that, but I know that Mom wanted her to be alive, and it tears me up even more when I understand the enormity of her circumstances of trying to fish her baby out of the water. Maybe she didn't get her out in time. Maybe Violet died in Mom's belly. I just will never allow myself to believe that she died at Mom's knowing hand. We will never know for sure, but I choose innocence as there is no way of proving such guilt. And that is a fact I can hang my hat on.

I cannot imagine having gone through these last weeks without Sydney and Jake by my side. There is such strength that comes from knowing you have capable people standing by, ready to catch you if you fall. Sydney had always been there for me, though I kept her in the dark about most of the agony of my life. I didn't want to dwell in this moment of grief any longer, so I willed it to pass while finding our way to the truth of my mother's life. It felt like I was scrambling to the top, setting my feet upon that calloused place, so I could finally see the greater world around me.

The counselor at school, Miss Snyder, got involved in my educational planning, as she tried to renew my interest in school. My anxieties of the first quarter had crept into my grade point average. She talked to me about my future, which was beginning to take some shape. I could feel the solid ground under my feet for the first time, part of a family who cared about my success. I had a lot of making up to do to make it through the semester without failing. Somehow, I mustered up the strength to face my schoolwork head on. I would pour myself into it. The distraction would help to push me through the ever-burning questions that lay deep in my mother's history, just underneath the hard edges of my focus on school. I would just put my head down and barrel through. It was that barreling that got me through most of my life. I could, surely, rustle up enough to get me the rest of the way through my freshman year. I felt determined.

Chapter 38

Right after New Year's, the forensics were completed on both Mom's and Violet's remains, so we were free to give them a proper burial. Since no adult relatives had been identified, the county would pay for it, and they would be placed at the old city cemetery in Tapton. Sydney drove me there so I could see it first. There were old headstones from the 1800s, with large evergreens dotted along the winding pathways, surrounded by well-trimmed grass. We walked silently among the old stones, the tule fog hanging close to the ground as we walked, reading about the lives of those who passed from unknown circumstances. That is the beauty of a cemetery. You read of the long and short of people's lives, not going through the pain of each of their struggles, only seeing their final resting place, peaceful and free from all that ails.

Sydney asked if I would like to have a memorial service. I decided just to take flowers to their graves when it was done. There was so much misery wrapped up in their ends, I did not see any reason to drag us all through the ache of a funeral. I knew that there would be people whispering and staring, finding me more of a curiosity than a mourner, and I wanted no part of it.

We went to a local florist to pick up two large bouquets. Mom's was a large bunch of sunflowers, with tall ferns, wrapped in a bright orange bow, just as I wanted. Violet's were pink roses, with baby's breath, and small green mums, wrapped in a giant purple bow. They were perfect. Sydney, Jake, Izzy and I went to their graves, unmarked, except for a brass plate with their identification numbers placed in the ground. They were side by side. Together for eternity. I asked for a few moments alone to recite a poem I wrote for them.

Your lives too short, though flowers bloom
The angels sow the seeds
Please rest your tender souls in peace
In the garden of eternity

I cried, feeling my sadness drip out of me. It felt like it was being released in some way, and I hoped that my grief was beginning to set me free.

Chapter 39

Sweet Violet was at rest, but Mom's mystery was still at the forefront of our lives. Jake had a new energy regarding her case. He was as determined as ever to get to the bottom of my mother's life story and get me free to move on with my life. All of our lives, as a family. He would be doing it under the table of course, since he had lost his official position as lead detective on the case.

Jake made an announcement that he wanted to take us up to the Sierras to go sledding, or maybe skiing, if we wanted to learn. He talked about how he spent many winter weekends up there in the snow with his boys when they were younger, speeding down the hills and sitting beside the fire at the Great Timber Lodge when the light would leave the mountain, which was the only thing that got the boys to stop racing for the ski lifts. I was excited about learning to ski, but Sydney was less enthusiastic. We decided to head up the next weekend, where Jake would teach me to ski and Sydney would wait for us, with a good book and a warm smile at that lodge.

I had never been up to the snow. The closest I ever got was the time that Joe Riley ran his old truck up to the higher elevations and filled the back heaping with freshly fallen snow. Chance had run over to get me and a few of the guys in the neighborhood to come and build soldiers out of snow that laid ready in their front yard. We rolled out their bulbous bodies, using carrots for noses, stones for eyes and mouths, and long sticks for arms. One wore an old coat of Joe Riley's. He was the leader of the band. The weather was cold and foggy, so our squad stood guard in their front yard for the day, as they slowly melted into the ground. I thought again of Joe Riley maybe being my dad. He had been a good fill-in on those days that I just needed somebody to stand in. And I was beginning to see that Jake could be a good one, too. I was filling my life up with better dreams, as time tried to gently ease my path forward.

As the excitement built up throughout the week, my mind kept racing back to Eagle Meadow, its beauty, and its lessons. So much had changed since that weekend I had spent in the mountains. I was beginning to feel like a different person from that boy who was so buried in the mire of my mother's life. But sometimes, I would still visualize myself back then, sunk down in the muck of Dewey Creek, my arms out front, pushing through the mire rising high above my head, as I tried to find my way through. But I felt gratitude for my new life and was learning not to hold too tight to the miseries of my past, with Sydney's help. Though I still felt the trudge of wading through the echoes of the unknown that lie deep in my mother's grave.

Our weekend in the snow was exhilarating. After a long morning of snow plowing and Jake's coaching on the bunny hills, we finally went up on a higher lift. The view from the sky was breathtaking, as the snowflakes gently swept across our faces. Jake smiled below his goggles, as we silently drifted up and out of the abyss of my former life.

I skied down that mountain, only falling a couple of times. Jake staying close, soaring by, then falling back to watch over me. He helped me up when I fell, and clapped with delight, poles dangling, as he watched me soar down the mountain, in the capable arms of my guardian angels.

After a long day, we headed back to the lodge where we found Sydney curled up in a large leather chair, her eyes closed, listening to the music of a pianist, that echoed like magic throughout the entire lodge. She jumped up with delight as we walked up, giving me a giant hug. "How was it?" she asked excitedly.

"It was great!" I said, proudly.

Jake went on about my prowess on skis. I was a natural, according to him, until I went tumbling down, which brought us all to laughter. We sat together by the fire of the large fireplace, taking in the music that accentuated the joy that enveloped our lives. We sat down at the restaurant and feasted on seafood pasta, the special, and a mountain of warm

French bread with real butter. The great food and quiet laughter at our table warmed me along with the fire.

As we stepped out of the lodge and into the crunchy snow, Jake led us through the trees to a vista, where you could see the entire canyon, trees holding their labored limbs, heaping with heavy snow. As we stood, ankle deep, we didn't speak, taking in the silence of the trees. We stayed the night at the lodge like a normal family. Well, almost. Sydney and I shared one room and Jake another. My thoughts carried me back up the lift to the highest mountain, as I looked off into the expanse, to see life's beauty, which was all stretched out before me. I could see the whole forest as I climbed out from below the trees.

Chapter 40

The next week, as we were sitting at our dinner table, Jake was unusually quiet. "You okay, Lovey?" That was Sydney's new *love* word for him.

He looked up, studying the ceiling, then over at her with a nervous grin.

Sydney smiled a knowing smile. "It's time." she said, nodding her head forward and tilting it slightly to prod him on.

"What is it now?" I was growing nervous watching them do their little dance of expressions.

"I have some information." He looked horribly uncomfortable as he glanced over at me and then back at Sydney.

"Okay." I said slowly, as if opening a door slightly to peak in, yet holding it firmly in case I wanted to slam it shut.

"It's a lot. It's big."

"What do you mean, *big*?" I questioned, looking deeper into him.

I began to feel nauseous from the weight, waiting for the shoe to drop.

"I've been combing over all the leads and got a major break."

"That's good, right?" My voice struggled to find its way out.

"Of course, it is. The truth is what we're after."

"Well, what is it?" I was cautiously curious, concerned by the solemn look on Jake's face.

"I found out Kat's story." He looked sad.

I gasped, from the shock of his words that I knew full well would come someday. All that we had been waiting for was now terrifyingly close. The well of my eyes began to fill, as I could tell, it was not going to be a good tale. "Maybe I don't want to know." My voice sounded far away.

Sydney reached for my hands and closed her eyes in kind of a silent prayer, as she breathed in slowly. Jake placed his hands over ours, and dropped his head, taking a deep breath, then looked up at me.

"Oh, Buddy. I know." His eyes started to glisten as they filled to their rims. "I wish we could all go off and live happily ever after, leaving all the past behind us. Believe me, I pondered this, but the truth is too powerful. It'll always find its way, no matter how far you run. I just want you to know that I love you. I love you both." He looked from me to Sydney, who was sitting tall holding herself strong for me. "What I have to tell you is a lot. We'll talk about it all together and you'll have the answers to all that you could've ever imagined, and more."

I hung in that space of silence before he spoke the next words, fearful of the knowing. My mind wanted to back-peddle. I wasn't ready. Things were looking up toward a wider expanse of living. My heart was in healing mode. I didn't want to go back to revisit anything in the past. Not today and maybe never. I was moving on. But truth was standing there in my way, ready to pounce or light my path in an unknown direction as my guardian angels held tight. Those with wings and those sitting with me at the table. The light of truth is so powerful, like the rays of the morning sun. You try to stare straight into it, but it stings, so you shift your eyes to see what its lightness reveals, all that was sitting right there in the darkness. It had been waiting to rise, waiting for us to find it, holding all the secrets of the universe, right there, just waiting. It was my time to know my piece of it. It could not be held back. *Ready or not, there it came, to light its light on me.*

Chapter 41

Mom's real name was Elizabeth Mary Dumont. She was born on July 3rd, 1941, in New York City to Celia and Thomas Dumont. She had a younger brother, Lars, and a younger sister, Violet, who was a baby when Mom left. Their family lived in Cleveland, Ohio, where her father worked as a commercial fisherman on Lake Erie.

Jake was able to find Mom's parents, living in Euclid, a little town up the road from Cleveland. Lars was now married and living in Detroit, with one child. Violet, in high school, like me. They explained that Mom had been suffering from emotional distress for some time. They had her in counseling, and she was on medication for a mental disorder. The medication helped, until one day when she was fifteen, she became hysterical and was inconsolable, then refused to speak. Her parents did not know what to do for her and called her doctor, who recommended that she be placed at the mental hospital for observation and further treatment. Her family was so worried and desperately wanted their happy girl back. They hoped it would be short-lived, as she would get the treatment she needed, under a doctor's care. It was there that they found out she was pregnant. Within a few weeks of treatment at the hospital, she began to walk through the halls singing, holding her growing belly, but never confided the details of her pregnancy. Her doctor expressed the importance of her family not to prod and recommended that she be taken to St. Mary of the Angels Mothering House in Wintonville, Ohio, a school and birthing center for unwed mothers. It was from there that she went missing.

Jake had the awful task of telling the Dumont's of the death of their daughter, an extension to their grief which laid claim on them so long ago. They had tried to find her, to no avail. They had little hope left, and now, all was lost. They had been devastated for so many years by their daughter's disappearance, that the news of her death seemed more of the same grief that they would forever carry, for their Elizabeth, knowing she was never coming home.

They asked about me, and Jake told them that I was with a family who loved me very much. He broke down as he shared those words. Then he told Mom's parents about the death of their grand baby, Violet. It broke them even more. Violet had loving grandparents, and an aunt for whom she was named. It was a small glimpse of the promise she would have had, had my mother stayed in the loving arms of her parents.

It all sounded like someone else's story. I could barely sit there with it. Like a movie you just want to turn off. But it was the truth, and I had to know it.

"Levi." Jakes voice startled me, as I was running it all through my head. "Buddy, there's more."

I stared through him, feeling Sydney's hand squeeze tighter, still on mine, sweaty. *Dear God, no more.*

"I wanted to tell you about Elizabeth and a bit of her life first, so you could better understand."

I blinked in rapid succession, trying to make sense of his words and where he was going with this. "Understand what?" The words drug off my tongue. *What more could there be?*

"Kat did something, Buddy." He took a full breath of air through his nose and breathed it out, making a windy sound. "I'm sure she didn't think through the consequences of what . . . what she was about to do before she did it, or the hurt she would cause by making the rash decision that she made, but she did something terrible . . . unforgiveable."

I knew about the terrible things that she could do. I had lived with it all of my life. I buried my face in my hands, thinking of Delano, and felt so grateful that he was now buried in the ground. My poor mother had to endure so much from him and his evil wrath. I adjusted my seat and sat up tall, taking a long deep breath. Sydney did the same and grabbed both of my hands, squeezing ever so gently, smiling to try and comfort me. I lifted my gaze solemnly toward Jake, my gut in a wrench. "Maybe I don't want to know."

Jake's eyes were pained. "I wish it was as simple as letting the truth just lie there still but you need to know."

My voice quivered. "I know. I have to hear it so I can reconcile with it." He and Sydney helped me to understand that fact. I took another long and shuddering breath sucking my lungs full of air.

Jake took a quick breath and let it out fast. He still had some things to learn about how to take a healing breath. "Okay, Buddy. Let me start from the beginning."

Chapter 42

Jake circled around the few clues that he had, having put away any hope of learning more from the Medallion Motel. The baby bracelet and onesie were his only viable clues. Then he remembered the old *Wintonville Weekender* newspaper that we found in Mom's things. He had not yet looked it over as he had planned to before the situation with Violet took a wrong turn and sent him in another direction. There was a slight chance that Mom may have saved the paper for something other than the Sputnik article. He had to sneak the paper out of the official evidence locker, having been yanked from the investigation that meant so much to him.

There was a small article in the paper that caught Jake's eye. It was tucked down at the bottom of the second page, below a large advertisement for women's hosiery, as if it had no authority to scream, having been overshadowed by Sputnik. It was placed along the bottom, so small, that it appeared as a decorative fringe to the ad. The minuscule size of the article made it seem trivial, not worth the ink with which to articulate it.

Baby Abducted From Home For Pregnant Teens

It explained that a minor was suspected of kidnapping an infant from the St. Mary of the Angels Mothering House in Wintonville. The police were investigating. It was short and gave no names, as all parties were minors.

From Jake's official position as sheriff's detective, he made some calls to the St. Mary of the Angels Mothering House. *It was a bombshell.*

He found out that a pregnant minor, Elizabeth Mary Dumont, was a student there. When she was about six months along, she went into early labor. She labored long and gave birth to a stillborn baby boy. She was devastated, according to the reports.

The day after she gave birth, a young woman with whom she shared a room at the Mothering House, *Lily Boudreaux*, gave birth to a healthy baby boy. The following day, Elizabeth Dumont and Baby Boy Boudreaux went missing.

His words wrestled with my ability to soak them in. I just sat there blinking, trying to catch up with the truth that was trying to find its way to me.

"Levi, Baby Boudreaux . . . is you." It hit me like a rock. A straight shot from Mom's sling.

My jaw dropped from my face, as I stared at him. "What are you saying?" *Even though I heard every word.*

He was visibly shaken, as was Sydney. All three of us on a spinning wheel, holding on for dear life. "Buddy." He hesitated, "Kat was not your real mother."

I stared past his words. Then gasped for air, at the shock.

He spoke slowly, to soften the edges of his words, so they wouldn't cut so deeply. "Kat did not give birth to you. She stole you from your mother, changed her name, your name, everything, in order to keep you both hidden from those who were searching for you."

I sat silent, blinking rapidly, my heart racing to pale my face. Staring at nothing, and into my own mind, as I played it all out with his words, like pictography, with Mom as a bird, stealing a baby like a stork, flying away over the mountains and into the deep, sling shot in hand, where I must have been her only hope. Her not knowing that she was stealing mine. "Are you sure, Jake?" I stared into the forest.

"Yes, Buddy, I'm sure. The baby bracelet that we found in the locked box with Violet, was yours. It bore the name of your mother, *L. A. Boudreaux*. It was on your arm the day that you were taken. Your real mother is Lily Alyce Boudreaux, who was sixteen at the time. She was beside herself when you were abducted."

My real mother. I was *abducted.* The words seemed too storybook to be true.

"At first, I thought that the bracelet may have been Kat's real name, but I was wrong."

"Could you be wrong about all this? It just doesn't seem possible."

"I know. I felt the same way. But I wouldn't have told you if I'd not proven every word to be true."

I was trying to hold myself together.

"You were born on October 3rd, 1957."

I stopped before blurting out that I was born on November 12th, realizing that it was yet another lie that I was told.

"Levi, the birthing center had a copy of your birth certificate. I just want to prepare you. Lily named you."

He handed me the document, and I read it slowly, barely able to breathe.

St. Mary of the Angels Mothering House

```
Name of Baby: Angus O'Malley Boudreaux
Date of Birth: October 3rd, 1957
City of Birth: Wintonville, Ohio
Mother of Child: Lily Alyce Boudreaux
Date of Birth of Mother: May 1, 1941
State of Birth of Mother: Louisiana
Father of Child: blank
```

Everything rose from the page, as if rolling like a scroll, from a different time, and a different life. Like the lines of a play. Someone else's story. I studied it. That there was no father listed, was just a blur. I read over the lines again, and again. She gave me a name, a different name, an unfamiliar name. It was unfathomable. The reality struck like a knife in my back, as I felt physical pain strike from where the phantom blade penetrated my body.

"Oh, Honey." Sydney's calming voice broke through her own grief and her gentle hug brought me back to the comfort of her, my back still throbbing from the knife's edge.

"Buddy, I wish I could have prepared you better somehow. There was no other way to handle it, but to walk straight in with the truth." Jake's face wore his anguish.

My head dangled from the weight. "I know. I had to find out." My sense of self was falling to shreds from the unravelling of all that I had ever known. I was being stripped clean down to the bare bone, hovering in time and space as if in another dimension.

"Levi? Buddy?" Jake spoke from far away.

His voice called me back from my mental flight, as I sat in the certitude of what felt like fantasy. I looked through the ocean of Mom's secrecy on which we had sailed. A heavy surf rose up with each word, "Oh my God, Jake. I can't even imagine her losing her baby like that." A vision of Violet flashed before me. "Do you think she's still looking for me?"

Jake looked at Sydney. "We'll find out." He got up and gave me a big bear hug and walked outside. It was then that I realized that the life-changing news he had to share had begun to unravel the new little family that we had become. By solving Mom's case, he had begun to collapse all the plans for our future together. I closed my eyes in disbelief, as the truth began to sink in on me.

Chapter 43

Jake's original task was to find my mother's official birth certificate and her family, which he did. The chief was irritated that Jake stayed on the case, but relieved that it was solved. The coroner was pleased as he could finish up his job with accuracy, tie everything up in a neat little folder, and place it in the archives for dust and time to bury it in the annuls of history. Mom's family was found. Bodies were buried. His task complete, while my life story lay unraveled on the floor.

Chapter 44

Jake and Sydney helped me to work through the wreckage and reconciliation of my mother's life, and mine. There were many days of hopelessness and wanderings of my mind, as the truth tried to find a footing. I felt more sorry for Mom than mad, which Sydney said was a very healthy way of dealing with my memories. Mom did not have the capacity to handle what life had thrown at her. I always knew that. I thought it was her inability to handle being a mother. All I knew for sure was that her hiding was the only way she knew to free herself from the unbearable truth of her life. All of it. Her illness, the unknown circumstances of her pregnancy, her obvious psychological collapse, the intensity of her crime, what she took from my real mother and from me, and her addiction that she used to bury it all. Mom's life had become a ball of destruction wrapped up in a giant chain of deceit that held her tight, driving her clear down to her early death. And my real mother was left with an empty crib. I would never wish her to know of the horrors experienced by the child she had lost.

I started dreaming of Lily, imagining her walking along a beach, throwing seashells into the sea, her white dress flowing with her steps, her bare feet setting in the sand at the edge of the foaming water. The salty air touching her lips as she whispered to the gods to bring her baby home. Gulls purring overhead, trying to tell her that I had been found. I dreamed that I would run to her along the sand as she turned to see my familiar face, the one she named Angus. She would peer into it, knowing it was me without a word. I longed for her to know, for her heart to be unbroken, and for me to know my mother, Lily.

Jake set out to find her.

Chapter 45

Sydney and Jake, and others, I would find out later, coordinated a plan to help me through the latest devastating news that had found its way to me. They thought it best for me to talk with a therapist to help support me through yet another turnaround in my life. I didn't much like the idea, but Sydney was adamant. She took me to appointments, sat with me while I cried and listened. I wondered if she and Jake thought that I might go mad. From the book that I read on the subject, a professional may be needed to help pull people free from their mental illness. They assured me that my situation was totally different. I was not *unwell*. They just wanted to be certain that I had all the tools I needed to maneuver through the tumultuous circumstances of my life the best way possible. They were there to make sure I was working through it all in a healthy way. I was sure that Sydney was all that I needed, but I humored them by being open and letting all my sadness fall out to be reckoned with straight on, not waiting for it to hit me well down the road, which can happen to people, I was told.

My therapist, Dan Curtis, felt more like a friend. I really liked him and felt compassion for him. He was in a wheelchair, having been paralyzed in a car accident. I immediately understood that he had been through his own share of tragedy. His situation had the power to make me truly listen. He knew what he was talking about. I was sure of that. He didn't want me to go back and revisit my earliest childhood trauma, which I was grateful for. He didn't want me to let that define my life. According to him, I was the resilient young man who made it through that time. He wanted me to stand right there on my own strength, trusting my own coping skills, which had served me well. The past was gone, and the future would be designed by each brand-new day. Worry and regret would only stand to rob me of the beauty of it. Terrible things come our way, no matter who we are. Truth and honesty would never lead me astray, though it could not guarantee *no pain*. It's important that we lean ourselves toward purposeful good which will hold us up when things go awry. Otherwise, we just bumble along haphazardly, bumping into whatever life throws at us. He said I had built a tower of intentional good around myself with my deeply connected friendships, visits to the library to explore the greater world around me, my writing and my music, which could raise me clean out of a storm. All of this supported me along the way, no matter what played out in my surroundings. I could always lean on the love of those around me and from that within me, which was the gift of life itself, he said. He wanted me to be proud of me, and I was learning to.

Dan also sat with me through my grief and loss, and my uncertainty about my unknown mother (and father, if I had one at all.) I had never cried so much. I worked through the forgiving of my mother at the very deepest level. Dan felt that I needed to come to terms with her life and death, not waiting for that grief to unfurl later on in my life. Even though she stole so much from me and my real mother, I could still feel empathy for her. I believed that it was Delano that made her do it all. I could place my blame square on him, leaving only my compassion there with my mother. I laid it over her like a soft warm blanket, which was a visual comfort to me.

It helped me to see Mom as a child, the young Elizabeth. I felt empathy for that girl who was fighting for her own survival, and mine. I could never hold that against her. If she had known that Delano could have been caged, that may have saved her. But he was left to become a charlatan who was responsible for our deepest despair. He was the gatekeeper of the truth, raising his ugly head to bite it back to the far reaches of my mother's mind. And he was gone now, never to return, nor would the innocent child whose mind he stole, Elizabeth Mary Dumont. I mourned the deep loss of the only mother I had ever known.

Raindrops Fell by Leviticus Strong (For Elizabeth)

You lay in silence, as raindrops fell
To your face in its heavenly gaze
The holy grail of a promised peace
Slipped you silently away

You did not see your beauty
You did not know your song
May you dance in the arms of the angels
As the songbirds sing along

You did not know your virtue
You did not dream your dreams
I see you dancing softly
As you skip through a babbling stream

Raise your heart to the heavens that hold you
Lift it high in the air as it flies
May you rest now, Mom, from running
As love replaces your lies

Your breath grew soft and lowly
As it left your body torn
Soar off to heavens great glory
Where the child in you was born

Chapter 46

Dan thought it would be a good idea to write Elizabeth a letter. I toiled over it, writing and re-writing what I wanted to say. I wrote to her about my feelings; the angry ones, the sad ones, all of them. Little did I know that I was sorting through each of those emotions; holding them, living with them, and then rectifying with them, until I finally whittled it down to the words that I would leave with my mother, Elizabeth, forever. Dan sat and listened to all of the many versions of it. He did not judge them or me, but encouraged me to just let them flow, which I did. After several weeks of writing and re-writing a zillion times, I finally completed it to some satisfaction.

I stood at Elizabeth's grave holding the final version of my letter, standing solemnly for a moment as a light breeze rustled through the trees. The scent of pine wafted from the evergreens as they waved gently overhead. I felt empowered. The letter would put a period on a great portion of my life. The one that Mom had claimed for herself out of desperation. With the letter, I was claiming the rest of my life for my own self.

Dear Mom,

It has taken me a long while to write this letter as the full story of our lives is finding its way to me. I've been so sad, confused and angry about all the sorrow you sowed. This conflicts with the guilt that I wasn't able to save you. I'm sorry that you never got the help you so badly needed. You were just a girl, scared and heartbroken, and I know you didn't understand the breadth of the devastation you were creating in the lives of others when you ran with me. Though your deeds can never be forgiven, I'm not going to riddle you with blame. I'm still sorting through the mess of my emotions, trying to get them all neatly tucked away in their rightful places. I want you to know that I will always love you. There's something unconditional about it. Kind of like that of loving a child I guess. No matter what wrong they do, love is just bigger than that. My love for you just is. And I'm walking a new path, wearing a different stride, than the boy who lived with you among the reeds, and I'm creating the space I need for the truth of my life, including my real mother, Lily. She deserves that special place that is held for the mightiness of her position. It hurts so much to think that you stole her child, and that I am that child. I'm glad you're not here to endure the consequences of all that you've done. It would have been a more painful end for both of us. I hope we're able to find Lily, and maybe I even have a dad out there somewhere too. I have carried the dream of finding him for my entire life, and now it includes my real mother too.

So today, I breathe in the freedom of letting you go, as you float away into the arms of the angels. Go on now, Mom. Set yourself free.

Remember, I'll always love you,
Levi

P.S. You should know that my real name is Angus and I will now and forever call you by yours, Elizabeth. It's a pretty name and it belongs to you. I hope this will free you to live out eternity as the beautiful girl you were always meant to be right up there in heaven. And I hope your little babies are right there in your arms where they have always belonged.

Tears rolled off my cheeks as I stared down at the letter. Then I looked up at the blue sky imagining her hovering there with the angels reaching out to her, handing over her babies, who had been in their safekeeping. I pulled an old matchbook from my pocket and peeled a small cardboard match from it. I firmly pressed the head across the striker with my thumb as it sparked to a flame. I held it to the letter as it darkened and curled into itself. I kneeled down and laid it on the small bronze plate with a number that marked her grave. As I watched, it slowly fell to ash. I didn't want to hold any hate for her for what she'd done, and I was told that it would only serve to keep me in the bondage of that hate. I released her with the dying of the flame, so she and her transgressions could melt away into my past. I felt my own release from her heavy grip as she began to melt away. As I stood, I looked up at the sky again and the vision of her was gone. I looked over at the flowers I had placed on hers and Violet's graves. I hoped there really was a heaven, especially for the innocent. And even Elizabeth was innocent, by reason of insanity, if the law is true.

Chapter 47

All the while that my life was spinning like a top, I stayed in therapy and continued to go to school. Izzy was my rock. She kept me going. I could talk to her about anything or nothing at all. I knew the importance of school and my future. She was a straight-A student and had visions of college. I had never even thought it a possibility for myself, but she encouraged me to think about it, which gave me a purpose and distraction that I so badly needed. I felt some promise in myself that I didn't want to let go of no matter what. I had a lot of bad days, but worked in some good ones too, as the toil of life and education found its way within me. I realized that life had just been happening to me as I side-stepped through the mine fields of my life. There was a growing awareness that I could actually begin to steer my own ship in a purposeful direction, even amid the uncertainty that surrounded me. No one knows the future, but you just can't sit around waiting for it to show up. I wanted to make mine something good, on purpose. And thanks to Izzy, I finally understood that about myself.

One day, we got a freeform assignment to write about something that was important to us. I put my thoughts to paper. The grade mattered less than my understanding of the subject.

TRUTH IS, by Levi Strong (*Angus O'Malley Boudreaux, if I told the honest truth.*)

Truth is unchangeable.
It is known at the basic level of the universe.
Something that can never be shifted.
It just is.
There is no motive or well-thought-out plan.
There is just truth, lying there still to be discovered, if not already known.
Truth is unyielding, as it stands on its own merits, no effort to make it so.
It can be glorious and painful to learn.
But it is as real as the dawn.
Truth is.

Chapter 48

Jake hauled in big bags of food from the Jolly Cone. Big Bang burgers were our comfort food. As we settled into our meals, Jake announced, "I've got some news." His eyebrows lifted, as he hesitated.

"Well, are you gonna tell us, or make us guess?" That was our usual banter, making light of things. I smiled. Jake stared at me warmly, with that slant of his mouth that let me know that he was bringing me more truth, steering me toward that next limb, guiding my steps, when I was ready, so I could keep my balance. He and Sydney were good at that. "You know that finding Lily was next? Right?"

I kept a steady gaze on his eyes as I hunched over my plate of food. I didn't take another bite but set down my burger and wiped my face with my napkin. "Did you find her?" I asked through a full mouth. My voice slow, as I visualized her walking down the beach.

"We did, Buddy. We found her." Jake's lower lip began to quiver, as his chin bunched up tight.

My mind raced. Was he sad or was he worried? Was she alive or dead? The anticipation of the answers momentarily bound me up like a straitjacket.

He smiled back, having already wiped his hands from his mess, and gathered his words. "I contacted the Wintonville Police Department, who handled the investigation on your abduction.

My abduction. I would never get used to it.

"Buddy, they had enough information to track down Lily. She made it easy, as she kept them informed for a long while, after she married, whenever she moved."

I started to tremble, staring, dumb struck at the words as they slipped from his lips.

"They found her." Jake let out a quick whimpering sound, as his mouth tried to regroup.

Sydney sat, her eyes glimmering, as she stood on her great strength, having lived through so much heartache herself and having helped so many others who were so deeply wounded in their lives. She was handing us that strength. I felt her support, and her devotion to my well-being was a steady warmth that rested gently on me. I could see her anguish, but her strength was unyielding.

I could barely breathe, but then inhaled deep to catch hold of myself, as Sydney kissed my forehead then sat back down, grabbing Jake's hand and mine. There were a few moments of silence, as thoughts swarmed around the room, my guardian angels standing watch, protective and hopeful, as Jake continued. "The Wintonville police detectives contacted Lily and went over everything with her. They gave her my number for her to call, which she did straight away."

"You spoke to her? You spoke to Lily?" I just couldn't wrap my mind around it. "What did she say? How did she take it?" I felt excited and then an ache as it crossed my mind that she may want no part of me. I was wounded and so much different than the baby, Angus, that she had given birth to so many years ago.

Sydney answered. "She's overwhelmed with joy, and relief, Honey. She's been searching and praying for your return since the day you were taken." Sydney tried to hold back her emotion. I stared through her as my mind raced to the vision of Lily standing there alone without her baby, then back to Sydney's unconditional love for me. It laid so heavy, as I toiled with the magnitude of it all.

"Buddy, to our great surprise, she lives right here in San Francisco," Jake said, trying to sound excited.

My eyes blinked a million times in one second, as I realized how close I had been to her, there in the city, the day Sydney and I strolled along the pier and wandered through the museum. We were breathing the same air.

Sydney's voice broke my trance. "She wanted so badly to jump right into the car to come to you, but also understood that you have been through so much. She didn't want to inundate you by pouncing on in without your getting a chance to soak in what you've learned. She put trust in us and Dan as we all conferred on what was best for you and we knew you needed time to settle into the fact that you have a different mother. I want you to know that this was the most unselfish thing I have ever witnessed, Lily's loving care for your best interest, after all this time of her waiting." Sydney melted through her last words, as did I.

Lily was my mother. *Mother.* The word had become a new term completely, it represented something totally different than it had before. It wasn't meant for Elizabeth. It was meant for Lily, my real mother, who I had only known for one short day, before I knew anything else at all.

I realized that we all needed to be ready for the news. None of us wanted to deal with the reality of the situation. We were all just trying to navigate through the wake of Elizabeth's ill-fated deception, as our futures all hung in the balance.

"I have so many questions." My head was swimming in them. "Did she say anything about my father?" The question seemed cruel, as I blurted it out, like it bounced right over the top of Lily, making it seem like she didn't even matter.

Jake looked to Sydney who smiled with her eyes and words. "We know you have so many questions, as do we, but instead of jumping in on her, we will leave this to the two of you to inform and discover. You should be doing the asking and she should do the telling as you find out all that you need to know. It's your birthright to hear it from your own mother. What we know for sure is that she is as beautiful a person as you, which was no surprise. She's waiting patiently to see you whenever you feel you're ready."

Jake smiled at Sydney, then me. "I'm so happy for her to have found you after all these years, and for you." *Why then did he look so sad?* I already knew the answer. And the mix of emotion was almost more than I could bear.

We talked well into the night. Jake tried to make us laugh, even when we cried. Sydney and Jake expressed their love for me, as well as for each other, and assured me that they would be there for me no matter what, for the rest of my life. We would all be straight with each other, all of us. Lily was already on board, waiting in the wings. I could stand there on the soft cushion of truth that they all laid out before me. They would guide me gracefully over steady ground, as we walked into the open meadow of truth together. I understood the enormity of my good fortune.

Somehow, I had been waiting for this day all of my life. Now, I stood on a catwalk, edging out into my future. Sydney, Jake, and Dan, my spotters, standing with arms outstretched, lest I fall. They had been guiding me onward, past the swamp, toward the lilies of possibility. They were preparing me for this. Though I felt a jilt of abandon, as I knew my future was now pulling me away from the refuge of Sydney and Jake. They were both happy and sad for all the right reasons. Sydney told me that nothing would ever change with us. We were bonded for life, all of us. The unfolding of the existence of my birth mother was the icing on our very fancy cake. I could have it all, wrapped in the support of so many. It was miraculous to feel the comfort of it, and yet, still a solemn understanding as I stood over the former abyss, which had been filled with the fertile soil from Sydney and Jake's healing hands. Now the planting would begin. The orchids of my life would reach up from the heaviness of the earth that lay ready. From that steady ground, I would soon hear the voice of *my mother* for the first time that I would be able to recall, though I felt certain that she whispered sweet words of affection and devotion as she coddled me on the day that I was born.

Chapter 49

Sydney and Lily thought it best for me if we started with a phone call. Sydney handed me the number. It was nearly impossible to fathom that those simple digits would take me to the voice of some far away story, the truth that lay wait for me.

I sat with the numbers, staring at them, unable to pick up the phone as the butterflies in my stomach were all circling at once.

"Would you like me to dial her up for you?" Sydney offered.

I pondered it. "Yeah, I think it'd make it easier." *I hoped.*

"Okay, whenever you're ready, I'll call." She grabbed me and hugged me long. We both took a deep breath, and busted out laughing, as we did it in unison, which had become our thing. A thing that I would carry with me forever, the healing breath of Sydney.

"Okay, I'm ready." The butterflies were threatening to bolt.

With each number that she dialed the anticipation grew to where I felt faint by the time she placed the phone to her ear. "Hi, Lily? This is Sydney." She listened. I was woozy. "Yes, I'm so happy to speak to you again too . . . He's well . . . He's an amazing young man, which you already know." She winked at me, grinning. "Yes, the day has finally come . . . He's right here with me . . . I know, it's unbelievable . . . He's excited to speak to you too."

She made that last part up. It was more like overwhelmed. I was about to fall right out of my skin.

"Okay, I'll look forward to talking to you later. I'll pass you on to Levi." Her eyes were pinned to mine. She handed me the phone. I stared more deeply, my eyes widening as I grit my teeth, anxious. She smiled big, raising her eyebrows, a tear rolling down her cheek. She took another long deep breath. I followed her lead, then took a trembling grasp of the phone.

"Hello?" My voice broke from the advancement of my adolescence and the frog that was dancing around in my throat.

"Levi," she whispered, then hesitated. I heard her take a breath. "It's so good to hear your voice." It was my mother. A stranger. Her voice was soft and melodic, gently moving into my brain, like poetry, and memory, never to leave.

I tried to hold on to her words, as she spoke, but my mind could barely comprehend, as it spun around unable to slow down enough to follow. My mouth was dry from being held open, trying to listen, as I held tight to the receiver, unable to speak.

"Are you there, Levi?"

My nerves finally released me. "Yeah. I'm sorry. Yes, I'm here." Lily tried to keep the conversation moving, but it was of no use. I was shaking like a leaf. My brain was in tatters.

"I know that you must have so many questions," she said tenderly.

"I do." It just blurted out. I desperately wanted to ask about my dad, and wondered if she, too, had no idea who he was, just like Elizabeth's fictional tale. "I mean, I do wonder about . . . everything really." My face grew warm as the burning questions about my father's existence ignited inside me, but I knew better than to ask. Not now. It just didn't seem right to barge on in with such questions.

"Finding you . . . It seems like a miracle." Her voice grew faint.

Her words touched me to where I could not speak, yet again. "Yeah." It was more of a whine than a word. My emotions caught fire as I began to fall apart.

"I know this is so difficult for you." Her words went almost to a whisper. "You don't need to say anything. I've spoken to Sydney several times and just want to tell you one important thing that I know you've been yearning to hear. It's about your father."

I held on to my breath to listen more carefully. My hand began to shake as I buried the phone into my ear to hold it steady.

"I named you after him."

I was done, as the water rushed over the dam. It's all I ever wanted to know. I had a father. He was a real person. She gave me his name. I began to sob uncontrollably from the release of my quest to know that I had a dad. It blew right in on me as I buckled over, losing all control of myself. Sydney raced in and grabbed the phone, kissing the top of my head as she stood behind my chair, laying one hand on my shoulder so I could lean into it.

I heard Lily's faint voice echo from the phone, "Levi?"

Sydney lifted the receiver to her ear, standing strong behind me. "Hi, Lily … Yes, he's okay. Just a little overwhelmed with the wonder of it all. He'll be fine … Yes, I know. I know you did. It's always hard to know what's best … I think you're right … Of course, I can. I think that's a good idea. It'll help you both … Okay … Then, we'll make a plan … Yes, he really is … I know. He's gonna be okay … Okay, I'll tell him. I'll talk to you later. It was a good first step. You take good care now and have a good night … Okay … B-bye."

I was still bawling. "I wanted to ask her more about my dad," I said nasally.

"I know, Honey." She walked over to the sink and got me a glass of water. "There'll be plenty of time to ask all your questions. Don't worry."

"What'd she say?" I started feeling bad for Lily as I had not spent any time longing for her because I never even knew that she existed. I just bounced right through her to my constant infatuation with my dad. It wasn't fair, my preoccupation with him over her. It wasn't fair to her at all. I wailed again from the ache of it all.

"She'd like to talk to you again when you feel ready, but she doesn't want any pressure on you. Just take your time. Be patient with yourself. And maybe you can start thinking about meeting each other face-to-face soon." She shot me a look of assessment.

I just stared at her, wondering.

"How does it make you feel, thinking about seeing her?"

"I'm kind of nervous about it. Especially now that I've been such a bawl-bag."

She chuckled. "You're not a bawl bag. You're a sensitive young man who is facing some very big life changes. I think you're handling yourself quite well." She smiled wide as she tousled my hair with her fingers.

"I would hate for her to see me like this."

"You just be yourself. She'll love everything about you. You think on it. She wants you to be comfortable. You have all the time you need. She's on your side."

"I guess." I got up and walked straight to my room and threw myself across my bed, drowning in my unrelenting emotions. The call had been so much harder than I expected. Sydney came in and checked on me as I laid face down in my pillow. "You go ahead and cry, Honey. You've got a lot in there to get out. I know that was hard, but it was a good first step for the two of you. It'll be alright, Honey. I promise you. It'll all be alright."

After my tears ran dry, and my mind came back to myself, I went into the bathroom to wash my swollen red face. I looked a mess. Sydney was in the kitchen fixing dinner.

I sat down at the table. "Should I call her back? I feel bad."

"Listen here, young man. You have nothing to feel bad about. Nothing. You hear me? And if you want to call her right now, you absolutely should, but you did nothing wrong."

"I kinda made a fool of myself."

Sydney dropped her shoulders and looked sideways at me. "That's not possible. You were feeling the enormity of it all and her only care is for what is best for you. That's the truth."

I sat there in the kitchen with Sydney as she saw me through the astonishment that felt so much like grief. I decided to talk to my mother again the next day. We would discuss a time to meet. And my lifelong wonder stayed there steady, working on me. *Where in the world was my dad?*

Chapter 50

I spent most of the day at school thinking, about Angus. Maybe he never even knew about me, or maybe he did, and didn't want anything to do with me from the very start or maybe he was even dead. I let my mind carry me around all day, doing that kind of worst wondering. I had her number in my pocket and went to the phone booth on campus at lunchtime to call Lily, but there was no answer. My burning questions had to wait.

After school, I watched Izzy's basketball game in the girl's gym. I loved watching her move across the court with her confident stride in her short-shorts. Though I sat there tapping my feet with impatience as my mind kept floating back to Angus. I decided to run on home before the end of the game, as I had grown more and more anxious to call my mother and learn the truth about my dad before I wrenched my gut into a permanent snarl.

I smelled fried chicken and ran straight for the kitchen when I got home. Sydney was finishing up the frying and I started mashing the potatoes with the masher.

"I'm starving," my belly cried.

Sydney laughed, "Of course, you are."

I grabbed the plates and silverware and placed them on the table. Jake arrived with a smile and an apple pie that he got from a Girl Scout bake sale on the way over. Sydney finished the chicken and made the gravy. I was sitting in my seat with my fork in my hand when she laid out the spread.

"I was talking to Lily this morning." Sydney pierced a drumstick with her fork.

"I'm gonna call her tonight." The words tangled with my already full mouth of food.

"Good, we were talking about you two getting together."

"Can I meet Angus, too?" I peeked at her for a sign.

"She's got word out that she's looking for him," Jake said.

"Can't you help?"

"You know I am, Buddy. We're both making calls."

"I was thinking today that he might be dead." I threw my worry out there.

Sydney looked at me sternly, her eyebrows drawn down in the middle. "Don't you go borrowing trouble, Mister. There's absolutely no sign that he's *not* alive. These things just take time, as you know better than anybody. I know you want to learn all about your father, and you will. In the meantime, you can learn all about your mother right now. She really wants to see you. I think it's time you meet, don't you?"

Sydney tilted her head and smiled slightly with her eyebrows raised.

I was still shoveling in my food. "I do, I'm tired of wondering about every single little thing."

"I bet you are. It'll be nice to have all your questions answered."

"Yeah, it still doesn't seem real though, that I have another mother."

"I know." She got up and got me another napkin, as I had my other one spun into a little ball of grease.

"Thanks."

"You're welcome. Can you imagine how anxious Lily is to see you?" She was pushing on me a little.

I raised my eyes to meet hers. "Yeah, I know." Dan had been talking me through it all, but I was still in a tizzy.

"Lily's husband, Sam, has been battling cancer." Sydney just threw it at me.

It struck me, pulling my mind into those words. Cancer. I let out a groan, understanding the helplessness of seeing someone you care about fall ill: watching, waiting, wondering. I had considered that Lily might have a husband but had not deeply mulled it over. My gut circled round to wallow in the familiar place where my sorrow rests. I envisioned a woman sitting in a chair next to a hospital bed as I turned my incessant yearning for my father around to face her.

From the beginning, learning about Lily had sent me into a state of confusion where I had to reconnect with the reality of who I truly was and who Elizabeth was *not*. I didn't want another mother. I had already had one and that didn't work out so well for me. I was looking so deeply inside my own self that it was hard to pull up a vision of her. It wasn't fair to her that she was a complete surprise to me, someone I would need to get used to knowing about, being all that she was, such a huge person in my life that I could hardly comprehend the greatness of. It was so far reaching that my mind was fraught, instead of feeling the miracle of her. Finding my dad had always been my quest and my wildest dream. Now, after hearing my mother's voice and learning of her life situation, she was becoming more real, and I could see more deeply into her sadness: losing me all those years ago, waiting and wondering, and now her husband's illness. I understood the devastation of it all and realized that I was a light that rose from the darkness of her deepest despair. I felt the power of it.

We finished our dinner, and I cleared the plates. "I need to call Lily." I pulled her number from my pocket where I had carried it around all day. "But I don't know what to say."

"Just say *hello*. She'll be glad to hear from you." Sydney shot me a supportive grin as she took a deep breath. I did the same and breathed a long exhale from my mouth as I steadied myself. Sydney and Jake stepped into the living room to give me some privacy.

My hands were shaking as I picked up the receiver and dialed, holding the phone to my ear, flying myself toward Lily with every ring. My stomach began to ache from the greasy chicken and a sense of dread as my self-absorbed curiosity spun around with my sympathy for her and her husband Sam for all that they were going through.

She picked up. "Hello?" I scanned her familiar voice.

"Hi, Lily." My voice quivered.

"Hi, Levi." She knew it was me even before I could tell her.

"Sydney and Jake told me that you've been trying to find Angus." As soon as I said it, I felt a stab of guilt for jumping to my selfish wish, when I knew what all she was going through.

"I'm hoping we'll be able to get word to him soon."

"Yeah . . . and Sydney told me about your husband being sick. Is he doing better?"

"He is, though the treatments left us wondering for a while. They knocked him down pretty good, and now he's trying to build himself back up again before another round."

I didn't quite know what to say. "I hope he feels a lot better soon."

"Me too. Thanks for asking about Sam." I could hear the heartache that lingered there in her and started to imagine Sam and wanted to know more about him and my mother, and Angus.

"He's got several more treatments and we think he'll feel a whole lot better when that's behind him." Her voice got small.

"I really want to see you." I wanted to say what I thought she wanted to hear. It was all that I could offer in an effort to comfort her. It wasn't totally selfless as I felt myself being more drawn to her.

She grabbed her air and sniffled. "I'd love that. Would you like to come to San Francisco? Or I could come to you."

"I really like San Francisco. I went there a while back with Sydney."

"Well, why don't we plan for you to come here to the city?"

"Yeah, maybe Sydney and Jake can drive me over."

"I'll talk to them about that." There was a lift in her voice. "You've just made my day."

"Do you want to talk to Sydney?"

"I do, but I have something else that I want to tell you first."

"Yeah?" I held my breath in anticipation.

"You have a brother and a sister, Alyce and Sammy, who are here waiting for you, too."

I let out my air and closed my eyes as my mind soared off. I had never really considered having siblings, except for Violet. "Oh my God," I whispered under my breath. I held on to their names and tucked them close. "Alyce and Sammy," I repeated slowly. "I can't believe it." Tears were moving in on me and I felt a pang of sorrow for all that I had missed, and for them having the threat of losing their dad while I was just beginning the hope of finding mine.

"I've told them about you, and they're really excited to meet their brother."

Brother. I was a brother. I couldn't speak as I tried to calm my seesawing breath as it bumped the air into and out of my lungs.

"I look so forward to seeing you soon."

My words finally formed. "How old are they, Alyce and Sammy?"

"Alyce is six and Sammy's four."

"Hmm. They're so little."

"Well, Alyce would think otherwise. She's six going on sixteen," she chuckled. "Sammy has a great sense of humor already, just like his dad."

I wondered how I might be like my dad.

"Shall we get Sydney on the phone and make a plan so you can meet this silly bunch?"

"Yeah. I'll get her."

"Keep my number handy and call whenever you'd like. I love you, Son."

I mumbled with a whiny voice as my emotion tore loose again. "You . . . too." It felt so small and wrongly put. I was feeling a sense of something, but I didn't quite know how to say that I loved her. It kind of felt too soon but I could feel a connection with her, something fresh and new, yet it felt like something that had always been there somewhere. I was stepping out into the light of her and felt an ache to see her and my siblings. They were still fighting a war for Sam as they meandered through. I was rising up and taking solid steps outside the mine field of my own worst days. I could feel myself being pulled toward them and their great fight for Sam.

I put my hand over the receiver. "Sydney?" She was standing just outside the doorway. "Lily needs to talk to you. I wanna go see her. I need to go." I felt my determination building.

Sydney hugged me and grabbed the phone, as I stood there springing up and down on my toes, waiting to meet my own mother and my sister and brother, and Sam. They were drawing nearer to me.

We planned to meet on Saturday. Sydney and Jake would drive me to San Francisco to meet my family. We would meet at Alamo Square Park, by the *Painted Ladies*, the old Victorian houses on Steiner Street. It would be just two days, though it seemed so long to wait. School was important to them all, and me, if I looked down deep, so I didn't argue about waiting.

I called up Chance to tell him what I had learned about everything. It all sounded like a fable. He was flabbergasted.

"Dang. I hope they can find your dad." Chance understood my longing.

"Yeah, me too. I always wished that I had a dad and now I have a whole family who's been out there looking for me."

"I guess I never thought about *not* having my dad."

"Yeah, I used to dream about Joe Riley being *my* dad too."

"Now that would've been something, us being brothers."

"Yeah, that's what I thought." We both chuckled, him not knowing that it was not so long ago that I had held on to that dream.

I quickly ended the call so I could dial up Izzy. She asked more about how I felt about it all. She sounded more like a counselor, a good listener. Before we hung up, she asked how my history project was coming along. I changed the subject by asking about hers, which she explained was already done. Then I confessed that I hadn't even begun mine. She reminded me that it was due on Friday. My gut gurgled as it twisted with that gnawing ache of procrastination. I told her that I just didn't have it in me to start. I had planned on writing about Sitting Bull since I already knew a little bit about him. Izzy said she would help me, and it would be good to keep my mind tended as I waited anxiously for Saturday. *A win/win* she said.

We planned to meet up at the library the next day after school, to journey more deeply into the life of Sitting Bull, a distraction from my own. My interest in the project was forming as my stomach began to feel the relief of finishing my paper. I was grateful that Izzy had jumped in to rescue my grade from the delay tactics of my life's winding road.

Chapter 51

I met Izzy by the gym, and we walked over to the library hand in hand. I liked being with her. She put my body in a tailspin whenever she was close, making me shiver.

"How are you holding up today?" she asked.

"I feel a little unsteady." She had no idea that my wobbliness was partially due to being right there next to her. We took our time getting to the library, catching up and holding on to each other. We found ourselves alone in a small vacant courtyard beside the library and had a short make out session that made me want to do all kinds of sensational things with her. She seemed to be melting into me, when she quickly pulled herself away just as I was about to lose my ever loving mind.

"Stop," she said, holding her hands to my chest but not pushing me away. We were both breathing heavily.

I backed up and stared at her beautiful face, her blue eyes floating. She started to cry.

"I'm sorry. Did I hurt you?" I asked, concerned, as I wondered if my amateur French kiss felt more like a freight train as I was losing myself.

She moved back in and hugged me, laying her head on my shoulder, putting my brain and my body in more jeopardy.

"No, you didn't hurt me. I just can't," she whispered.

"Can't what?" I wanted her to can, can, can.

"Be losing control of myself like that."

"Well, I kinda liked it." I smiled, tilting her chin up gently with my fingers and kissing her lips.

"Momma told me this would happen," she said, pulling back and looking grim.

"What? What would happen?" I questioned, though I knew full well what she was talking about.

"It's easy to get carried away when you let your guard down."

Don't I know it. "I kinda liked your letting your guard down." I grinned.

She smiled and punched my arm like a buddy. I grabbed her in a bear hug and rocked her back and forth, my body still on high alert. I could barely make out Jake's words that were trying to tap me on the head, but I understood fully, my responsibility to back off and it was nearly killing me. Maybe there was still hope that she would provide some mutual agreement someday so I could run out and use my twenty dollar bill for some mutual protection. My body was begging.

"Come on, we've got a lotta work to do, Levi." Izzy grabbed my arm as she yanked me from my desires and led me to the library steps, where we marched up and into the history of Wounded Knee. We buried ourselves for the rest of the afternoon, after I finally settled on down.

Book after book, we read all that we could about the history of Sitting Bull and his people. The librarian told us about a current event happening that very minute at Wounded Knee, where his people were still trying to get the government to face their broken promises, a situation that begged my attention away from my own life's melodrama and Izzy's body.

As we read the stories, we shared snippets with each other. So many innocent people had been pushed from their land, into desolate corners of the country, out of the way of the settlers who felt that their own lives were worth far more than that of the Native people. So many died because they were *just too free* in their own homeland. It disgusted me to see it in writing and imagine it, the truth of our history. I read a quote from Sitting Bull:

"For us, warriors are not what you think of as warriors. The warrior is not someone who fights, because no one has the right to take another life. The warrior, for us, is one who sacrifices himself for the good of others. His task is to take care of the elderly, the defenseless, those who cannot provide for themselves, and above all, the children, the future of humanity."

He was dedicated to his people, like a father.

"Let us put our minds together and see what life we can make for our children."

He and his people were a gentle folk, until provoked. They took care of their own, living on the land which was their birthright. Then they were rounded up and killed. To maintain their aliveness, they had to walk into the corral of reservations where they faced extreme poverty and racism that held them tight within those borders. They were pushed so far out into the Badlands that there was no way to earn the money necessary to uphold the European lifestyle that was forced onto them. They hungered for food and a sustainable life, all the while trying to hold on to the last bit of their heritage that was trickling away.

We read about the undoing of people's lives, as their independence was robbed from them. The Native American Indians being treated *less than* for not being *civilized* like their counterparts, who were the ones trying to kill them off. They sterilized the women on reservations without their consent so they would have no more Native babies, then their other children were ripped away and put in boarding schools, where they were not allowed to speak their Native languages, while being molded to their captors liking. It made me think about what Elizabeth did to me. Ripping me from my mother's arms and denying me my birthright of knowing who I was. She only cared about her own selfish desire to have a child and did not allow herself to consider the torment that she inflicted on my real mother, and me. That comparison hit me like a rock. I could see Delano standing over her shouting orders, just like Custer, without a care.

As we continued reading, we got into the history of the slaves, and how they were treated like animals, as less than human, too. Given no right to their own liberty. Learning more about the depths of the upheaval lit a fire in me. We talked about the current racism held by some folks. Izzy knew of it firsthand. I always felt a strong burn whenever I saw its ugliness. We talked about bigotry, trying to understand where it all came from. We figured that it was like a long-honored family custom for some people, thinking that their own lives and lifestyles were all that mattered. Like there was some kind of inflated value placed on *their kind*, with *outsiders* being a big zero, especially if they looked or lived differently from themselves. We tried to come up with an answer for how to untangle that kind of deceptive thinking that crept through families from generation to generation. Our only answer was for every person to learn the history and walk through the worst of what we've done to others, trying to see their own selves standing in the very shoes of those they hate.

I was wishing that the likes of Johnny Brindle, who wore his white skin as an armor, could see himself as an Indian or a Black boy so he would know that skin was just a covering, with the true person sitting right there inside it. I understood that in there, we are all the same. Johnny was just a boy, like any other boy, who wore the brunt of his bigotry. I could see the sameness in all of us, sharing our hopes and dreams as part of the whole human race, each shade adding to its beauty. Being punished for being *different* from another was something I just could not understand. It was like being slapped around for coloring inside the lines with all the colors of the rainbow.

All these findings and notions became my history project. I drew a pencil drawing of Sitting Bull's face and wrote on the bottom of it: *Sitting Bull is us.*

Izzy called her mom from the payphone at the library, and I called Sydney, to let them know we were running late, as darkness was falling quickly. I walked Izzy home, well, actually ran, as she just grabbed my hand and took off running away from any chance of her losing her guard. We giggled like two little kids. She was fast! When we reached her house, I stepped inside to say hello to her family, still panting. I tried not to make too much eye contact with Izzy's mom for fear that she might be able see all that I wanted to do with her daughter right there in my eyes. I took a different look around their house, as it was buzzing with energy from the fullness of them. It was hard to believe that I also had such a family, of my very own, who were waiting for me in San Francisco. I realized how much I wanted to see them.

When I stepped outside to leave, Izzy followed me out and hugged me as I held on to her, never wanting to let her go. As I walked down the steps, I looked back at her, seeing her in a new light. She looked more like a woman than a girl. I stared for a moment as she smiled at me, waving.

"Goodnight, Levi. See you tomorrow."

"Okay." She took my breath away as I turned to head toward home, longing to hold her deep into the night.

Chapter 52

I called Lily when I got home from Izzy's. I was mentally exhausted, but it was good to touch ground and I wanted to hear her voice again. She asked me if I liked to listen to music and I told her all about my quirky record collection, everything from Beethoven to Bob Dylan.

She giggled. "It sounds like you have the same taste in music that I do. I haven't found anything that I can't appreciate yet."

"Yeah, me too."

"Do you play any instruments?"

"I have a harmonica that I mess around with, but I can't say that I'm a player."

"Don't sell yourself short. If you're playing at all, then you're a musician. That's how we all start, just playing our music. Writing and art are the same. If you write, you're a writer. If you make art, you're an artist. It's as simple as that."

I'd never heard it put so simple like that. Maybe I was a musician and a writer, and maybe even an artist from my

Sitting Bull sketch. It's funny how uncomplicated she made it feel to be something that I already was without even knowing it.

"I was inspired by Bob Dylan to play the harmonica."

"I understand that inspiration completely. I hope you'll play for me some time."

"I don't know about that."

She laughed easily. "Only if you want to but I'll be dying to hear you, you know."

She let me off the hook then snatched me back to wonder if I could ever play in front of another person. "Do you play an instrument?"

"I do. I teach piano and pluck around on the guitar. Sam's a great guitar player and writes a little. I like to think that he's the Sonny to my Cher when I sing along with him. But trust me, we're not that good." She laughed, which made me smile clear inside thinking of them singing together.

The lyrics *Baby Don't Go* came to me, as a reflection of Lily's hope for Sam.

"We could use a harmonica player in our little ensemble."

"I better get a little more serious about my playing before I try something like that."

"There's nothing serious about our playing. We just have fun."

I started thinking about it and felt a little encouraged.

"Would you like to say hi to Alyce and Sammy? They've got something to tell you."

I didn't know if I was ready but ignored my reservations. "Yeah, I would."

She put them on the phone so we could chat. They shared their excitement about their dog, Daisy, who had just had five puppies. They were going to name them even though they knew they could not keep them all. They would still need names, Sammy explained, and since there were five, we could each name one. Alyce had done the math, considering the size of our family. I asked a lot of questions about the pups and chuckled as they shared the joy of them. It felt good to hear the ease of their laughter. Sammy had a great laugh, which tickled me every time. I felt like I was peering out from the mountaintops over a brand-new world.

Alyce settled on Dolly for the pup in her charge and Sammy named his Levi Angus, after me. Alyce told him he couldn't use my name, but he was steadfast in his decision. So, it was so. Lily explained to me that Sammy had melded my two given names together, trying to understand who I was in the light of who I had always been. She hoped I didn't mind, which I didn't. It kind of had a ring to it.

I named my pup Samson. I wanted to return a namesake to Sammy. Alyce got upset though, because she didn't have a namesake too, but our mother quickly fixed that by naming hers, Floralyce. I didn't have a lot of experience with little people, but I was starting to get the hang of it.

Sam got on the phone. He made me laugh as he was naming his pup *Lily of LaMancha*. He said it was good to be taking care of the most important family business of naming those pups. They all made me feel a part of something bigger than myself.

That night I lay in bed with all of the fresh stories of Sitting Bull and the injustice that still sat on the heads of the Indian people. None of the wrongdoing had ever been undone. I imagined Sam, who was fighting for *his* life. I envisioned him sitting there in a teepee with Sitting Bull, smoking a peace pipe, working on the saving of life itself. Then I let my sleepiness carry me away as bullets began to fly, me running from house to house trying to save all the women and children, scooping them up in my arms and taking them to safety, right along with Sam. Sitting Bull was holding cover with his rifle, the last rifle of the Lakota Sioux. This was his final chance to save his people. Then he was gunned down by a soldier who stood there unfazed, fulfilling the command of Delano, a monster, who stood right beside him shouting the order. Sitting Bull was out of bullets. Sam was running with a baby in his arms, holding it high above the water, as he crossed a creek to hand me my dead sister, Violet, before being hit by a bullet and landing at my feet.

I snapped myself back to reality, as I was being carried off into a horrible nightmare. None of it was real. Well, except for the fact that Sam *had* been struck with the reality of cancer and both Violet and Sitting Bull were undeniably dead.

Chapter 53

I turned in my report on Friday and was grateful to Izzy for helping me to see it through. I not only got it done but was proud of it for saying something that was heavy on my mind.

When I got home, I called my mother and spoke to Alyce and Sammy again. They went on about the pups, our connection to each other. Sam got on the phone, making me chuckle with his quick wit, making light of things through the heaviness of his fight for life itself. Lily told me that she would meet with me alone at first on Saturday, so we could talk to each other without distraction. We would meet up with Sam and the kids later, as the kids would absorb me with all the stories of their lives and pups. I was a little nervous, but I was learning the ropes of being a big brother to little people. Something that I wanted to be good at.

Saturday finally arrived as we set out for the city. I was a little giddy and nervous as we were all coming to terms with the new reality of our lives, each of us finding our way through. We still had a lot to work out, but we were all gonna be okay. Just like Sydney said. I felt it, too. I had spoken with Dan a lot about my future, knowing that it would be with Lily, my mother. It was the way it was supposed to be. It was agonizing at first to think of leaving Sydney someday, but Dan kept reminding me that we wouldn't be leaving each other but would be supporting each other in our best lives, as they took flight. Each of us reaching for our own star. I felt a great comfort knowing that Sydney had Jake and he had her. I could have never left her alone. It would have been too much to bear. Izzy's dad would be moving his family sometime in the next year, too. I had been preparing for that reality. It was gonna be messy no matter what, but it helped that Izzy and I would both be moving on, though we would have to rip ourselves from each other. I guess it would have been even harder had I been able to break that twenty dollar bill, which was still standing on the ready in my wallet, in spite of every scream from every cell in my body to spend every bit of it.

We drove over the San Francisco Bay Bridge, the day sunny and crisp, as Spring forced its way early, showering its light over the skyline of the Bay. Lily had shared with me the night before, that there were many of my kith and kin who were awaiting our reunion. There was much excitement in the air, as they all wished to be there, but understood that each would have their time. We would be filled with deep emotions. Me, coming to terms. Lily, answered prayers. And Alyce and Sammy would want me to themselves for a while to share the joy of their pups with their long-lost brother. They had been talking about me, bringing me to life in their lives, as I would finally arrive as a real person, their big brother. I wondered about the agony they suffered from my being gone from their lives for all this time. It would be a hole, much like that of Mr. Cooper's, but theirs was filled with an undying hope that had finally rung true. I guess I had always had the hole, but it was buried deep down and had to be opened up, like a fresh wound, in need of healing.

We would stay the night with Lily and Sam. They had a little downstairs apartment for guests. Jake had planned on he and Sydney getting a hotel, but Lily insisted. She expressed that we were all family now. I was glad that we would all be together. Sydney and Jake were still my spotters. I needed the comfort of them.

We came into the city early, as the traffic can be unpredictable, with a constant array of community events drawing in the crowds on most weekends. We drove down the Embarcadero, as we showed Jake all the places that we enjoyed on our visit a few weeks ago. We circled by the Palace of Fine Arts, as I stared in awe as it slowly came into my view. It looked like an ancient city sitting on the lake's edge. I smiled as we passed it, pinching myself. We found our way around to the *Painted Ladies*, standing tall in the mid-morning sun, as they shimmered from the warm glow of the morning light. They were built back in the 1800s and smiled out upon the many tourists who made it a point to drive past. I tried to calm the butterflies, as they circled around with anticipation.

Lily would be wearing a bright yellow shawl, and I was wearing my favorite green shirt so we could spot each other. I strained my neck in search of her as we parked along the street. I slid out of the car and opened Sydney's door for her. She stepped out and gave me a firm hug, holding on. Jake joined us as he wrapped his arms around us. We held tight for a moment, then took our deep breath forward, and stepped onto the fresh cut green grass, the scent rising to fill my mind with its healing power. I stood tall, looking out, scanning the view for yellow.

I quickly set my eyes on my mother, standing in the warmth of the sun looking up into the sky at a kite flying high in the air, her shawl floating across her shoulders and along the length of her arm as she used it to shade her eyes from the sunrays.

She spotted us as she turned our way, raising her hands high, the yellow shawl lifting on the breeze, in a billowing dance with the air. I was being swept toward her, my arm lifted to wave, as she moved steadily toward me. I focused on the reality of her. Each step pulling lightyears of loss toward the surface. Her floating with her shawl, as it enveloped her small frame, the curls of her dark brown hair, lifting in the breeze above her shoulders. Each of us were wearing my lifetime of hopes, as we walked, entranced, and into each other's arms, holding on. We wept freely for the 15 years that separated us. Lily pulled herself back to look at my face, as I towered over her. She shook her head, "You look so much like Angus." Her words struck me as did the glistening of her turquoise blue eyes that were rimmed in red. She looked over at Sydney and Jake, who were standing back silently holding each other, in their joy and in their greatest hopes for me. Lily placed her arm around mine as we walked over to them.

"This is Sydney and Jake," I said, as if they needed an introduction.

Lily and Sydney embraced.

"Thank you for taking such good care of him." Lily smiled warmly at Sydney.

"It's been my greatest pleasure."

Lily then gave Jake a big hug. "It's nice to finally meet you."

"You too, Lily." Jake readjusted his hat and smiled at her.

We all made small talk as the magnitude of the moment held tight to me. There were still so many questions floating around that begged for answers, but this was not the time to blurt out my insides. We were all trying to fill the space around us with ease. I was grateful, but my emotions were tangling up, as I could feel the joy of possibility for me and my mother, and then a sense of abandon for Sydney and Jake, as their life planning took a wide turn. Then the ever-wondering about the whereabouts of my father. The weight of it laid heavy over me until I looked around and marveled at these people, who gathered around me like I was a newborn star.

Sydney and Jake announced that they would have no trouble finding the house and would meet us there later for dinner. They had their own reservations for lunch that left

Lily and I to trek off on our own. It was our time to learn more about each other.

We walked along the streets of the city, taking in the views and crisp air. Lily wore a smile that stayed steady on her face. She hailed a cab that took us to the water's edge where we sat on a bench with the view of the Golden Gate Bridge before us. The sun felt warm on my shoulders.

"I have something for you." Lily reached into her large knapsack and pulled out two giftwrapped albums.

I opened them up to find Neil Young's *Harvest* and *The Godfather Soundtrack*. "Thank you." I hugged her. Her hair smelled like flowers.

I looked at the list of songs on the back of each album cover. "I can't wait to listen to them."

"I hope you'll like them.

"I already do."

"Here, I'll put them back in my bag for you."

I handed them over as she tucked them back in.

I told her all about Izzy, Chance, Joe Riley and Miss Olive. She listened, holding on to my words with a pleasant expression.

I didn't want to talk about Elizabeth. That would be for another day.

"I'd like to put my feet in the water." I had never touched the ocean.

My mother smiled at me, then started pulling off her shoes. We both rolled up our pant legs and walked calf deep into the chilly, healing water of the Pacific Ocean. We stood there until my feet and legs began to feel some warmth, as my heart was trying to save me from the cold. She stood firm with me as we peered out over the water, pulling in the freshness of the air and the awe-inspiring view of the open ocean flowing into San Francisco Bay. The gulls were singing toward the harbor in a distant call that was more like music filling the air. We trudged back to our bench, rubbing the sand from between our toes as best we could, pulling our socks and shoes back on to warm our frigid feet.

"How long since you've seen Angus?" My question burned its way out of me.

"It's been a very long time. Since before you were born."

That took me aback. *Did my father abandon her?* My golden vision of him threatened to fade as I considered this. "I hope he didn't hurt you."

"Oh, Honey. No. I mean, we were both hurt. We were so young . . . we loved each other with all we had, which just wasn't enough to get us through. We tried though. I hope you can find comfort in that."

I did, knowing that she was not much older than me when she was saddled with the idea of becoming a mother. I couldn't even imagine it and wondered so . . . about Angus.

"Can you tell me . . . ?" I couldn't finish my sentence because I didn't quite know how to ask it.

She finished it for me. "Our story?"

"Yeah."

"Of course, I'll tell you. It's *your* story too."

I sat in silence as she shared her memories with me:

Lily was born and raised in New Orleans. Angus had immigrated with his family from Ireland when he was sixteen, the year before she met him. When she started high school, he was a senior at the same school. She said he walked up and spoke to her that very first day and she was smitten by him. It wasn't long before they were going steady. She wore his class ring, wrapped in yarn to hold it onto her left ring finger. She twirled her wedding band as her mind took her back. They enjoyed the hops and dance halls together and did a mean jitterbug, lindy and swing. They loved everything about the music and dance scene in New Orleans. They even snuck into the Club 809 in the French Quarter one night to watch Chris Owens and the Maraca Girls. Lily's eyes lit up as she pulled in the memories. I was sitting on the edge of my seat, envisioning them dancing through the streets of that magical city I had only read about. They had a lot of fun during that time. Their happy-go-lucky lives were filled with music, dancing, fish fries, crab boils and ball games. Angus was a mighty good shortstop, making the papers after most of his high school games.

When Angus graduated high school, Lily's mom offered him a job at their family restaurant. He was a waiter extraordinaire, she said. Everybody adored him, especially my mother, Lily. They were making plans for their lives, her even figuring on how she could graduate early and start her life with Angus.

One day, one of Angus's buddies asked him to go down to the Army recruiter's office, where his friend was going to sign up. After the recruiter was done mesmerizing the two with the grandeur of military service, Angus had signed up too. He didn't even know that he was eligible, him being an immigrant and all, but the recruiter pulled him right on in. He was as surprised as everybody else that he then belonged to the Army. He had some regret when he was quickly hastened to boot camp within weeks of signing on. He left for Fort Benning, Georgia, in January of 1957, when Lily was starting her last semester of her sophomore year. Soon after her sixteenth birthday, Lily had determined that she was about four-and-a-half months pregnant. She had been writing to Angus about her suspicions and her little bump confirmed it. She and Angus began to make plans, not telling anyone. By that time, he had finished boot camp and was in training for his deployment, wherever that would be. On his next leave, he would fly home where they planned to sneak off and get married. They were gonna be a family, with me in their center. They had it all figured out until everything started falling apart. As he was flying home to make her his wife, her growing belly had gotten her shipped out to her Aunt Gloria in Ohio, where she would be forced to attend St. Mary of the Angels school for unwed teens. Her tear-stained letters and he had passed in flight. Angus went straight to her home when he landed. Her parents were upset about their pregnant daughter and just told Angus to leave. He called Lily's best friend, Nora, who told him where she was. She gave him her Aunt Gloria's phone number, but he got no answer. Out of desperation he placed a call to St. Mary of the

Angels, but they would neither confirm nor deny that she was a student there. Finally, after a couple of miserable days Angus reached Lily at her Aunt Gloria's house. He got her address and flew straight to Ohio with just days left of his leave. They had planned to slip off to get married before he headed back to the base, but Ohio would not allow them a marriage license without her parent's approval, which they did not have. They considered an escape for her and an AWOL for him, but thought better of it, as they could not risk their baby's father being a kidnapper and a military criminal. They determined that he had to go back to base in order for them to have any chance at a future together. They tore themselves apart as he pushed himself back to his duty. Soon after, he was shipped out to Germany. They exchanged letters of their undying love for each other and plans to marry as soon as he returned from his yearlong deployment.

I was born on October 3, 1957. She said that I was *perfect*. She spent that first day holding me, feeding me, and telling me how beautiful our lives would be. I was like all her dreams wrapped up into one, she said. The next morning, she sent off a letter to Angus, shouting the news of my arrival. She dreamed of him opening it and racing through the barracks to shout that he was a father. His son, Angus O'Malley Murphy II had arrived. After feeding me that morning, a nurse took me back to the nursery while Lily filled out my birth certificate. The clerk who brought in the paperwork, gave one last effort to convince her to give me up for adoption. They had been leaning heavily on her since her arrival at the school, but she adamantly refused, yet again. Once she got the certificate completed, the clerk tore it up and made her start over, telling her that she could not give me my father's full name because they were not married, and she could not list him as my father for the same reason. The clerk demanded that my last name had to be the same as my mother's, Boudreaux. While she was tormenting and finished up the document, I was being ripped from my crib in the nursery. The following day, after an extensive search of the ward and the area around the birthing center with no sign of me or the girl who was believed to have taken me, Lily wrote the letter to Angus that I was gone. She wept from her remembering, as did I for the knowing.

Lily was devastated and returned to New Orleans without me, the baby she longed for. It took several weeks for Angus's next letters to get back to Lily, as they found their way from Germany to Ohio, then were forwarded on to her parent's address in New Orleans, where she lay, childless, waiting word. The first letter was adorned in promise, a love letter to their newborn son. She reached into her bag and pulled out the letter, written on Army stationary. She handed it to me, and I slowly unfolded it with trembling hands. It read:

My Dearest Lily,

I am the happiest man alive! I'm a dad! And you're a mother! We're parents! Our little Angus is a very lucky boy. There will be no other child who will be so loved. Hold him close for me and whisper in his ear that I love him and will be there as soon as this damn duty is over. Well, maybe don't say the damn part. I wish I could be there with you. I imagine you holding him and telling him about our greatest hopes for him. He will be the smartest kid in school because his mother is a genius. And there is no doubt that he is the most handsome baby in the nursery. Kiss him for me and please send me a photo as soon as you can. I need to look into those eyes of our boy. I am heading out on an exercise mission so it will be a couple of weeks before I can write again but know that I love you more than the stars up in the sky my beautiful Lily. Take good care of yourself and our boy. I need to get this letter off. I long for you.

Forever yours, Angus

She wept while I read the letter and I nearly folded over reading it. I could feel the hope in him, in both of them. It tangled me up to feel it, along with the realization that it all came to a devastating end. I sat quietly with the letter. It came from my father's hand. We sat there with it, mourning over it, like it was the very first day. A moment that we had to go through, together.

His next letters, which she did not bring, expressed his sadness for not being there for her and me. He felt handcuffed on the other side of the world, as his child had been stolen from his mother's arms. Lily touched her grief again, remembering his words.

They tried to hold on to what they had and their great hope of finding me, but their devastating loss, the spinning of time and the distance between them pulled them further and further apart, until all letters finally drifted to a stop. Their young love could find nothing left to hold on to. I understood that when things fall apart, they just slip right through our fingers. Their dreams unraveled and fell into the sea between them. She said it felt like every good thing had fallen from the earth, even the depth of her devotion to Angus, which slipped further and further away right along with me. They never spoke or saw each other again.

She finished up high school and headed off to college in San Francisco, where she met Sam. They got married while he was in medical school. He was a pediatrician with a practice in the city. She said that he wore a giant red nose to greet his new young patients. "How could I not love a man like that?" she giggled. She taught piano lessons while continuing her schooling with plans to teach when her young ones were ready for such a commitment by her. All was up in the air, as they hoped and prayed for the saving of Sam.

I sat in awe. "It's so much to take in," I confessed.

"It hurts to say it all out loud to you," her voice quivered.

"I really wanted to know."

"I know you did. I was prepared to tell you. Sydney told me that you'd want to hear it."

"Yeah, I've learned that I need to hear the truth so I can come to terms with it, instead of always wondering."

"You're right about that. The truth is important, even if it hurts. I have something else for you." She reached into her purse and handed me a photo. "This was taken the last day that I saw your father. Aunt Gloria snapped it for us."

I stared into it and pulled out the image of my father, who was towering over Lily with his arms wrapped around her. She was leaning into him holding his hands in front of her, her bulging belly filling her dress. They were both smiling at the camera with all their hopes still intact. I studied it.

"Can you see the resemblance?"

I could, but couldn't speak, seeing his face for the first time and the promise of us right there before me.

We sat there in silence, as I stared at the image, my eyes dripping with threat of a deluge biting at my nose.

Finally, I gathered myself. "I think I see it, the resemblance."

"You have the same smile and eyes, and your hair's the same color, with that sparkle of golden amber that shimmers in the sunlight."

I imagined the photo in color and could see it all.

"We think Angus might be in Montana."

"Oh, you got some news?" My pulse perked.

"I spoke to his ex-wife, Loretta, who said that he was doing some research out there last she heard."

I tilted my head, wondering. "What kind of research?"

"She said it had something to do with fish habitat and the environment. He was writing a book on the subject. Something to do with flies.

"Flies?"

"Yes, the food of fish."

"Hmm."

"He was working for a newspaper in Chicago before he left."

I envisioned Angus walking away from the tall buildings of that large city and finding his way through the flora and fauna of the forest, like in Eagle Meadow. Then I quickly changed the subject. "Do they have children?" I wondered if there was any room in his life for me, though it's funny that it was not a question that I had for Lily.

"I didn't ask. That'll be for you to learn from your father." She smiled at me.

"Yeah, so much to learn."

We sat in silence breathing, then she shared more about her mom and dad, my grandparents, Peter and Claire Boudreaux. "We had a hard time, when I was younger, after my losing you and then Angus. I was bitter and wanted to blame them for all of it, which I did, for a long time. I don't even know how they put up with my anger. But as I got older, I began to understand that they only wanted the very best for me. They were scared for my future and flying blind, doing what they thought was best, and then it all turned out so wrong. They apologized to me for not keeping us safely at home. Had they known the outcome, of course they would have made a different decision. But life isn't like that, is it?"

"Nope." I shook my head and smiled a knowing smile.

"My parent's regret and my blame has been hard on us and our relationship, but we've worked through it. I finally apologized and stopped condemning them. And they forgave me for dragging my sad self around and taking everything out on them. I was quite a mess. Something that I'm not very proud of."

"I've been a mess myself and am learning to forgive, too."

"It's a good skill to let go of blame. There's a healing quality to it."

"Yeah. I can see that."

She smiled looking out toward the bridge as we watched a boat slowly move toward the sea underneath it. Her tears losing their footing from the well of her eyes.

"Do they still live in New Orleans, your parents?"

"Oh yes, and they will never leave their beloved homeland. I don't blame them for that. Their little restaurant has been passed down from my mother's family for a couple of generations. The best Creole-cooking in New Orleans. And a whole slew of family that meet up there on the first Sunday of every month. It's a time-honored tradition." She had a far-off look in her eyes. "I miss that."

I smiled imagining it. A restaurant filled with laughter, and Creole, whatever that was. "What exactly is Creole-cooking?"

"Oh Levi. It makes my mouth water to even think about it. It's rich and luxurious food that crosses so many cultures: African, Native American and European. Jambalaya, Gumbo, Shrimp Creole. I could go on and on. Creole also describes my mother's family heritage perfectly as we are most certainly true Louisiana Creole, coming from a broad mix of races and cultures from West Africa, France, Spain and Native American. My father is French, and your father is Irish. You are the most perfect mix of all these amazing people and cultures."

My jaw dropped. "You mean I'm part African and Native American too?"

"Yes, you are. My mother has the family documents to prove it. What do you think of that?"

I smiled. "I've never been prouder." Sitting Bull would be proud too, and I could hardly wait to tell Izzy and Chance. Shoot, maybe we're all related!

She looked square at me and grinned widely. "Me neither. We'll make that trip to New Orleans where you can feast your heart and soul on all things Creole."

"I've never been there," I said, as if I'd ever been anywhere. "I'll look forward to that and eating some of that cooking, too."

Lily looked at her watch. "I bet you're hungry. Shall we go grab some lunch?"

I hadn't even thought of food until she started talking about Creole and my stomach lurched with excitement. "Yeah, I'm starving." *Always starving.*

We hailed a cab that dropped us off in front of a pretty hotel called *The Queen Anne.* It was much like one of the *Painted Ladies,* but larger in scale. Lily said it was a sight to see, so we ducked in to have a look. As we walked into the lobby, it was dressed in marble and dark wood. It was beautiful, as my eyes were drawn around the room to see old Victorian furniture placed in small groupings around the space. A grand piano sat in the corner, ready to serenade us, if someone's fingers laid upon it.

"Can you play something?" I asked my mother.

"Is there something special you'd like to hear?" She took my hand and led me to the piano. She sat down and patted the seat for me to join her on the bench.

"I like everything, as you know." I grinned at her and she gave me a knowing smile.

"Okay, how about Gymnopedie, Number One? It's one of my favorites." She shot me a warm smile as she spread her fingers gently onto the keys and began to play into all the spaces of the lobby. The music was slow, each note intentional, yet soft, as she stepped through them. My arms grew goose bumps as the sound floated around in me. I closed my eyes, taking in the simple music that formed the arrangement. It touched me to my core. I could feel something like magic swirling within me. When she played the final note, there was a gentle applause from all who could hear her. She closed her eyes and bowed her head in appreciation. "I've always loved that one, kind of a healer."

I understood how music could heal. I shared that same sense with my mother as our eyes dripped from the healing power of it.

We walked down the street to a little Italian restaurant where the aroma drew us in. I had a huge plate of homemade pasta with *Ragù Napoletano* sauce. The waiter shredded fresh cheese over the top and added cracked pepper. It was out-of-this-world delicious with its rich red sauce and several kinds of meats. Lily had a salad, though she just had to have a few bites of my pasta in a little plate after I went on and on about it. We talked and laughed with ease, especially when the front of her blouse was dotted with the rich red sauce.

"I should have tied my napkin around my neck or worn a big red tie with a fancy Windsor in hopes that it would catch it," she giggled.

"What's a Windsor?"

She held her giddy expression. "It's a nice plump knot for a necktie. When we go to the symphony some time, I'll tie one of those pretty knots for you." I didn't tell her that I didn't own a tie.

"The symphony," I muttered. "I'd like that."

She dipped her napkin into her water glass to rub out the sauce. "I shouldn't worry about it. It's a tribute to the chef when you wish to wear a fine recipe home from the restaurant. Sam does it all the time, with pride. It's like a badge of honor."

We both shared a good laugh, my mother and me. I was stepping into the light of her world, one that had always existed, feeling it expand around me. I was finding my way home, which wasn't really a place. It was the loving space that my mother and all the generations before her had always held for me, somewhere in that sacred space that holds us all.

Chapter 54

We walked out of the hotel like old friends, a smile permanently fixed to my face. My mother carried with her a warmth that filled me with ease. We strolled along the streets and into a small courtyard in front of a tall skinny house. It looked to be three stories. Each having a large bay-type window facing the street. It was painted orange with lively yellow trim. It was Lily's house. My mother's house. We stepped in the door and marched up a long flight of stairs to an open living room with a fireplace. There were fresh flowers spilling over a large vase on the coffee table. The floral scents grabbed my nose. She took my hand as we walked to the kitchen where Sam stood peeling carrots. He was thin and slight, wearing a Breton cap to cover his hairless head, one like Dylan and the Beatles fancied. I had looked up the name of it when I first saw a picture of Dylan wearing one. I fancied it too. Sam looked up with a broad smile and grabbed a towel to wipe his hands.

"Hi Honey. He's here." My mother's eyes flooded over as she looked at him, beaming. "This is Levi. Levi, Sam."

He looked deep into my eyes and shook my hand, then wrapped his arms around me. "I'm so glad you're finally here." Tears filled his sunken brown eyes as he looked into me. He was frail. I could see the devastation of his illness as it clung to him.

I tried not to blubber. "I'm glad to be here. It's nice to meet you."

"As much as I'd like to scoop you off to visit, the kids are in the backyard with the pups." He glanced at the back door, where I could see them through the glass, laying on the ground encircling the brood. "They've been waiting for you."

"I guess I better go on out then. Excuse me." I bowed my head and walked toward the door, staring through the glass pane at my brother and sister, laying there in the warmth of the sun. They were young and innocent, surrounded by so much hope. I walked out, as they both looked up at me. "Hi there."

"Angus?" Sammy yelled as he jumped up.

"Yeah. Hi Sammy." He bolted right up into my arms where he wrapped them around my neck, holding me tight.

"He goes by Levi, Sammy," Alyce said sternly.

"That's okay. I've got two names." Sammy released his grip as I placed him back on the ground.

I reached out my hand to Alyce. I wasn't sure if she wanted a hug. She grabbed my hand and I followed Sam's lead to reach around and hug her.

"You're our brother," Alyce tilted her head, staring up at me.

"Yes, I am."

"How come you left us?"

Her words caught me by surprise. "I-I would never leave you. I just got lost for a while." Her question gut punched me. *Did I say the wrong thing?*

"We've been waiting all day." Sammy began to jump up and down with delight, pulling us from Alyce's impossible question.

Alyce grabbed a pup and handed it to me. This is your Samson. We can tell by the white spot at the end of his tail. He's yours."

"Thank you. I've been looking forward to seeing him." I hugged her again in hopes of giving her comfort for my being gone for her whole life. Then I went over and sat down next to Daisy with the pup as she started licking Samson to ensure that he was alright in my care. Alyce and Sammy joined me as we sat there holding our pups, me in near disbelief that I would get to carry the role of big brother to them.

Sam and my mother came out and joined us, sitting in the circle, each introducing their named pups. Sammy giggled, kissing Levi Angus's soft snout, then holding him close. Alyce had Dolly wrapped in a tiny blanket, rocking her like a baby. Daisy went from pup to pup, as we comforted her with our gentle care of them. M'Lady flashed into my mind. She would have loved this circle and thoroughly enjoyed the shiny bowls filled with food and clean water. I gave her all the love I had, but she deserved so much more.

The back yard was small, yet filled with raised garden beds, ready for their summer vegetables to be planted. There were flowering fruit trees along the fence line, bursting with fruity scents. The sky was the brightest blue with soft billowing clouds floating through. I kept breathing, long and deep, taking it all in.

Sydney and Jake arrived a little later and we had a nice dinner with a long and easy conversation to follow by the fire. I read Alyce and Sammy a goodnight story after several games of *Go Fish*.

"Daddy's been sick," Alyce said. Her eyes showing her sadness.

"Yeah, but he's gonna feel a whole lot better soon."

She grinned ever so slightly. "That's what he says."

Lily hugged them both and I watched silently as she tucked them in. I had missed so much of what a mother's love can do but felt some comfort that my siblings would never know the darkness of a young life lived in the seat of loneliness.

After everyone went to bed, Lily and I sat on the sofa by the fire, talking.

"What do you think about moving in here with us?"

"I've been thinking about it."

"I'm glad. I'm sure you're feeling torn, and I want you to know that we're supportive of your friendships and loving relationships. They're your people, and we want them in your life. We would never take that away from you. You can see them often, either here or there. We understand that they're your family. We're *all* your family."

"Yeah." I stared into the fire feeling uneasy at the thought of leaving everyone I had gathered around myself throughout my lifetime.

"Just know that we want you here with us."

The fire held me in its trance. "I know," I whispered above my breath.

"I don't want you to feel any pressure, but also want you to know how much we'd love to have you here with us."

The fire would not release me. "I know. I've been preparing myself for it, thinking maybe after the school year."

"I'm sure you'd like to finish up there. I understand," she said warmly. "But if you decide you'd like to come sooner, we'd love that too."

"I'll think about it." I *was* feeling torn, knowing my fate was to be with my own mother. Something I was beginning to want.

"I'm glad you'll think about it. And Levi?"

I drew my eyes back from the fire, meeting her gaze. "Uh huh?"

"How would you feel about calling me Mom?" Her eyes glistened over, turning a brighter shade of blue.

"Well, it feels kinda weird, calling you by your first name when you are my own mother," I grinned. I had been preparing for that too, what I should call her.

She grabbed my hand. "I'm proud to be your mother. Always have been."

"I know. And I'm proud to be your son, too."

She smiled wide, taking a deep breath as we both returned our gaze to the fire, sitting in the warmth of who we were to each other.

Chapter 55

We returned to Sydney's which left me yearning to go back to my family. Meeting them changed everything. I wanted to be there, sit with them, laugh with them, cry with them and help them through Sam's illness. They needed me and I needed them.

I played my new records over and over. Each song burning into the memory of my new life and time with my family. I played along on my harmonica, feeling a little more confident in myself as a musician, though I still had a lot to learn.

Sydney and I talked a lot about my going to be with my mom, where I belonged. I was starting to pull myself toward my family and away from Sydney and Jake. It was subtle but necessary for me to detach my heavy grasp of their safety net, that supported me when I fell right into it. I loved them and forever would. They loved me and each other, which was the perfect perception needed to move on in our lives, apart, but forever together in our devotion for each other.

I felt a strong tug toward Izzy. It was like I had to tear myself away. I wasn't ready for that, but also knew that she would be leaving me soon enough when her family traipsed off to who knew where in the near future. I had to face the facts, but it didn't stop my dread.

Chapter 56

I had been packing my things all week, preparing to head to my family home when late one night, the phone rang. I jumped up from a dead sleep and met Sydney at the door as we raced for the phone. We were both nervous. No one ever called so late. I flipped on the light as Sydney grabbed the phone.

"Hello?" I listened anxiously. "Uh huh." She looked concerned and then her lips turned up to smile as she listened intently. "Oh, my goodness . . . Oh, thank God . . . Yes . . . Yes . . . He's right here." She passed me the receiver. "It's Lily." Her eyes sparkled.

"Hello?"

"Levi, Angus called. He called."

I was stunned, blinking her words in. "Oh my God." The words slid slowly out.

"Your father is sitting by the phone somewhere in Montana, waiting to give you a call."

I nearly jumped through the phone to hug her. "Oh my God. I can't believe it," I said, trying to believe it. Sydney was standing in the doorway of the kitchen with a knowing smile. She clasped her hands over her heart, then pumped her fists high in the air. I smiled at her, shaking my head in disbelief.

"I told him all about you. He's overwhelmed with excitement."

"Oh my God," was all I could say.

"I'm so grateful, Levi. For him, for you and for all of us. He wants to call you. Right now."

"He's gonna call me?" My heart began to race.

"Yes, I just wanted to prepare you first and didn't want you to fall over from the shock when he called unannounced in the middle of the night." She laughed, a sound that sung to me.

"I would have, you know." We both giggled, my mother and me.

"Okay. I guess I'd better let you go so he can call. I'll talk to you soon. Call me back when you can. I'm so excited for you, and him."

"Okay."

"I love you so much."

"I love you, too, Mom. Thank you for finding him."

"I'd do anything and I'm so glad for him to know that you're okay. It's a grand relief. All of it." Her voice was giddy. "You enjoy talking to your father. He's beside himself. Okay, I'd better let you go. Bye, Son."

"Bye."

Sydney was still standing in the doorway, smiling. I ran over to her and swung her around like a dance partner. "He's gonna call." My voice sung from the mountain tops.

"I'm so happy for you, Honey. So, so happy." Her eyes were dancing in the light as her tears swam around in them.

Before I could say another word, the phone rang. We both looked at each other wide-eyed and busted out laughing. "It's my dad." I could hardly get hold of myself. My dad was calling me. I held my hand above the receiver as it shook, took a deep breath, then picked it up. "Hello?" My voice cracked, as usual.

I held my breath to listen for the sound of my father's voice. "Hello, this is Angus Murphy. I'm calling for Angus. I mean. I'm sorry. Is Levi available?"

His name and him saying both my names, melted right into me. He spoke with a lilting brogue, like an Irish poet. It surprised me in a warm and comforting way.

I cleared my throat. "This is Levi."

"Is this really you?"

"Yes, it's me."

"You sound so grown up . . . I guess you are kind of grown up, aren't you?

"I'm getting there."

"I'm sorry that I wasn't home sooner. I just got word of you. I nearly fell right out of my boots."

"Me too, about you calling."

"It's almost unbelievable, finding you after all this time."

"I know. It's crazy." *I've dreamed of you my entire life.*

"I'd like to come see you. Lord. This is . . . oh . . . I haven't let you get a word in edgewise."

"That's okay. I'm just glad to hear your voice." *Finally.* "Where are you?"

"I live in Bozeman, Montana. I just got back from a trip. My mailbox was filled with letters that I needed to call Lily right away. My feet haven't hit the ground yet."

"Mine either."

"Oh, my boy. I can imagine. Lily said you only live about ninety some miles east of her. It's remarkable that you've been so close for all this time."

"Yeah. It is."

"I almost moved to California once. I guess, somehow, we must have known you were there."

I was losing my words as the enormity of my talking to my dad hit me hard. "Yeah," was all I could say.

"We've got a lot of catching up to do, young man."

"Yeah, we do," I managed.

"Sorry to call so late, but there was no way I could *not* call this very night. I am bouncing off the moon right now." He chuckled. "And I'm actually freezing my britches off. I haven't even turned the heat on yet. Oh, how I've missed . . ." He choked up, as did I. "Well, I'd better pull myself together here so I can go see my son."

I smiled. *His son.* "I'll look forward to it."

"Me too, my boy. Me too. I'll call again tomorrow to make some plans."

"Okay."

"You have a good night."

"You too," *Dad.* "Goodnight." I hung up the phone.

Sydney hugged me tight. I held on to her, not wanting to let go, trying to hold back my childish tears. *When would I ever grow out of being a bawl-bag?*

I sat on my bed and stared at the photo of my mother and father. My parents. The tide of my life was turning, having pulled so much sadness down under its wake, leaving the starfish of promise to bask in the glory of this new day. I thought back on my vision of me standing on the beach. My mother and Sam were standing there now, with Alyce and Sammy by their side. My father stepping out from the ocean, grabbing my mother's hand as I ran toward them all. It was like a fantasy. Like a wish upon a star, not a dream come true. I had never felt such hope. Good fortune had been circling in on me. My life was beginning to feel more like the miracle that it truly was.

Chapter 57

Angus headed west that very morning, early, calling from a phone booth in Pocatello, Idaho to talk to Sydney about his heading our way. He just couldn't wait, he said. Nor could I. I watched for him, peering out the window every few minutes for hours, when his truck finally pulled up just after dark. I ran straight for the door and stepped out onto the porch as he turned off the engine. The streetlamp flooded down on his truck as I stood, waiting for him to step out. It took a minute or so for him to see me, as he sat with his hands on the wheel, his head leaning forward, nearly laying on it. Then he turned and spotted me standing under the porch lamp. Everything went into slow motion, as the truck door opened, and I stepped toward my father. We were staring through the darkness, each lit by the light of the lamps dancing down upon us, as we reached each other and held on tight. Again, I felt the release of 15 years of wishing and wondering and waiting. Neither of us let go. I held on for dear life, as if he would melt away like an impossible dream if I let loose. Finally, I took a deep breath and released my grip on him. He was the man in the photo, my father, only larger than life.

He smiled widely as he held me arm's length to peer into my face under the lamp light. "Lily said you look just like me and I can see it, you handsome devil."

I laughed and blew snot out my nose, wiping it with my sleeve. My face dripping wet.

He threw his arm up around my shoulders as we marched toward the house. Sydney and Jake were standing at the door holding on to each other, watching my wildest dream come true.

Chapter 58

Four months later

Dad and I were standing knee-deep in the Yellow River. He had been teaching me to fly fish as we crisscrossed our way through Yellowstone National Park. I was getting the hang of the rod, flinging the line back and forth as I found my rhythm with it. I breathed in the clean air, filling my lungs, then let it out, as it held tempo with the dance. The water was singing its way over the stones it had carried there, echoing the gentle rush through the canyon walls. I caught Dad staring and smiled back at him as my line laid long on top of the water. Then my reel screamed as a fish ran the fly deep.

"You got it, Son," my father whooped.

I kept the line taut, reeling, as the fish fought for its freedom. As it neared the surface, Dad scooped it into his net. I reached in to release it from the feathered hook made by my father's hand, then lifted the fish slightly to see its iridescent colors shimmer in the morning light. I smiled at my dad as his eyes glistened, holding my gaze for a moment to burn it into my bank of memories. Then I gently laid the rainbow back into the water as it slowly swam away.

Chapter 59

My father gave me a sheet of paper from his wallet. It was yellowed and tattered, having survived the test of time:

My Lionheart (by Angus O'Malley Murphy, my father)

In the gentle deep places of heart beats,
Where I lean in the hope of your name,
We share the same sun, the moonlight,
A wellspring, we are of the same.

I endure the depth of my mourning,
Be safe, on the wings of a dove.
Hold fast to the hope born within you
It shall rise, as a sign from above.

The call of the lark, draws you closer,
Pulling, as onward, you climb.

May hope draw the ache from within me,
As the lark sings above, it's our sign.

The spaces still hold you, not empty,
As you sing from the heartstrings that draw me,
Your eyes bright as they spark from the knowing,
My tears falling, like rain, to your face.

I have sent you the birds as they follow,
Singing your Irish song.
Surely you hear, o'er the tempest,
As you peer through the shadows, steer on.

Your lionheart beats within me,
As I call you onward, to me,
Listen hard for the edict, oh mercy,
And bring forth me boy from the sea.

I envisioned him writing these words so long ago and know that it was he and my mother who pulled me toward them, as they longed for me, their son, his only son, to hear their cries, the silent echoes that sang to the knowing of the lionheart within me.

Acknowledgements

My work in *family finding* was a big inspiration for this story. When children feel connected to people who care about them, it can make all the difference, even in the darkest days. Thank you to all of those incredibly hard working people who make up the safety net that supports our most vulnerable children and families; those behind the scenes, and those who face the hardships head on. It is such a comfort to know that you are there.

I would like to thank my editor, Thornton Sully, for your thoughtful consideration of my words, and for your steady support, kindness and glowing encouragement. You asked all the right questions. Thank you, Thorn, for helping me to step out from behind my laptop and face the world with my story, with the confidence that my proper nouns were all in check too.

Thank you, my dear friend Daphne Short, one of the advanced readers of my story. You helped me tremendously with your thoughtful perspective as an advocate for children and your great eye for detail.

When I finished my first draft, my mother was one of the first to read it. I was wrapping up the final chapters, as we read them out loud to each other, taking turns. After the final words were spoken, we looked at each other with tears in our eyes. "You did it," she said. It meant the world to me. Thank you Mother Dear. And if anyone finds Sydney's character too good to be true, I will just say that you've never met my mother.

Thank you to Dad and Pat, for carefully reading through those rough first drafts, even though Dad called to complain that I had not prepared him for the fact that he would cry like a baby. And thanks, again, Dad, for taking the liberty of sharing my manuscript with vacationers at the lake. I was very touched by the notes of encouragement and well wishes from these strangers.

Thank you, my brother Russell Tiffin, for sharing your expertise in graphic design. I appreciate your incredible knowledge and very quick wit. Thank you for making me laugh.

Thank you, my sister Deanna Desvaux deMarigny, for reading my draft and for your insight on light and tone as I designed my cover. What a gift you gave to me.

To my children, Josh, Colby and Tiffiny. Thank you for your steady encouragement, for reading my words and for always asking how Levi was doing throughout my long journey to this book. And thank you for always being there for me, as I leaned on your many talents, big hearts and steady support.

To my grandchildren; Brier, Ellis, Riley, Hunter, Waylan, Calian, Holden and Hadley. Thank you for filling my heart with unending joy. Brier, thank you your sweet notes of encouragement that I have appreciated so much, and thank you for trusting me with your stories. You are an excellent writer. Though it may be a little while before the rest of you little beauties can read this story, your questions and curiosities about my being a writer and artist have been heartwarming. You each have made everything about my life so much better for you being in it.

To my extended family and friends, including those on Facebook and Instagram. I appreciate your kind words and interest in my writing. It is such a joy to see your notes of excitement for this upcoming novel. Many of you helped me to see that this big wide world of social media can be a positive and loving place of support. Thank you for that.

I was greatly inspired by music while writing this book, from folk to classical. It would soar from my studio each day, where I could hear Levi's voice echo in the melodies, lifting me up to that space where creativity flows. Thank you to the myriad of singers, songwriters and musicians who carried me to that higher place. And Bob Dylan, how could I not place you fictionally in my book. Your storytelling has touched my soul since the very first time I heard you oh so long ago.

To my husband, Randy Self. I could write another book about all that I love about you. Thank you for fueling me, literally, with the meals that you quietly placed in front of me at my desk as I wrote. And for that glass of wine that would slide in, along with a big smile, on some of my late night writing sessions. Thank you for all of the many things you do to show your love for me. We have spent most of our lives side-by-side and it is a joy to look back on the years, as we created a loving space together, that holds all of the beautiful people that we hold dear. I'm sure glad you liked me in the 7th grade. I liked you too, and still do.